HOT SEAL LOVER

NY TIMES BESTSELLING AUTHOR

LYNN RAYE HARRIS

HOT SEAL TEAM

Cover Design © 2016 Croco Designs
Interior Design by JT Formatting

www.**lynnrayeharris**.com

First Edition: June 2016
Library of Congress Cataloging-in-Publication Data

Harris, Lynn Raye
Hot SEAL Lover / Lynn Raye Harris – 1st ed
ISBN-13: 978-1-941002-15-5

1. Hot SEAL Lover —Fiction
2. Fiction—Romance
3. Fiction—Contemporary Romance

OTHER BOOKS BY LYNN RAYE HARRIS

HOSTILE OPERATIONS Team Series

Hot Pursuit (#1) – Matt & Evie

Hot Mess (#2) – Sam & Georgie

Hot Package (#3) – Billy & Olivia

Dangerously Hot (#4) – Kev & Lucky

Hot Shot (#5) – Jack & Gina

Hot Rebel (#6) – Nick & Victoria

Hot Ice (#7) – Garrett & Grace

Hot & Bothered (#8) – Ryan & Emily

Hot Protector (#9) – Chase & Sophie

HOT SEAL Team Series

HOT SEAL (#1) – Dane & Ivy

HOT SEAL Lover (#2) – Remy & Christina

PROLOGUE

City of Baq
Qu'rim
Middle East

"GOT A SITUATION."

The SEALs were gathered around the computer screen in the building they occupied near the edge of the city. The sounds of battle being waged in the desert filtered into the capital. Small arms fire, RPGs, and various other explosions sounded with alarming regularity. Not long now and Baq could fall to the rebels.

Remy "Cage" Marchand shifted his weight as he watched the man speaking on the screen. Colonel Mendez was the badass full-bird Army colonel who ran the Hostile Operations Team with an iron fist and an arsenal of high-tech weaponry. He had the approval of Congress, the budget of a military dictator, and the balls of an elephant.

In short, Mendez was just about the scariest motherfucker Remy had ever come across—and that was saying something considering how utterly nightmarish BUD/S had been. The instructors at Coronado weren't known for being pussies, that's for sure. Remy had never considered ringing out—okay, he *had* considered it. Everyone considered it at one point or another. Basic Underwater Demolition/SEAL Training wasn't your typical military boot camp. It routinely took down the kind of men you'd never think would quit.

But Remy hadn't actually pulled the cord on the bell that would have ended the torture. He had a feeling that Mendez, if he'd been in the Navy, wouldn't even have considered it.

"Need you boys to go get some American citizens from the Abu Bashar Hotel and put them on a plane before Baq falls."

Remy glanced at his platoon leader. Dane "Viking" Erikson didn't look too pleased, but then Baq was on a travel advisory list and had been for months. On the other hand, the State Department had only issued an evacuation warning for nonessential personnel a few hours ago. Private citizens couldn't be forced to leave, though they usually wanted to during crisis situations.

Typically, the State Department handled noncombatant evacuations. The fact that HOT SEALs were being sent to collect these people was interesting. Which meant there had to be more to the story.

"I'm sending over the names," Mendez said, "but you should know that one of them has a connection to HOT."

And there it was.

Remy's heart skipped a beat. He told himself it could be anyone—but the truth was it could only be one person. Christina Girard-Scott, Matt Girard's beautiful, damaged sister. Remy still wanted to kill the motherfucker who'd broken her heart and ruined her ability to trust in men.

Because of her asshole of an ex-husband, Remy'd had to watch her run away from him when he'd been convinced she was something special, that there could be something between them if only she'd give it a chance.

Mendez continued. "Christina Girard works for Girard Oil. She's there to close a deal with Sheikh Fahd ibn Aziz. She's also the Alpha Squad commander's sister. I don't have to explain to you what a disaster it would be if the rebels take the city and she's captured."

Holy fuck, this was a nightmare.

Christina might not know who her brother worked for, but she did know he was an Army officer in an elite unit. That made her a high-value target for the rebels—and for the Freedom Force, the terrorist organization that was widely considered to be the engine behind the rebellion—if they learned that information.

Remy glanced up, met Viking's eyes. The other man was looking at him with real concern in his gaze, which was surprising considering Remy had never told anyone about Christina and him. It'd happened so fast and been over so quick there'd been nothing to tell.

"We'll get them out, sir," Viking said, looking at the screen again. "We won't let anyone take Christina Girard."

No, they damn sure wouldn't. Because Remy would die before he let that happen…

CHAPTER ONE

Six months earlier…

"WOW."

Christina couldn't help the word that popped out when she looked up and saw the man striding with purpose across the grass. He was tall and muscular, like all these Special Ops types her brother worked with, but there was something more about this one that caught her eye. Maybe it was the tattoos on his arms and back. He'd removed his shirt and dropped it on the grass before picking up the volleyball someone tossed over, and Christina had to make sure her tongue wasn't hanging out as all that muscle rippled in the sunlight.

"What?" her sister-in-law asked, swiveling her head to look at the group of seriously fine military men playing volleyball in her backyard.

Christina took a sip of the sweet raspberry smoothie Evie had made and shook her head. "Nothing. Just a little overwhelmed by all the man chest on display."

She shifted in her seat, a little surprised and even, yes,

a little uncomfortable with the zinging sensations happening in the region of her lady parts as Mr. Muscles lifted the volleyball high in the air and then lobbed it toward the other side of the net. Seriously, her body had to pick now to perk up?

Evie laughed. "They are rather fun to look at, aren't they?"

She leaned back and patted her belly. It was soft and round with the babies growing inside. Christina felt a pang of envy. Not over the babies in particular, since she wasn't quite sure how she felt about bringing a child into the world, but over the general contentedness that Evie had with Matt. Not that it hadn't been rough going for a while. Evie had been in love with Matt since forever, and Matt had been stupid enough to nearly ruin the whole thing when they were teenagers.

Thankfully they'd figured it out. It had taken ten years, but Evie didn't look like she'd trade her happiness now for anything.

"Oh honey, I'm sorry," Evie said softly, and Christina knew her sadness must have shown on her face.

She sipped her drink and tried to look nonchalant. "I'm fine. Really. It's been three months since it happened."

Evie reached over and squeezed her hand. At least she didn't *tsk* or *cluck* or make any of those noises that other women tended to make when they realized who Christina was.

Christina Girard-Scott, wife of Benjamin Scott. Ben Scott, up-and-coming attorney who'd been running for public office on family values and a squeaky-clean life.

Squeaky-clean until Ben decided that kinky sex in a

restroom at a fundraiser was just the thing to do. Not that there was anything wrong with kinky sex if it was your thing, but the kinky sex hadn't been with *her*.

If it had been, maybe everything would still be okay—aside from the mortification factor of being caught, of course.

Instead, Ben had been caught with a woman named Chardonnay—seriously, Chardo-freaking-nnay for heaven's sake. Except that Chardonnay wasn't precisely a woman. She was an absolutely stunning drag queen who possessed the secret to creating beautiful knockers when in fact she didn't really have any at all.

Christina glanced down at her pitiful excuse for a chest and sighed. Dammit, outdone by someone who hadn't even been born with boobs.

Which, it turned out, Ben knew. He knew perfectly well that the person he was banging was a dude, as the audio recording had made evident when he demanded that Chardonnay fuck him in the ass with his big dick.

Christina shuddered. Dear God, what a mess.

She didn't have a single thing against being gay, but by God she drew the line at pretending to be something you weren't, especially when what you really were was a liar, a cheat, and a fraud. She'd actually argued with Ben about his stance on gay rights—and holy crap, he'd been such a hypocrite the entire time. He'd married her to pull off a political career, no other reason, and then he'd cheated on her with someone whose interests he'd actively campaigned against. It sickened her and angered her more than she could ever say.

And then there was the money. Oh yes, Ben had pretty much drained her trust fund in his quest for office. Apparently, getting elected took a *lot* of cash. As if having gay sex and stealing her money wasn't enough, Ben's actions had also made them the butt of late-night talk show jokes, tabloid fodder, and ensured that her coworkers were probably snickering behind their poker faces whenever she was in a meeting.

It hurt to think that all she'd worked so hard for took a secondary role to her position as the candidate's disgraced wife. It had been hard to leave the house in the aftermath of the scandal, but she'd forced herself to do so. Thankfully, it was getting easier all the time. The press had moved on from daily updates, and the only mentions in the tabloids now were when Chardonnay managed to gain some new publicity over the whole thing.

One thing was for sure, the drag queen's career was certainly on the upswing after the scandal.

"Hey, girls," Matt said, coming over and plopping down beside Evie. He was sweaty from volleyball, but he looked so damned happy that it made Christina's heart swell. He deserved to be happy. He'd protected her from more than she'd ever realized when they'd been kids.

He took a sip of Evie's drink, his gaze slipping over his wife's face. It knocked Christina in the gut to see how much her brother loved his wife. She wanted that kind of love in her life too.

She'd thought she'd had it, but she'd been wrong. Dreadfully, embarrassingly wrong.

"Glad you could make it today, Chris," he said, putting his arm behind Evie. "We haven't seen enough of you lately."

She shrugged as if everything in her life was perfectly normal. So long as she didn't fall apart in front of anyone, they couldn't worry, right? "Daddy's keeping me busy at work."

"Is he?"

Matt's voice was mild, but she saw the hardness in his eyes and her heart skipped. Of course she hadn't forgotten how Matt felt about their father, but she always hoped that one day the two of them would figure out their relationship. Not that their father had done very well at having a relationship with either one of them when it had counted the most. But he was clean and sober now, and things were different.

He'd never been violent, though he had been verbally abusive. Except she suspected that he'd sometimes taken his anger out on Matt in a physical way. It was the only thing she could think of that explained the animosity.

Yet she couldn't ask. She would never ask.

"There's a lot to be done in DC, and he doesn't like leaving Louisiana much these days. By the way, Misty Lee's planning their anniversary party at Reynier's Retreat—she wants him to announce his retirement."

Misty Lee was their father's fifth wife, also one of the ones he'd found in a strip club—except that Misty Lee was a gem and their father was head over heels in love with her. And she with him, which was somewhat of a surprise. But it worked for them, and that made Christina happy. Losing his wife—their mother—when Matt and Christina had been children hadn't been easy for any of them.

Matt's eyes widened. "Seriously?"

Christina nodded, happy to be talking about something other than Ben. "Yes, but I don't know that he's ready to give up the reins yet. Though maybe she'll get him to start considering it anyway. I expect, even if he announces he's going to retire, it'll be a couple of years down the road."

Like everything else in his life, their father hadn't always done a good job at Girard Oil—but that too had changed. He worked long hours, and he'd done a lot to keep the company in the black. That wasn't easy with the price of oil being so low these days.

Or with the trouble in the Middle East. Some companies were having trouble getting their supplies out, but so far Girard Oil hadn't been affected. The scandal with Ben had only made them more visible in the public eye—but not in a negative way, oddly enough. People sympathized. Girard Oil was a family institution, and one of the family had been hurt. They were angry *for* her, not at her.

"Are you ready to take over when that happens?" Matt asked softly, and her belly clenched.

"Why wouldn't I be?" She knew she sounded defensive, but no way was she letting anyone think she wasn't strong enough to weather her current difficulties. Besides, she wasn't sure her father planned to put her in charge anytime soon. Even if he retired tomorrow, there were others in the company more qualified to run it.

And maybe that would be better anyway.

No, stop saying that.

She worked hard at her job, and she'd worked hard to learn the business over the years. She might not have decades of experience, but she wasn't stupid. And she *was* a Girard.

Matt's gaze held hers for long moments, and she knew he sensed her turmoil. "You tell me, Chrissy."

Like everyone else, he attributed her mood to her personal situation.

"I'm fine. Ben and I were already finished, Matt. His public meltdown wasn't as much of a surprise as you might think."

Liar.

It had been a huge surprise, though it was true they hadn't actually had sex in about six months. She'd chalked it up to busy lives, etc., but really, who in the hell was she fooling?

Herself, that's who.

She'd been the only one who'd thought everything was perfectly fine. She'd thought they had goals, and while she'd missed the intimate contact, she'd thought as soon as everything calmed down and they spent more than a few hours in each other's company, everything would be normal again.

Matt frowned. "You hadn't even been married for two years yet."

"I know." She slid her finger through the condensation on her glass. What more could she say?

"Honey, if you want me to take some of the boys and go kick his ass for hurting you, we'd be happy to do it."

Christina hadn't expected that. It took her a second of wide-eyed surprise before she laughed. "I would love for you to go kick his ass, but I'm afraid you'd be the ones who got in trouble, not him."

Matt looked fierce. "He's not giving you any trouble in the divorce proceedings, is he?"

"No." Because her father was helping to make the divorce happen fast, which meant paying Ben to keep it uncontested. Not to mention that he'd already stolen all her money, so what was there to contest anyway? She'd liquidated her shares of Girard Oil by selling them to her father when she'd been raising funds for Ben's campaign. She had nothing left for her cheating ex to take, and he knew it.

Matt didn't know about the shares. She didn't want him to know either. If he did, she didn't know what he'd do to Ben. Since Matt was one scary badass these days, she didn't think it would be good. Or legal.

"Dude, you ditching us or what?"

Christina jerked her gaze toward the sound. It was the sexy tattooed guy who'd spoken. He stood mere feet away, tossing that volleyball back and forth in his hands, his muscles glistening with sweat.

But that wasn't what had her attention right now. No, it was his accent. It was unmistakably Cajun to her ears. Not thick, but with that certain cadence that someone from the bayou had. Matt had it. She had it to a degree, though she'd worked hard to lose it.

"Naw, man, I ain't ditching you," Matt drawled. "Crazy Cajun motherfucker."

The man snorted. "Takes one to know one, *mon ami*."

"Hey, you met my sister yet? Christina, this is Lieutenant Junior Grade Remy Marchand. Remy, this is my baby sister."

Christina offered her hand. He didn't take it.

"No, ma'am, don't want to get you sweaty. Pleased to meet you though."

"Where are you from, Lieutenant?" she asked in her best debutante voice.

"Near Lafayette, ma'am."

"Please. Call me Christina."

He grinned at her and her heart did a flip. "You play volleyball, Christina?"

She didn't bother to point out that she wasn't dressed

for volleyball in a dress and heels. "I'm afraid not."

He tossed the ball up and caught it. "Too bad. You coming, Girard, or what?" he said to Matt.

Matt kissed Evie on the cheek, kissed her belly, and stood. "I'm gonna wipe the floor with you, Marchand."

"You can try."

"Remy's easy on the eyes, isn't he?" Evie asked after the two men were gone.

Christina started guiltily. "Definitely so. But even if I wanted to—and I don't—I couldn't do anything about it."

"I understand."

Christina shifted in her seat. Damn tingly parts. "The divorce isn't even final yet. Not to mention, I'm a little wary of men and their motives right now."

Evie took a sip of her drink. "Well, whatever Ben's issues, I'm pretty sure Remy Marchand isn't into chicks with dicks."

Christina almost snorted her drink. "Oh God, I shouldn't laugh. I really shouldn't."

Evie grinned at her. "Honey, you have to laugh. It's that or cry—and that asshole doesn't deserve a single tear more."

Christina still ached—she would ache for a long time, she suspected—but yeah, her sister-in-law was right. Ben didn't deserve any more tears. He'd gotten enough.

"I wish I was the kind of woman who could take home a gorgeous guy like that and screw him silly," she said, watching Remy dart back and spike the ball. "Then I'd kick him to the curb and get on with life."

"There's always a first time for everything."

Christina shook her head. "No, I'm really not that brave."

Evie lifted an eyebrow. "You're Matt's sister. I don't buy it for a second, knowing that man the way I do. Tell a Girard he can't do something, and he'll be compelled to prove you wrong."

Christina laughed. "That's Matt, all right. Not sure it's me though."

Evie smiled. "Well, if you change your mind, you know where to find a whole boatload of gorgeous military guys, any one of whom would be happy to rock your world for a night."

Christina swallowed the knot in her throat. "I'll remember that."

She'd remember it. But she wouldn't do anything about it.

CHAPTER TWO

REMY FOUND HIMSELF looking at Matt Girard's sister more than he should. It had been a week since he'd met her at Matt's place, and now they were all hanging out at Buddy's Bar and Grill, slamming back beers, pizza, and wings, when Christina sashayed in.

She wasn't very tall, but she was rail thin, a wisp of a thing. She looked like a lawyer, dressed in a pencil skirt and heels, with her beautiful brown hair pinned in a bun at the base of her neck. She even wore a pair of glasses, which rounded out the whole lawyer look.

Or maybe she was a schoolteacher. He hadn't asked because, well, how could he?

She was pretty, though it wasn't just her beauty that attracted him. She seemed sad, vulnerable, like something wasn't quite right in her world. He didn't know what that was, and he wasn't going to ask about that either.

Though he wanted to. There was something about seeing her sad that bothered him. His damned savior complex coming to the fore again.

"You can't save the world, Remy," his sister had always said.

He knew that. Hell, when it counted the most, he hadn't even been able to save her. Remy swallowed down the bitterness that thought created. There wasn't a day that went by when he didn't miss his twin. She'd been an extension of him, the completer of his sentences, the other half of his entire existence in a way that only twins could be. He missed her like he would miss an arm or a leg, though that wasn't really an apt comparison. Never forgotten, always wanted. Always needed.

He took a swallow of his beer and concentrated his attention on Christina, shoving the sadness to the back of his mind and locking it up. It wouldn't stay there, but he could hold it back for a while.

She sipped a fruity drink at a high table with some of the other women, laughing when someone said something funny. He chalked his pool cue and watched her from beneath his lashes, his cock twitching with interest as she traced her finger around the rim of her glass, over and over and over.

As if she sensed him watching her, she turned her head and their gazes met. He thought about looking away but decided he wasn't going to do it. He met her gaze boldly, let her see the raw interest there. She didn't look away.

And then she did, her lashes dropping as she turned on the chair and faced Olivia Blake—wife of Alpha Squad operator Billy "the Kid" Blake—who sat across from her.

Remy went back to his pool game, but he didn't stop stealing glances at Christina. She wasn't wearing a wedding ring, though that didn't necessarily mean anything. Some women didn't wear them.

When she stood up from the table, he thought she might be leaving, but instead she headed for the back hallway and the restrooms. Before she disappeared, she turned and looked at him. He didn't know what that look meant, but he wanted to find out. He stopped dawdling, sank the rest of the balls in the pockets, and his teammate groaned.

"Cage, dammit, that's the fifth game in a row you've won."

Remy grinned and put the cue back in the wall rack. "Then you need to stop challenging me, don't you?"

Cody "Cowboy" McCormick rolled his eyes and peeled off a twenty-dollar bill that he then slapped on the edge of the table. "You've soaked me for a hundred bucks tonight."

Remy took the twenty and shoved it in his pocket. "I didn't tell you to keep coming back for more, did I? Your choice, Cowboy."

"Yeah, whatever." Cowboy picked up his beer and ambled off as two other guys waited for the table.

Remy took the opportunity to head for the restrooms. He wasn't sure if that look had meant anything at all. Hell, maybe it hadn't. Maybe she'd been looking at the table behind him, the one with her friends. Or at her brother, who stood at a bar table with his teammates, heads thrown back as they laughed about something.

He stopped in the darkened hallway and told himself this was crazy. Christina hadn't been looking at him, and he wasn't the kind of guy who followed women into restrooms.

Public-bathroom sex was not his thing. Not at all.

Not that he thought Christina was the sort to engage in such a thing, especially with her brother fifteen feet away. Or maybe she was. Maybe she liked a little danger.

The ladies' room door opened and she walked out, pulling up short when she saw him standing there. Her eyes widened slightly and she swallowed as if she were a little nervous.

"Um, hi again," she said.

"Hi."

"I… I…" She closed her eyes and shook her head. "Dammit," she muttered.

Remy didn't know what to say, so he didn't say anything. She'd sort it out eventually.

Her head lifted, and she looked as if she'd turned on a switch somewhere deep inside. A switch that people like him didn't have. He knew she came from money. Hell, everyone in Louisiana knew the Girard name.

But that hoity-toity superiority thing had never set well with him before, and it wasn't going to start now. No matter how cute she was.

She was every inch the elite debutante as she stared down her nose at him. No mean trick since she was several inches shorter.

"I'm sorry if I've given you mixed signals. The truth is I have no idea what I'm doing." She spread her hands, dropping her gaze from his. "You seem nice. No, you seem sexy and appealing, and I'm going through a divorce, which I'm sure you know. He cheated on me, and well, I think I'm doing this for all the wrong reasons, so maybe you should just turn around and go."

Okay, now *that* was different.

And he should definitely go.

But he wasn't going to.

Her speech didn't make a helluva lot of sense—why would he know she was getting divorced?—but he got the gist. Her rat of a husband had cheated on her, and she wanted to get back in the saddle. Prove she was still desirable. Yeah, that kinda kicked him in the chest in some weird way, but at least she was honest about it.

Which was new since he didn't usually run across women who talked about their motives straight up.

"He's a stupid fucker, Christina. You're gorgeous, and even if he decided he didn't want to be with you anymore, he should have had the balls to tell you that. Cheating is a dick move."

She blinked. And then she started to giggle. *Oookay*, girl was definitely not playing with a full deck here tonight.

She slapped a hand over her mouth and tried to hold the giggles in. He found that he wanted to laugh too—but he couldn't. If he did, he'd be as cracked as she was. Especially since he really didn't know what they were laughing at.

"Oh God," she said after a moment of helplessly gulping air to calm herself. "You must think I'm insane."

"I'm beginning to wonder," he said, but he grinned to soften the words.

She searched his face as if she expected to find an answer there. "You really don't know, do you?"

"Know what?"

"About my husband? About the drag queen?"

Remy thought that if eyebrows could climb a face, his were doing it right now. "Honey, I have no idea what you're talking about. But I've got to admit it's intriguing."

Christina pressed a hand to her middle. She was slightly built, but she had curves. She smiled at him and he felt like someone had knocked him in the back of the head with a hammer. Damn, she was pretty.

"You must not read the papers. Or watch much television."

"I'm in the Navy, *cher*. I don't have a lot of time for gossip. HQ tells me what I need to know, and then I go to work fixing the bad stuff."

She darted her tongue out to lick her lower lip, and his groin tightened. Jesus.

"Well, you're probably the only person I've run into who has no idea then. I find that rather refreshing. Except now you want to know what happened, so there goes your ignorance of the situation." She sucked in a breath. "Nevertheless, you can google, so I'll give you the gist."

She leaned toward him. He wondered if she was drunk, but she didn't sway or have glassy eyes, so he decided she wasn't. She was just fond of the dramatic.

"Ben—that's my rat-bastard soon-to-be ex—got caught getting fucked in the ass by a guy with boobs bigger than mine at a political fundraiser. So there you go. Google away for your amusement."

Honestly, she didn't know why she was telling him that. Or why she'd been giving him looks all night. What was she going to do? Haul him into the bathroom and take a page from Ben's book? Bang a hot guy in a public restroom just to get back at her soon-to-be ex who didn't care what she did?

No, she hadn't thought she was going to do that at all when she'd caught Remy's gaze right before disappearing into the bathroom. She didn't know why she'd looked back at him, except that they'd been playing some sort of eye-tag game all night. She'd been sitting at the table with Evie and the girls, feeling his gaze on her as she sipped her appletini.

And yes, the alcohol started to slide into her veins, making her feel good. She'd only had two—it didn't take much since she was such a lightweight drinker—but she'd suddenly felt like she could conquer the world.

Or at least conquer one gorgeous, dark-eyed Cajun with tattoos that she was dying to see again. So she'd kept looking up, meeting his eyes. Encouraging him even while she asked herself what the hell she was doing.

Now he was looking at her with a heavy frown on his handsome face. She'd expected the same mixture of horror and pity she got from most people. She hadn't expected anger, which was what was going on in those dark eyes. He was pissed *for* her. She liked that.

"Like I said, he's a stupid fucker. Are you okay?"

Christina blinked. Now that wasn't something most people asked. Oh, they did ask, but not like that. Not like they meant it. It was always syrupy sweet, unless it was her family asking, and designed more to elicit information than anything.

But Remy Marchand seemed to mean it.

"I… Yes, I'm okay."

"That's good, *cher.*"

"Do you want to get some coffee?" she blurted, her heart pattering in her chest.

Oh God, now wasn't that a stupid question? He would want to get away from her, not have coffee with her.

He grinned that sexy grin of his. "Yeah, I'd like that."

"Really? You don't have to say yes because you feel sorry for me. I get that most people do, but I really hate—"

She didn't expect him to reach out and touch her, his fingers curving around her neck as he stepped closer and lowered his mouth to hers. The contact of his mouth was shocking, in fact.

And delicious. He didn't kiss her hard, didn't try to shove his tongue into her mouth. He just moved his lips against hers, lightly and sweetly, and she found herself melting against him, her hands coming up to clutch at his T-shirt.

Her body started tingling again. The wetness between her legs was a surprise only because it happened so fast. She didn't even know this man. In fact, she should be pushing him away, not pulling him closer.

Christina made a sound in her throat. It was frustration and need all rolled into one. She wanted him to deepen the kiss, to give her more of him, but he didn't. He lifted his head, breaking the contact, and she clung to him, suddenly dizzy.

"I don't feel sorry for you," he said, his deep voice a cross between a growl and a caress. "I want to have coffee with you, Christina."

She sucked in a breath, ridiculously ready to cry for some reason. Instead, she uncurled her fists from his shirt and tried to smile.

"Well, then. Coffee."

"Yeah, coffee."

"Now? Or maybe you'd prefer tomorrow—"

"Now, *cher*. I want coffee now. With you, just so you're clear."

"Great. Okay. I'll get my purse and say good-bye."

"Yeah, you do that. Meet you out front in five minutes."

CHAPTER THREE

THEY RODE IN separate cars and met at a coffee shop tucked away on a side street. They were far enough from Buddy's that probably no one would find them there. Then again, why did he care if they did?

It was coffee, for fuck's sake.

Remy was still processing that kiss. He didn't know why he'd kissed her, except that he'd just felt an overwhelming urge to do so. Her lips were sweet and soft, and when she'd clung to him, he'd wanted to squeeze her tight and not let go.

"So," she said, running her finger around the rim of her cup, not making eye contact. "Here we are."

"Here we are."

She looked up a few moments later, puzzlement creasing her forehead. "This is awkward, isn't it?"

Remy took a sip of his coffee. Strong and sweet, that's how he liked it when he had a choice. Out in the field, he'd take it run through a sock if that's how it had to happen.

Which sometimes it did.

"Is it?"

Her brows drew together. "You aren't a man of many words, are you?"

"I can be. Right now I'm busy figuring you out."

She snorted. "There's not much to figure out. My husband dumped me in a very public and humiliating way. It's still the butt of late-night jokes sometimes. I'm confused and lonely and maybe even a bit desperate."

"Desperate?"

She shrugged, but her gaze dropped again. "You know. For sex. It's been about nine months now."

And didn't that just make his cock start to harden?

"Are you normally this blunt?"

He knew Matt fairly well since the SEALs had joined HOT, but they weren't teammates. And while Matt was direct and blunt when he had to be, he was a guy. In Remy's experience, women weren't usually so forthcoming.

"Actually, no. And maybe I should be. Maybe if I'd been blunt with Ben, I wouldn't be in this predicament."

"Blunt how? *Get that dick out of your ass, fuckwad, because we're married?* How do you think that would have worked out anyway?"

She shook her head, but she didn't look sad. Just resigned.

"Of course that wouldn't have worked. But maybe I should have been more blunt back when we were dating. I should have asked why he always wanted the lights out and why he always wanted me on my hands and knees. Or ninety-nine percent of the time, anyway. Is that normal? Or does that sound like a guy who's gay and pretending not to be, because he sure as hell was never interested in my breasts—though he seemed to like Chardonnay's pretend ones just fine."

Jesus. Remy wanted to laugh at the twist of humor she put into her words, and he wanted to shut her up with his mouth. The shit she was saying was making him harder. He liked the idea of her on her hands and knees. He'd like to take her that way.

He'd also like to press her down into the mattress, her tits mashed to his chest, and fuck her until she screamed his name.

Remy reached for her hand, mostly to keep from kissing her in the middle of this coffee shop.

She bit her lip when his fingers twined in hers. Her gray eyes gazed into his, and he felt a kick somewhere in the pit of his stomach. Every last protective instinct he had was snapping into gear. He told himself she wasn't in danger, but that didn't seem to stop the feelings coursing through him.

"I told you the man's a jackass. If you were mine, I'd strip you slowly, kiss every delicious inch of you, and fuck you with all the lights on. Because I'd want to see everything. Your breasts, your belly, your pussy—and those gorgeous eyes of yours when I made you come. Yeah, *that* I'd want to see most of all."

A flush stained her cheeks even as her mouth dropped slightly open. "I can't believe you just said that to me. Or that I really, really want you to do it."

God, he wanted to do it too.

"Baby, you're hurting. You aren't thinking straight right now. Much as I want to do every last thing I just said, I think the right thing to do is maybe have another date or two first, don't you?"

"I… I don't think dating is for me right now."

He lifted her hand to his mouth, pressed a kiss on her soft skin. Then he let her go again because touching her electrified him. "Two more dates, Christina. Real dates where I pick you up and take you to dinner, maybe a movie. We can get to know each other. Make out some."

She stared at him for a long moment. "You're strange, you know that? Most men would go for the easy sex."

Yeah, he was strange, at least right now. But she intrigued him—and he hadn't been intrigued in a long time.

"I like easy sex as much as the next guy. But I'm pretty sure you'd regret it in the morning, and the last thing I want is to be a regret."

"I don't know what I'd think in the morning, quite honestly."

"How about we drink our coffee and talk about the kinds of things people talk about on a date?"

She sat back in her chair and gave him a look that smoldered even though he didn't think she intended it to. He really wanted to pull the pins from her hair and see it down like the day he'd met her.

He studied her. Her white shirt was buttoned all the way up to her neck, which was kind of ironic considering the conversation they'd been having. Her breasts were small and round. Every once in a while he saw a hint of lace as she leaned forward and her bra was outlined against the thin cotton of her shirt.

Her fingers were long and elegant where they gripped the cup, her nails done in that French thing that women liked. Her lips were full and kissable—which he knew from firsthand experience—and her eyes were sad and soulful.

"So tell me about you, Remy," she said. "Who is Remy Marchand and what does he like?"

He shrugged, slightly uncomfortable with the thought of talking about himself. Because tragedy was such a part of who he was, and he didn't want to go there yet.

"I'm a Navy SEAL. I like blowing things up and stopping the bad guys, among other things."

"Is your family still in Lafayette?"

"Yeah."

She looked at him expectantly. "That's it? Just yeah?"

"Nothing to tell, really. There are a lot of Marchands in Lafayette, and I'm probably related to most of them."

Which was as much as he was saying about his family. Remy thought of his mother, barely living since the hunting accident that had killed his father last year. He sent money home to supplement the social security she got after Dad died. He knew she had what she needed, but his sister Emma said that Mom hadn't left the house in two months now.

There wasn't much he could do about it, so he sent money and hoped Emma would figure it all out. If anyone could get his mother out of her blue period, it would be Emma.

He knew it didn't help that Roxie had been in the ground for the past four years. His family hadn't been the same since that had happened, and they all knew it.

Remy clenched his fist beneath the table, helpless anger welling inside him all over again at the fate that had befallen his twin.

He should have known what was going on. And he

should have fucking stopped it.

Too late.

"That must be nice, having so many relatives," Christina said softly, staring at her cup again. "There's just Matt and me and our dad now—and his wife, whom I love like a mother even if she's not much older than I am. Granny died a few years ago, and our mother died when we were kids."

"I'm sorry."

"Well, it happens, doesn't it? People die. One day, poof, gone."

Yeah, people died. One day they were vibrant and alive, and the next some asshole with emotional problems shot them dead. And you thought, *Fuck, you should have told me, Roxie.*

And then you thought that you should have fucking known the dude you'd grown up with, the guy who'd been your best friend, was an abuser and unstable. But you never knew it, and now it was too fucking late.

"Hey," Christina said, and Remy focused on her again. She was frowning at him. "Are you okay?"

Remy cleared his throat and picked up the coffee. "Yeah, fine."

She didn't look convinced. "You looked so fierce there. I thought maybe I'd said something."

"No, you didn't say anything. It's fine. Really."

He reached for her hand across the table again, threading his fingers through hers. One simple touch and he already felt calmer. What was it about her?

He didn't know, but he wanted to find out.

"So, we're doing this again. You, me, dinner. When's a good day?"

She dropped her gaze to their hands. "I don't know if there is a good day," she said softly. "My life… it's crazy right now."

He snorted. "*Cher*, I'm a SEAL. Believe me, I understand crazy."

She lifted her head. Their eyes met, and something kicked in his gut. Maybe it kicked in hers too, because she gave his hand a light squeeze.

"Okay. Saturday night then."

CHAPTER FOUR

WHY HAD SHE agreed to go on a date? Christina stood in her bathroom, staring at her reflection in the mirror and asking herself for the millionth time if this outfit was the one.

She'd changed four times. The dress she wore now was too flowery, too virginal. It was cream with little pink primroses all over it. She'd paired it with kitten heels and a white cardigan because it was often cold in restaurants.

Then she'd put on her mama's pearls—and she looked like a damned '50s housewife. June Cleaver or Mrs. Cunningham, maybe. Starched and perfect when she was anything but. Why couldn't she loosen up a bit? Her father had married a succession of strippers after her mother died, yet her feminine role model had been her grandmother. Not that she needed to dress like a stripper, but the point was that none of those women had dressed like strippers on a pole while married to her father, either.

They'd been young and sexy, which was what she should be.

She had just ducked back into her closet to find yet another outfit when the doorbell rang. Her heart lodged in her throat.

Damn, no time.

Why had she given Remy her address? She should have insisted on meeting him at the restaurant, but she'd had a moment of weakness and thought it would be nice if he picked her up.

She'd learned over the years how to talk to people, how not to be a total introvert, but that didn't mean she didn't need a kick out the front door. Left to her own devices, she could think up a dozen reasons to call off an outing.

She took a deep breath as the buzzer sounded again, and strode toward the front door. A quick peek through the peephole verified the man standing on the other side.

And oh dear Lord, her pulse quickened at the sight of all that muscle and leashed strength outside her door. Ben had not been strong, not like that. He was tall and lean, lightly muscled. Nothing like Remy Marchand.

Christina swung the door open and pasted on a smile. "You're early."

His gaze slid down her form, and her heart responded by beating even faster. When he looked into her eyes again, a slow grin spread across his face.

"Military habit. Damn, you look good, Christina."

She had to fight an urge to giggle. What the heck was that about? She was so not a giggler. *Nerves.*

"Like the Junior League look, do you?"

"Didn't realize it until tonight, but yeah, I do. At least on you."

"Do you want to come in?"

His gaze slipped over her once more. "I'd love to, but I don't think it's safe. You'd better get your purse and lock up. If I come in, I don't think we'll leave anytime soon."

And there it was again, that glorious tingle between her thighs. It had been too long. Too, too long.

"Remind me again why that's a bad idea?" she asked.

"Because you need to eat, that's why. And so do I."

Christina got her purse and locked the door. Remy escorted her down the steps and out to the pickup truck sitting by the curb. He opened the door and helped her inside, then went around and got in the driver's seat.

"Where are we going?" she asked.

"A little place I bet you haven't been to before. There's a town on the Chesapeake Bay where you can get the best seafood you've ever had in your life."

"Isn't that sacrilege considering where you're from?"

He laughed. "Yeah, probably so. Still, when I can't get back to Louisiana, this place reminds me of home."

"You know they steam the crabs here, right?" Of course she knew that he knew they didn't boil crabs in Maryland the way they did in Louisiana, but teasing him was fun. It was easy being with Remy. She liked that.

"Yeah, well, we'll have to make do, won't we?"

The ride to the restaurant took about an hour. The little town sat on the bay, its picturesque harbor filled with sailboats that bobbed in the current. It was different from her place in DC—quieter, more peaceful.

She could use some peace in her life right now.

Remy parked the truck near a dilapidated restaurant, then came around to help her out. They walked to the shack hand in hand. It was nice. Kind of weird, but nice. She hadn't been out with a man other than Ben in about four years now.

Once they were seated, the waitress brought laminated menus. The restaurant was definitely more of a dive bar than a fancy joint, but the smells were heavenly. Remy ordered a seafood platter and a beer. After deliberation, Christina ordered the same. Why get a salad just to impress a man? She was done with impressing anyone but herself.

"Hungry?" Remy asked with a grin.

Christina shrugged. "Maybe so."

"Going to enjoy watching you pick crabs apart in pearls and a dress."

"Wouldn't be the first time," she said a touch smugly.

Remy laughed. "I suppose that should come as no surprise, you being a Girard and all."

Christina's heart thumped the way it always did when someone mentioned her family name in connection with her upbringing. If they only knew the hell that being a Girard had been. But when you had money, nobody cared that you were lonely and ignored or that your father was cold and uninvolved in your life.

And then there were the times when he'd screamed at Matt for no real reason she could tell. He'd screamed at her too, but not often. Matt usually took the brunt of it. Once he'd left for West Point, she'd expected their father to take his anger out on her instead.

He'd only done it once. She remembered him screaming at her, calling her names—and then Granny was there and he went quiet. Christina had fled the room, so she never knew what Granny said. But Granny came and stayed with them after that. She stayed until the school year was over—and Christina's father had never yelled at her again.

"Hey," Remy suddenly said, his forehead creasing in a frown. "I didn't mean that as an insult or anything."

Christina forced a smile. "No, I know. It's just..." She sighed. "Sometimes what looks really great on the outside isn't so great on the inside. Money doesn't make you happy."

"I've never had any, but yeah, I can see where that would be true. I hope it wasn't too bad."

The waitress brought their beers then, and Christina sipped hers straight from the bottle. It was a small rebellion since she'd always been told that ladies asked for glasses and poured their beer if it wasn't draft. *Sorry, Granny.*

"No, not bad. Just a bit lonely, I guess. Matt was always doing his own thing. Our father wasn't home a lot—and when he was, he was drunk. I already told you our mother died when we were young. I spent a lot of time with my grandmother. She lived in Baton Rouge, and her house was like a refuge to me. Except for the part where she insisted on sending me to Junior Cotillion. But heck, Matt had to go too, so there was that."

Remy took a drink of his own beer. "I never did anything like that."

"You didn't miss anything really."

Her phone rang, startling her. She hadn't been expecting a call, which meant it was probably work.

"I'm sorry," she said, fishing in her purse. "I'm working on an important business deal, and I need to check this." Answering a phone during dinner was something she'd learned *not* to do in Cotillion, but sometimes she had to for the sake of the company.

Remy shrugged. "It's okay."

She took the phone out and glanced at it. She debated answering but decided she could take it later.

"It's my father," she explained as she put the phone away again.

"Do you want to take it?"

"No, it can wait until later. It's probably something business related." But not related to her deal, because he wasn't involved in that. He never called her about anything important. It was either mundane business stuff or something to do with Misty Lee and the party. She was betting on Misty Lee.

"You work in the family business?"

"Actually, yes. I trained as a petroleum engineer, though I'm more on the business side of things these days. I'm responsible for seeking new business and making sure Girard Oil presents a good picture to our potential partners. Not very exciting compared to what you do."

"And what does a petroleum engineer do exactly?"

"Well, we try to find more efficient ways to extract oil and gas. Before I moved to business development, I spent a lot of time in the lab and a lot of time in the field testing processes and equipment."

His gaze sharpened with interest. "Did you ever go out of the country for the job?"

"Sometimes. Russia and the Middle East mostly, though I've been to South America as well. I still go to those places, though I'm typically meeting with potential new clients."

"Does your company hire security for when you travel to those regions?"

The food arrived then, and they were quiet while the waitress set down the plates and asked if they had everything they needed. After the waitress had walked away again, Christina picked up her mallet. Remy was still watching her.

Waiting for an answer.

"You sound like Matt," she said. "And the answer is that it depends on where I go. I'll take a bodyguard when I go to Qu'rim, for instance."

"Qu'rim?" His voice had grown deeper, his brows arrowing down into a hard frown.

Christina cracked a crab. "We're working on a deal to import Qu'rimi oil. There's a sheikh I've been working with who is very keen to expand his business interests outside the country."

"You can't go to Qu'rim, Christina. It's dangerous. Volatile."

Christina glanced up at the tone of his voice. It had hardened quite a lot over the last few words.

He waited until she was looking at him before he continued. "Qu'rim is at war with itself, and no one is certain from one day to the next who's going to win. There's no guarantee this sheikh will even have any oil if the rebels win the war. Civilians shouldn't be traveling there. Hell, the State Department has issued enough warnings to circle the earth three times if they were all laid out together."

Christina frowned. "It's not that many warnings, and you know it. Besides, we're still working the details. I may not go at all if Sheikh Fahd doesn't agree to our terms." And while she knew there could be problems if the rebels won, Sheikh Fahd's wells were in the north, far from the fighting. He also had a port where the crude was loaded onto barges and shipped out. She wanted his crude for Girard Oil's refineries. It was a gamble to take his business, but it was also a buyer's market right now, and he was sitting on a lot of oil. If she could get it for the right price, it would be an important acquisition for the long term.

She thumped another crab and it cracked satisfyingly. Then she pulled out the sweet-tasting meat and popped it in her mouth.

"It would be better if you didn't. Could be years before Qu'rim is safe."

She laid the mallet down. Remy's gaze was intense, hot, and it made her belly clench. She barely knew this man and he barely knew her. But there was a powerful attraction between them, that much was clear.

Yet there were some compromises she would not make. She'd done her time trying to please a man, trying to be what he wanted her to be, and she was finished. Remy Marchand was a fling, if it happened. A sex partner to make her forget the shitty hand Ben had dealt her.

She was honest enough with herself to admit that. Remy was man candy, not a meal. She didn't want a meal, anyway.

And she really resented his trying to tell her what to do, even if she knew it came from a place of real concern. Matt had said much the same, in fact.

"Thanks for your advice, Remy, but this really isn't up to you. I hope that's not too blunt."

His eyes sparked. "You've certainly been nothing less than blunt since I met you. Don't stop now, by all means."

Christina folded her hands on the napkin in her lap. If ever there was a time to draw the line in the sand, this was it. "All right, if you insist. I'm not looking for a relationship here. I'm not even officially divorced yet, quite honestly, though it's merely a formality now. Not that it matters since Ben is most definitely not interested in reconciliation. But I can't start dating right now, and I don't think I really want to. I don't have anything to give in that department."

He didn't speak for a long moment, and she started to squirm.

"So it's sex or nothing, huh?" he finally said, his eyes hotter than ever.

A sudden urge to run erupted within her. Instead, she faced him squarely. "Pretty much."

He nodded slowly, deliberately. "All right, *cher*. We'll do it your way. But don't say I didn't try."

CHAPTER FIVE

REMY WAS PISSED, but he wasn't going to let her know it. They'd finished the meal, had a nice walk along the dock, and now they were in his truck again and on the way back to her place.

Sex. All she wanted was sex. Hell, he should be completely down with that—and he *was* down with that, no doubt—but he was also feeling a bit jacked that she only wanted him to fuck her.

Christina Girard was a lady. A beautiful, elegant lady in a flowery dress and pearls who wanted him to bare her body and make her forget about her dick of an ex.

He knew all about her asshole husband now. He'd googled her just like she'd suggested. The tale was sordid, and she was most definitely the injured party.

Christina was damaged by what her husband had done. He got that, and he got that it was too soon for her to think about something else. But for the first time that he could remember, he wanted to know a woman. It wasn't love or anything like that, but it was more than just sex for him.

He wanted it to be more, but she didn't. And that pissed him off.

He didn't know why she'd picked him out of the guys who'd been at Buddy's that night, but she had. He could either do what she wanted and hope it went further once she realized how good they could be together, or he could walk away.

He was seriously considering the merits of both as they drove. Christina talked to him about her job because he'd asked, but a lot of it was white noise for him. He pulled the truck up in front of her place and put it into park. He did not shut off the engine, however.

And he didn't take his hands from the wheel.

It was dark and her porch light was on. Manners dictated he walk her to her door, but he couldn't quite make himself do it just yet. If he could just sit here and get his disappointment and anger under control, it would all be okay.

She was silent and so was he. Then she unclipped her seat belt. It was louder than he expected it to be, and he turned his head to look at her. She was sitting there looking so sweet and pretty, her eyes big and innocent, her dark hair falling over her shoulders.

"Do you want to come in?" Her voice was small, tentative, and he knew she was feeling the strain as much as he was.

"I shouldn't. But I'll walk you to the door."

"All right."

He turned off the truck and got out. She got out of her side before he could go over and open the door. She met him on the sidewalk in front of the truck, and they walked up to her door slowly. They didn't touch.

And then they were there on her porch and she gazed up at him, those eyes tempting him all over again.

He thought about giving her a peck on the cheek, telling her to call him when she was ready for something more, but she took the choice away from him.

Before he knew what she was planning, she closed the distance between them, stood on tiptoe, and curled a hand around his neck. He bent to her automatically, though he hadn't intended to.

She kissed him. It wasn't a sweet kiss, or a goodnight kiss. It was a hot, wet kiss that had him yanking her against his body and thrusting his tongue into her mouth. One touch and his control evaporated like dew in the desert.

Her arms wrapped around his neck and her body arched into his. Goddamn, it wasn't supposed to go like this. He'd been planning to walk away, no matter what he'd said to her earlier about playing the game her way.

But his dick was hard and his body felt electric in a way he couldn't recall feeling before. He must have felt this way at least once in his life, but damn if he could remember when.

He pushed her against the door, molded his body to hers. She responded, her hand slipping down his chest, his abdomen, over the bulge in his jeans.

She moaned as she ran her hand over him, and he shuddered with the force of the need cresting inside. He was an animal, a hard male animal who wanted nothing more than to take this woman and find his pleasure in her body.

Still, he managed to step back, to try to inject some sense in this situation. He held her by the shoulders, their bodies no longer touching. His body ached for hers, but he had to be strong.

"Think about what you're doing," he said, his voice hoarse.

"I *am* thinking about it. I want you, Remy. It's been so long and I need this." She sucked in a breath then. "But if you don't want me—"

A little sob escaped her throat, and Remy stiffened. "Christina, it's not that. I want you. I definitely want you. You felt the evidence… But damn, honey, I want to be more than a revenge fuck, okay?"

Her eyes glittered with unshed tears. "I want more too. But I'm scared. I'm scared it's too soon and I don't know what I'm doing. I'm scared you aren't what you seem to be, and that tomorrow you'll walk away—I'm scared of so many things."

Of all the possible things she could have said, this was the one thing he couldn't resist. He slipped his hands from her shoulders, cupped her cheeks, his thumbs gliding over her cheekbones.

"You don't have to be scared with me, Christina. I'm not walking away."

"We don't even know each other," she whispered, her eyes still glittering as a hot tear slipped over the edge and spilled onto his skin.

"We know enough, don't we? There's something here. It may be inconvenient. It may be unusual. But it's here, and we owe it to ourselves to figure it out, don't you think?"

She didn't say anything for a long moment. His heart

felt like it slowed to nothing, but then she nodded and it started to beat again.

"Stay with me, Remy. Come inside and stay with me."

"*Cher*, there's nowhere else I'd rather be."

CHAPTER SIX

CHRISTINA DIDN'T QUITE know what she was saying, but she knew she couldn't let him go. Not tonight. Not when it was vitally important somehow that she climb back on that horse and remember what it was like to be wanted.

She unlocked the door with trembling fingers, the big man behind her making her shiver. Not from fear.

From need. From want. From anticipation.

She got the door open and stepped inside. Remy was right behind her, closing the door and locking it before he turned to face her again. She stood in the foyer with her heart pounding and her knees shaking, wondering if she'd bitten off more than she could chew.

It wasn't too late to tell him she'd changed her mind, that she couldn't do this.

But, oh, how could she say no to this man?

She let her gaze run over him, looking her fill. He was tall, broad, his heather-gray henley stretching over muscles that were glorious to look at. He was clean-shaven with a strong jawline. His hair was dark, cropped short because he was in the military, and his eyes were a piercing blue as he watched her.

He didn't look safe at all—but he looked like someone who would keep *her* safe. Someone who wouldn't let anything bad happen to her.

Looks were deceiving. Ben hadn't looked like the kind of man who would cheat and lie and stomp on her heart. He hadn't looked like he'd steal all her money and make a mockery of her love.

He'd done all those things. No, you couldn't tell a damned thing about someone just by looking at them.

Or by touching them. Hell, you couldn't tell anything at all. You just took your chances every day and hoped you weren't wrong.

And when you were wrong? Well, you got your guts ripped out and stomped on.

"Second thoughts, *cher?*"

Her pulse kicked at the evidence he could read her so easily. What was it about him? What was it that drew her even while she should be running in the opposite direction?

"These days, always."

And that was the other thing about him. She couldn't help but tell him the truth. She always said what was on her mind, though she was typically the sort of person who considered all the angles before speaking. Not with Remy. With him, she just kind of laid it out there.

One corner of his mouth lifted in a grin. He was so sexy it hurt. Really, truly sexy. And he wanted her, which was thrilling and frightening all at once.

"I love that you're so blunt with me. Tell it like it is, Christina. Always tell it like it is."

"I'm not usually this direct," she admitted. "But for some reason, I can't seem to be anything but honest with you."

"Good. Let's keep it that way, all right?"

She nodded.

"Now, how about you tell me if you want me to get in my truck and go home or stay here? Either way, I'm calling you tomorrow."

Christina's heart thudded. Yes, she was scared, dammit. And yet the idea of him leaving made her chest tighten. The only way she was getting through this was by forging ahead and doing it. She closed the distance between them and slipped her palms over his chest, thrilling at the hard peaks of muscle.

"I don't want you to go, Remy. I want you to stay right here and make me feel good about myself again."

His arms went around her, but he held her loosely. "I want to do that for you, baby. But you've got nothing to feel bad about, okay? Your soon-to-be ex lied to you about his sexuality. His inability to be faithful to you has nothing to do with you and everything to do with him. You got that?"

His words made warmth flare in her chest. "Yes."

He tipped her chin up with his fingers, stepped in closer. "One more thing, baby, and this one is important."

"What?"

"If you're doing this to get back at him, don't do it. He won't care and you will, so think about that for a minute."

Oh God, if her heart wasn't so bruised and battered, if

she weren't completely convinced that she was never trusting a man again, she might just fall in love with Remy Marchand.

Except that was impossible because she'd known him for barely over a week. Nobody fell in love in a week. And definitely not when they were still reeling from the last relationship they'd been in.

That was called rebounding, and she wasn't going to rebound.

"I won't say that getting back at him never occurred to me," she said softly. "It did, precisely three seconds after I met you the first time. But you're right, Ben wouldn't care even if he knew. The only thing he cares about is himself. If I offered to take him back tomorrow, he *might* come running—but only because it might salvage his political career, no other reason."

"Damn, baby."

She loved the quiet condemnation in his voice, the way she could hear everything he didn't say just by his tone. She'd always been careful what she said to people who knew her and Ben, including her brother and Evie. But with Remy she could say whatever she wanted. He didn't know Ben, and he didn't care about him. Not that Matt and Evie cared about him either, but they cared about her in a way that meant they got really angry whenever the subject of Ben came up.

She took Remy's hand and led him up the stairs to her bedroom. When he reached the threshold, he stopped. She turned and watched him looking at her bedroom.

It was utterly feminine, with soft white and pink flowers on the coverlet, frilly shams, and white furniture mixed with antiques. The floors were wood overlaid with

Oriental carpets. There was a television on a dresser, and the remnants of her frantic wardrobe search earlier lay across the bed.

She went over and scooped up the clothes, dropping them on a soft pink Queen Anne chair. Remy still hadn't moved.

"Too girly for you?" she asked, arching one eyebrow as she did so. Yes, she was nervous—and yes, this situation was funny considering the way he looked at her room like someone had set off a Strawberry Shortcake explosion.

His gaze met hers then and her heart skipped. God, he was pretty. So masculine and beautiful. Definitely not the kind of man who belonged in a Laura Ashley/shabby chic boudoir.

"It's pretty girly, yeah. But it suits you."

She ran her hand over the coverlet automatically, smoothing out wrinkles. Ridiculous considering he was here to mess the bed up as much as possible.

"In case you're wondering, Ben never slept in this bed. It was our guest bed. When we split up, I moved out and took this furniture with me."

"Yeah, I was wondering." He stepped into the room then, his dark form at odds with the frilly decor. His hands were shoved into his jeans pockets, and a little thrill ran over her at the idea of undressing him.

She realized she'd picked up a pillow and held it to her middle. She set it down carefully, fluffing it as she did so, her throat suddenly dry. Remy was too smart to think she'd been straightening it in the first place. She didn't know why she even tried to make him think the action was deliberate when they both knew it wasn't.

"Come here, Christina."

She swallowed—and then she walked over to him. He reached for her, curled a hand around her waist, and tugged her in close. Oh, she loved the strength of him. The way he took charge of the situation.

"This is what's going to happen," he said, his voice a growly rumble. "First, I'm going to kiss you until you melt. Then I'm going to undress you and lay you down on that pretty bed where I plan to explore every inch of you with my fingers and tongue. Sound like something you'd enjoy?"

Christina's belly tightened with need. "Yes," she whispered.

"Good, because that's not all. I'm going to lick you, baby, thoroughly and deeply, until you come hard on my tongue. Then you're going to ride my cock until neither one of us knows our name anymore. I plan to be here for hours, you understand? In you, on you, under you—*cher*, I want it all before I'm through. If this doesn't work for you, you need to tell me now."

Oh God. Her heart thundered and her ears burned, but yeah, she needed every bit of that right now. Every bit of Remy.

"It works for me."

He smiled a slow, wicked smile. "Glad to hear it, *ma petite*."

CHAPTER SEVEN

REMY KNEW SHE was nervous. But she wanted this, that much was clear. Her pretty eyes dilated, her bottom lip dropped, and her tongue darted out to lick it. He practically groaned.

Yeah, there was something special about this girl. Something that made the need hammering through him practically hurt. He wanted her, and he wanted to make her happy. He didn't want her to regret a moment of this.

His gaze lifted and slid over the room. Goddamn, it was so frilly and girly it ought to make his skull ache, but it fit her. Christina Girard was a lady. A soft, gentle lady who didn't deserve the shit being heaped on her by her asshole of an almost-ex-husband.

It was a wonder her brother hadn't pounded the guy into the dirt yet. Then again, it was probably a good thing considering what he was capable of—what all the HOT guys were capable of.

Remy had planned to start kissing her right here, but

he bent and put an arm behind her knees, sweeping her up and into his arms as easily if she were a feather. She gasped softly, her arms winding around his neck as he carried her the few steps to the bed. It was totally unnecessary to pick her up considering how close the bed was, but there was something about doing so that felt right.

He put a knee on the bed and laid her back on it, coming down on top of her. He could feel her heart hammering in her chest in the moment before he lifted himself up and put a little bit of space between them.

He kissed her gently, softly, but she didn't seem to want soft. She lifted her head and kissed him harder, her tongue demanding where it stroked against his.

All right, he could change the pace if that's what she wanted. He held himself up on his elbows, his hands cupping her face as he devoured her mouth.

She moaned as she met him eagerly, their tongues tangling and bodies straining to rub against each other.

Shit, he was hard. So fucking hard that every shimmy of her hips sent an ache arrowing into his balls and up to the base of his spine.

Her hands glided down his sides, around to cup his ass. She pulled him harder to her, and he began to get the idea about how this was really going to go. No leisurely kisses while he stoked the fire. No working up to undressing her. No slow burn for Christina.

She wanted to go up in flames right away. Well, hell, he could do that.

He got to his knees, reached for the belt at her waist, and unbuckled it. Christina sat up and he found the zipper at her back, slid it down until she could slip her arms free of the dress. Another few seconds and he lifted it over her head and tossed it aside.

Her bra and panties were white and lacy. Sensible, but still sexy. And fuck him, she was still wearing those pearls.

She must have followed his gaze because she reached for the clasp. He put a hand over hers, stopping her.

"Leave them on, *cher.*"

She blinked, but then she smiled. "All right."

He'd have never guessed it, but there was something about the idea of being cock-deep in a woman wearing pearls that turned him on.

He reached behind his head and grabbed a handful of the henley, pulling it off and dropping it. Then he pressed Christina back into the bed and attacked her mouth again. She moaned as she wrapped her arms around him, arching her body up to his.

And oh, he so got it. Because they were skin to skin for the first time. Yeah, she still had her bra on, but he could fix that. He reached beneath her and unsnapped it, lifting it off before lowering himself again.

This time there was nothing between their torsos but hot, silky skin. He glided a hand to her breast, cupped the small roundness in his palm. Her nipple was a tight peak that he rubbed back and forth beneath his thumb while she gasped into his mouth.

When he couldn't take it a moment longer, he tore his mouth from hers and sucked her nipple, flicking it with his tongue as he drew her deep.

Her fingers curled into his shoulders. "Oh, Remy. Damn, that feels good…"

He feathered his fingers down her body, over her soft skin, before sliding beneath the waistband of her panties and into the slick heat of her sex. She bowed beneath him as he found her clitoris and stroked it.

"Oh my God…"

She made a choked sound, her body stiffening, and then she cried out. He was so surprised he had to push himself up and look at her. Her cheek was turned into the pillow, her eyes were closed tight, and her skin flushed a pretty pink.

"You came," he said. "Jesus."

"It's been a long time," she whispered. "What can I say?"

A hot, possessive feeling flooded him then. He wanted to cherish her, make her feel as good as possible for as long as he could.

"I need to taste you," he said hoarsely, slipping her panties from her hips and down her slim legs.

She was looking at him again as he knelt over her, her eyes glittering, and he knew she was close to crying. It made him hesitate.

"Do you want me to leave?"

She shook her head.

"Are you gonna be okay, baby?"

She nodded.

"You need me to give you some time?"

He didn't know what she needed, but he knew that the look on her face was breaking his heart. Like she was shocked she could still feel pleasure or that anyone would want to give it to her.

Jesus, what a mind fuck it had to be when the person you married turned out not to be the person you thought they were.

"Take your pants off, Remy. I'd feel better if you

were as naked as I am."

"Honey, that's not a problem at all, trust me." He started to undo his belt, but she suddenly sat up, folding her knees under her, and reached for the strap.

"Let me."

"All right."

She flicked the belt open and then went for his button fly. It was sweet torture to have her hands brushing his hard cock through his underwear, but he managed to survive. When she got the last button undone, she leaned in and pressed her mouth to his pec while shoving his jeans down his hips.

Remy hissed at the touch of her tongue on his skin. He threaded the fingers of his right hand into her hair and cupped her skull as she explored him.

"You're so beautiful, Remy," she said, her voice vibrating against muscle and bone. "So big and beautiful."

She swirled her tongue around his nipple at the same time she wrapped a hand around his cock, and he hissed in a breath once more.

"Christina, dammit…"

"Fair's fair."

Before she could do any more damage to his control, he put his hands under her arms and picked her up, tossing her back on the bed and pouncing on her.

He caught her arms, ringing her wrists with one hand and pushing them above her head. If she'd shown the slightest ounce of hesitation or fear, he'd have let her go.

Instead, she hooked her toes in his jeans where they were lying around his knees and pushed them farther down. He kicked them off, and they disappeared over the side of the bed.

"I pray like fucking hell you have a condom in this place," he growled as she arched her hips upward and his cock glided along the wet seam of her sex. He'd deliberately not put any in his pockets because he hadn't been intending to do this with her yet.

Her eyelashes lowered a moment. "I bought a box the other day."

Relief coursed through him. "That's good, *cher*. Real good. But we're not going to need them for a little while yet."

He released her wrists and slipped down her body. She let her legs fall open as he settled between them. He studied the pretty folds of her pussy—the slick pink inner lips, the plump outer lips, the tight dark curls she'd trimmed into a triangle.

When he met her gaze, she was watching him with the tip of one index finger in her mouth. The pearls gleamed against her milky skin, and her breasts rose and fell a little quicker than usual.

Remy gave her a wicked grin. And then he did what he'd been trained to do—he stormed the gates and attacked with everything he had in his arsenal.

CHAPTER EIGHT

CHRISTINA HAD THOUGHT she knew what she was getting when she'd invited Remy into her bedroom. An orgasm or two, a romp in the sheets with a super sexy SEAL—she still didn't understand how SEALs mixed with what her brother did since he was in the Army, but clearly they did—and the satisfaction of knowing she was still desirable.

What she hadn't expected was how it was going to *feel* when he touched his tongue to her neglected flesh. She couldn't remember the last time she'd had oral sex, but she remembered that it wasn't something Ben seemed to enjoy.

Well, no shit, of course he hadn't enjoyed it. It was a wonder he'd ever managed it at all.

But this, oh God, *this* was nothing like she'd ever had before. Remy Marchand spread her with his fingers and then licked her clitoris with the kind of skill that suggested he'd done a lot of this.

No, don't think about that!

And really, it was impossible to think about anything except the way his tongue felt gliding over her. He nibbled and sucked and licked while she panted and grabbed handfuls of the covers in her fists. Every stroke of his tongue was torture—and revelation.

Oh, she hadn't had nearly enough experience for this. She'd had lovers in college—well, okay, two. And then she'd had a couple of semiserious boyfriends when she'd moved to DC and gone to work at Girard Oil's branch office here. And then there was Ben, which made a grand total of five.

Five lovers, and not one of them had *ever* made her feel quite the way she felt right now.

"Remy," she gasped as her body tightened.

"Hang on, honey," he murmured before spreading her open and curling his tongue around her clit again and again.

Christina saw stars that time. A wave of pleasure rippled outward from her sex, spread through her arms and legs, sizzled into her toes and fingers. She sucked in air, tangled her fingers into his hair, and held him against her as she rode his face to get precisely what she wanted.

He gave it to her. Every toe-curling, body-shattering moment until she was spent. Until she collapsed on the pillows and proceeded to feel embarrassed that she'd been so, well, forward.

Ladies weren't forward. She could remember Granny saying that to her. Often.

But oh, how forward she'd been with Remy Marchand. Not just tonight but, well, all the time. So uncharacteristic of her—and yet it felt natural with him.

The sexy man in question crawled up her body, stopping to spend a little time on her nipples before arriving at eye level. He was grinning like the proverbial cat that ate the canary.

And her heart gave a strange lurch in her chest that surprised her.

"Feel better?"

She closed her eyes and stretched. "I'm so relaxed I could go to sleep right now."

His fingers slid into her body, his thumb skating over her sensitive clit, and she nearly came unglued.

"Not that relaxed, I'm guessing."

His eyes sparkled in the lamplight and she blinked. Lamplight? She turned her head, surprised the lamp was still on. Ben always wanted the lights out. And maybe she had too, come to think of it. But she'd been so into Remy that she hadn't even considered the light.

"Okay, maybe not," she conceded. "What's next, Cage?"

It was his turn to blink. "You know my code name."

Yes, she did. Because she'd listened to every snippet of conversation about Remy Marchand since meeting him a little over a week ago. "It's not a secret. You guys call each other things that aren't your names. Besides, yours is easy. Cage for Cajun, am I right?"

"Yes, ma'am, that'd be correct."

"They call Matt Richie Rich. Which I'm sure you know. But it's not very original, is it?"

His gaze slipped down her body and her skin tingled. "Christina, baby, you're babbling. Do you honestly care what your brother's team calls him or doesn't call him at this very moment?"

He had her there. She rolled her head from side to side. "Not really."

"We can discuss names later… But first, either you tell me where to find those condoms, or I'm going back for seconds."

Her breath hitched. "I don't think either of those options is bad for me."

"Or me. You taste sweet… and I love the way you moan when you're coming, you know that? Such a proper lady."

Damn, but he made her feel good inside. So warm and happy. Crazy. And probably just a temporary sensation due to the very out-of-character way she'd jumped into bed with a man she barely knew.

"My granny would be happy you think so, God rest her soul. She worked hard to make sure I became a proper lady."

She reached for the drawer of her nightstand table and pulled out a box. She'd felt self-conscious when she'd gone into the drugstore for these the other night, but then she'd also thought, *What the hell?* A woman needed to be prepared these days.

Remy took the box with a wicked grin. "I look forward to making the lady scream before the night is through."

Her heart jumped at the promise in those words. "I want to scream, Remy. I really do."

He opened the box and ripped off a packet, tearing it and removing the condom. Tossing everything aside, he rolled it on, then settled between her legs again.

His fingers feathered over her cheek. "I suppose I could do this with a bit more finesse, but the truth is I want you too much to show restraint. You okay with that?"

Christina nibbled the inside of her lip just to make sure she wasn't dreaming. "What precisely does that mean, Remy?"

"It means, honey, that I'm about to lose my fucking mind. That I'm going to push inside you and fuck you harder than I probably should—unless you tell me it's too much, in which case I'll go easy on you. Then I'm going to explode, and I'll probably make some noise when I do. After that, collapse is likely—but only for about five minutes while I wait for the strength to do it all again."

Oh, the things he said made her squirm—in the very best way. Her body was still languid from her orgasm, and yet she was unsatisfied too. She *needed* more.

A little pinprick of fear pierced the bubble of her happiness, reminding her it wasn't a good idea to get addicted to this man. She couldn't trust herself right now, couldn't trust her heart or her head. Men were unhealthy for her long-term peace of mind at the moment.

Remy dropped his mouth to her neck, sucked the skin over her throat. "You okay with that, Christina? Or you need a bit more foreplay?"

She tugged on his hair until he lifted his head and looked at her. "If you give me any more foreplay, I may say something very unladylike."

He laughed. "Oh honey, I definitely want to hear you say something unladylike. Lots of things, in fact. But yeah…" He pushed forward then, entering her in a long, slow glide. "I'd much rather get down to business."

Being inside Christina was every bit the heaven he'd hoped it would be. Her eyes dilated, her jaw went slack, and the grip she had on him tightened as she arched her body up to meet him.

Remy had to be still for a long moment just to regain his equilibrium. He'd fucked a lot of women in his life, been semiserious with one once, but he'd never felt quite like *this* before. As if the next breath he took had to happen with her beneath him. As if her not being there would be the end of him somehow.

It was crazy and unreal—and he didn't fucking care how nuts it was. He only wanted to feel everything he was feeling right now for as long as he could.

He started to move deep inside her, drawing his cock out of her body and then pushing forward again. No matter that he'd said he was going to lose control when he got inside her, no way would he hurt her. No way.

Her legs wrapped high around his waist, her slim ankles resting on his back, and he reached down to cup her ass in one hand, lifting her even more.

"Oh," she gasped, her eyes closing, her teeth nibbling her bottom lip.

"Fuck," he whispered, licking that lip, sucking it between his teeth as he increased the pace.

"Yes," she moaned into his mouth. "*Yes.*"

"Kiss me," he ordered, and she obeyed, her tongue slipping into his mouth and tangling with his.

Her lips were so sweet, her tits so perfect, her pussy a world of pleasure he was getting lost in. The control he'd held so tightly slipped until he was pounding into her faster and harder, until they had to break free of the kiss to gulp in air, until the world narrowed into a dark point in the distance he had to reach.

His release slammed into him like a hard crash against a concrete wall, taking his breath, his strength, his ability to form words. He felt Christina coming around him, her body gripping his tight, forcing more pleasure into the moment than he'd thought possible.

He poured his body into hers until there was nothing left, and then he rolled to the side, relishing the cool air where it hit his sweat-dampened skin. His throat was scratchy, and he knew it was because he'd shouted a stream of dirty words as he came.

He didn't know what to say, hadn't quite processed the gravity of everything he was feeling. This was more than random, emotionless fucking. But how much more? What else could it be when they barely knew each other?

He didn't know, but he knew it was. He reached for Christina's hand, threaded his fingers through hers, and squeezed. She squeezed back, but her heart didn't seem to be in it. He propped himself up on an elbow and gazed at her. Her eyes were closed tight, the corners of her mouth turned down in a frown, and that made his heart skip.

Dammit, he should have had more control.

"Baby, was I too rough? You okay?"

She opened her eyes and turned her head to look at him. And then she smiled, but it didn't quite reach her eyes the way it had earlier.

"I'm fine."

"You sure?"

She lowered her gaze. "Physically, I'm fine. I'm not sure about the rest."

He tipped her chin up with a fist, searching her eyes. They shimmered and his chest tightened.

"Christina. Baby. It's a lot to process, yeah?" He skimmed a thumb over her soft bottom lip. God, he wanted to nibble that lip. And then he wanted to get lost inside her sweet body again. "We don't have to do anything you don't want, okay? You need me to leave, I'll leave. Need me to stay and hold you, I'll do that too. Just tell me what you want."

She wrapped her fingers around his wrist. "Why do you have to be so wonderful, Remy Marchand?"

He grinned, hoping to ease her pain. "It's the way God made me, honey. It's part of the DNA."

She laughed and the vise around his chest eased just a little bit. "You're too much, you know that?"

"Yeah."

"I wish I'd met you a long time ago." Her eyes were troubled. "I'm a little gun-shy about men now… not that we're having a relationship or anything. I get that. But how do I know what I can handle? What's safe?"

"Baby, if everyone knew that, nobody'd ever get their heart broken, would they?" He pulled her into his arms. She didn't resist, and he thanked God for that. "Let's just take this a day at a time, okay? Tonight it's you and me. Tomorrow is a new day. We'll see what happens then."

She burrowed her head against his chest. "Okay."

Remy ran his fingers up and down her spine. He didn't quite know how he was going to do it considering how skittish she was—understandably, of course—but he *would* convince her that she wanted to be his.

One shattering orgasm at a time was as good a place as any to start.

CHAPTER NINE

Baq, Qu'rim
Present Day

NIGHTFALL BROUGHT TWO things, one of them beautiful and haunting, the other frightening. Christina awoke from her nap to the sounds of the Muslim call to prayer ringing from the mosques of Baq. She lay in bed and listened to the melodic words she didn't understand, knowing that the citizens of Baq would be preparing to pray.

The second thing that had awakened her was the sound of gunfire and explosions. Christina sat up, her heart pounding as one explosion sounded particularly loud just then. The war was coming closer to the city.

She climbed from bed and pulled on her clothing—a light dress and sandals because of the heat. There was also an abaya and a hijab for her hair, but since she wasn't seeing Sheikh Fahd until later, she didn't put it on yet.

She grabbed the remote and flipped on the television. CNN International blared to life with coverage of the war in Qu'rim. Baq was supposed to be safe, but the fighting had taken a turn in the past few days and the rebels were close to the city now. The king's troops were struggling to maintain their hold on the city, but the US State Department had ordered noncombatant civilians out of the country.

She knew that, and she had a flight out in the morning. Commercial carriers were still flying into Baq, but only during the daylight hours. Before she left, she needed to get Sheikh Fahd's agreement on her proposal, which was why she had a dinner meeting with him in the hotel restaurant tonight.

She'd turned her cell phone off earlier because Matt wouldn't stop calling her, but now she turned it back on and waited for the inevitable blowup. Yep, twenty missed calls and a boatload of texts.

Matt: Chrissy, answer the goddamn phone.

Matt: Get the fuck out of Baq. NOW.

Evie: Sweetie, Matt's driving me insane. Please call or text him. I know you're fine because, well, I just do. But put the man out of his misery.

Matt: Screw Girard Oil. You're more important than a fucking business deal.

That last one made her smile. This deal was important to Girard Oil, as they all were, especially in these days of low oil prices. Sheikh Fahd needed a place to sell his oil, and Christina wanted to be the one he sold it to. But if she couldn't get the deal inked tonight, she was going home empty-handed.

Then she'd start working on the Russians while still trying to tempt Fahd long-distance. She typed in a quick text to that effect—well, not the part about Fahd and the Russians—and then went into the bathroom to fix her hair and makeup. Her phone dinged.

Matt: Don't ignore me like that again, C. I'm bigger than you, and I have no problem spanking your ass.

Christina: You just try it, Mattie. I have a knee and I know where to use it for maximum effect.

Matt: Just come home and we'll pretend this never happened. Where's your bodyguard, btw? The old man said he sent one with you.

Christina: He's been sick since we arrived. Stomach bug. Poor guy.

Matt: I don't fucking care if he's dying. He shouldn't leave your side for a second.

Christina sighed. Then she typed out, *They aren't all like you, big brother. He's a rent-a-cop, not an Army commando.*

Because while she didn't know precisely what her brother did, she knew it was pretty intense. Just like Remy.

And didn't that name in her head just call up all sorts of memories and regrets? She'd only had one night with her smoking-hot SEAL lover, but it had been a pretty spectacular one.

You could have had more, girlie. He wanted more.

So had she, but she'd panicked. And then she'd run. She hadn't stopped running either. But he'd stopped calling, which was what she'd wanted.

Or had she? Because damn, these past couple of months with no communication from Remy sure had felt lonely. And futile in a way. The day she got the formal divorce decree in the mail, she'd nearly picked up the phone and called him just to have someone to talk to.

Instead, she'd packed a bag and gotten onto a plane to Brazil where she'd met with some oil executives and pitched them a partnership with Girard Oil.

Christina sighed. This was her life now. Girard Oil. Travel and business. It filled the hours.

Matt: If you'd told me you were going to Qu'rim, you could have had one of Jack Hunter's guys.

Jack was one of Matt's former teammates. He'd married pretty much the biggest pop star in the world, and then he'd gotten out of the military and started his own personal security business. She didn't doubt Jack's people would be more than competent.

Christina: If I'd told you I was going, you'd have tossed me into your basement and thrown away the key.

Matt: Probably. LU. Be safe. Get home.

Christina: That's the intention.

When her phone didn't blow up with more texts, she breathed a sigh of relief. The television continued to blare dire news, however—and when another explosion rocked the city, Christina gasped as the hotel building shook. Her heart hammered as she ran over to the window and peered out. The sky was orange in the distance. Below the window, traffic snarled. Trucks piled high with people and their belongings sat in tangles while the drivers honked and yelled.

Christina lifted her phone and dialed. A man answered just when she was ready to give up.

"Yeah?"

"You doing better?" she asked Paul, the big dude who'd accompanied her from Texas when she'd stopped at Girard Oil HQ in Houston before leaving for this trip. She could hear the television in the background, and then it went silent.

"Somewhat. We need to get out of here, ma'am. The city is under blockade from the rebels, and someone just said the airport's been cut off."

Shit.

"All right, then what's the plan?"

He was silent for so long that she rolled her eyes. Honest to God, Matt or Remy would have had ten backup plans already. Though, on the other hand, she needed to be fair to the guy. He was sick—but at least he had current information that she did not.

"We need to get a car. Get on the road. Drive to the next town where we can get a flight."

Christina cursed silently. She *should* have called Matt before she'd come on this trip. She didn't know what Jack Hunter's guy could have done differently, but she had no doubt he wouldn't have waited for her to ask what the plan was.

"The next town is a two-hour drive in decent conditions. In these conditions, I imagine it will take days," she said.

"I don't think we have much choice, ma'am."

So polite, but he sounded a tad irritated with her right now.

A sudden thought occurred to her, and she almost wilted with relief. "Sheikh Fahd must have private transportation. I'll ask him for a ride to Acamar or Dubai, or wherever he's going."

Christina wrapped up the call—Paul did not offer to accompany her to Sheikh Fahd's penthouse suite, which she knew Matt would not approve of—and slipped the hijab over her hair. Fahd was modern enough that covering her hair instead of her entire body would satisfy him.

She tucked her phone into her purse and swung that over her shoulder, intending to head straight for Fahd's suite. At the last second, she grabbed her briefcase. Maybe Fahd would be ready to sign the papers too. She could get him at a weak moment—like between explosions.

The thought amused her, which was a good thing right now. She knew Fahd was too shrewd to allow anything to derail him.

Christina jerked open the door and bit back a scream at the sight of a very large man with his fist raised to knock. He was at once familiar and foreign, and her heart pumped so fast she felt light-headed. He lowered his fist to his side.

"R-Remy?"

She hadn't seen him in six months, not since that hot night in her bedroom, but her heart and body knew Remy Marchand even if she would rather they didn't.

He didn't look anything like he had the last time she'd seen him. He'd been wearing his henley and jeans, leaving her house after a hot night of sex and promising to call her later—which he had done, she knew, because she had the unanswered messages to prove it.

Now he was menacing. Tall and broad as always, but this time he was dressed all in desert camouflage, a mean-looking rifle slung over his chest, and sporting a helmet with what looked like a camera on the top. There was a mic curving around his cheek, and he wore a vest that appeared to contain ammo. There was also a gun in a holster strapped around his thigh and what seemed to be kneepads on his knees.

"Wh-what are you doing here?"

His mouth—that gorgeous, sensual mouth that had taken her to such heights—curved down in a hard frown. "This is a fucking war zone, Christina. I'm rescuing your ass."

She couldn't help the hot flush of anger that rolled over her then. "I don't need rescuing, thanks."

He pushed into the room and shoved the door closed.

"Objective acquired," he said into the mic. "Awaiting instructions. … Copy."

When he looked up at her again, his expression was dark. "Afraid you do, sweetheart. The airport's closed for business. The rebels have cut off the route. Soon they'll have the airport in their possession—and that's bad for us."

Her heart was thrumming from so many things, but the one thing that seemed paramount was just how shocking—and confusing—it was to see him again. And not just see him, but see him as the badass warrior he really was. He'd been sweet and tender with her. Handsome, yes, but not dangerous.

This man was not sweet. He was a lethal combination of training and testosterone. More dangerous than anything she'd ever encountered.

She lifted her chin. “I’m on my way to see Sheikh Fahd. He has a helicopter. He’ll take me with him when he goes—”

“Wrong.”

He made her trip over her tongue for a second before she found it again. “He will. I’m going to see him now.”

She started for the door, but Remy stepped in front of her. His hand rested on the weapon slung across his chest, and he looked absolutely menacing as he stared her down.

“You can’t, Christina. He’s gone. Left about three hours ago, like a sensible sheikh. You’re on your own.”

His gaze was challenging. Superior. It made her want to punch him. And kiss him, God help her. “I have Paul.”

Remy’s gaze narrowed. “Who the fuck is Paul?”

His voice was like a whip between them, cracking hard against her senses. He was not a man to be toyed with, that was for sure.

“My bodyguard. He’s across the hall.”

“Across the fucking hall? Jesus.” He picked up the radio clipped to his vest and pressed a button. “Do we have a Paul on our list? … Well, we do now. Bodyguard. … Yeah, guess somebody overlooked him.” He glanced at her. “Paul who?”

“I…” She shrugged. “I don’t know.”

“He’s across the hall from Christina Girard. … Yeah, copy.” He let go of the radio and gave her a hard look. “Call him and tell him to get over here. Now. You’ll have to leave your suitcases.”

“What? Why?”

“This ain’t a fucking vacation, baby. It’s an extraction. Take what you can carry. If you can carry a suitcase for miles through the desert, then be my guest. But nobody's carrying it for you. Not even Paul, so don't think of asking."

Christina drew herself up, hurt, furious, and confused. Seeing him was doing a number on her senses. Knowing he was pissed at her only made it worse. "What makes you think I'd expect him to do that? Did I ever give you the impression I was spoiled?"

He snorted. "The impression you gave me turned out to be a lie, so what do I know?"

His words pierced her. Maybe she could have handled the situation between them better, but she hadn't and there was no sense stewing in regrets. "Remy, I—"

"Save it," he bit out. "Call the bodyguard. The time for talking is over between us."

Tears pricked her eyes, but she did as he said. She dialed Paul, told him to come to her room, and slipped the phone into her purse again. God, she'd fucked up so badly. She'd only been trying to protect herself when she'd fled town after that night, but clearly she'd done a rotten job of it because she wasn't feeling safe at all right now.

She felt as bruised and battered inside as she ever had. Maybe more so considering she hadn't given Remy the benefit of the doubt before deciding he'd betray her the way Ben had.

But after being burned so badly once before, how could she trust another man not to do the same thing? Ben cheated. Her father had been a serial womanizer until he married Misty Lee. Matt was devoted to Evie, but look how many years it had taken him to get his head screwed on right.

She just didn't have room for that kind of drama in her life anymore. Besides, if she got a hankering for babies, she had her new nephews to play with. Cuter twins had never been seen on this earth, she was certain.

"Do you have any pants? Best to put those on instead of a dress." Remy's gaze settled on the abaya draped over a chair. "Wear the traditional clothing over everything once you've changed."

She wanted to argue with him, but what was the point? He was right, he was in charge here, and arguing was stupid. Did you argue with the fireman who came to pull you from a burning building?

No. You also didn't argue with the badass Navy SEAL who was trying to pull you from a war zone.

She went to her carry-on suitcase and took out jeans and a white button-down shirt. She didn't really have all that much with her, nothing of importance other than her briefcase and wallet. She'd learned to travel light when on these trips, so losing her clothing wouldn't be too terrible even if it was wasteful.

She slipped into the bathroom to change. When she was finished, her eyes glittered in the mirror as she lifted her head to stare at herself.

Damn it, why did she always get it wrong? She'd fallen for Ben and he'd been toxic. Then she'd decided a one-night stand with Remy was a good idea—until the intensity of what happened between them rattled her so badly she had to run away rather than face it.

She'd felt drawn to him in a way she simply couldn't handle. It had been too soon. She couldn't trust him—couldn't trust herself. She'd needed distance.

Yet here she was, facing him after six months and feeling like someone had ripped out her guts. It wasn't easier seeing him now, and it should be. She should be completely unaffected.

She was *far* from unaffected.

She heard voices and figured Paul must have arrived. She shrugged the abaya over her clothing, straightened the hijab, and jerked open the door.

Remy looked even more annoyed if that were possible. Paul was there, also looking annoyed. Seeing the two men standing together, she wondered how on earth she'd ever believed Paul was capable of being her bodyguard on this trip.

He wasn't precisely fat, but he wasn't toned either. He looked like one of those guys who worked out but still ate chili dogs and cheese fries. A bit of a gut, but with big arms and a thick neck. Like he'd been a football player at one point in his life.

He was shorter than Remy by about six inches, which made her realize just how tall Remy was. Six-four or six-five at least.

"You should have been here with her the instant you learned about the airport." Remy's voice was tight.

Paul puffed up his chest like a rooster. "Don't tell me how to do my job, asshole, and I won't tell you how to do yours."

She thought Remy might explode, but instead he just shook his head. "Motherfucker," he said softly, "you have no idea what the hell I do. But I guarantee you it's more before breakfast than you do in a month."

Paul puffed himself up again. "I'm an ex-Marine, buddy. I get it."

Remy took two long steps, cutting the distance between them.

Paul reared back, bumping into a chair and nearly falling. "What the fuck?" he demanded.

Remy grabbed him, spun him around, and at some point relieved him of the weapon he had holstered inside his jacket. After Remy checked the gun and shoved it into one of the many pockets in his vest, he looked at Paul in disgust.

"It's *former* Marine, dickhead, or simply *Marine*. Never ex. Don't pretend to be something you aren't. It's an insult to all who've served."

Paul rubbed his wrist where Remy'd grasped it. Then he blew out a breath. "I tried to join up but didn't pass the physical. I wanted to go, but they wouldn't take me. So maybe I don't have the right, but I wanted it."

Remy appeared to relax slightly at that unexpected bit of honesty. "Understood. But don't claim it when you didn't earn it. That's not cool."

Remy turned to where Christina stood just outside the bathroom door. "You ready?"

"I think so."

"Then let's roll, kids. We're going to meet up with my team and get the fuck out of here. All you have to do is keep up."

CHAPTER TEN

JESUS, WHY HAD he volunteered to be the one to get Christina? His gut churned and he wanted to say about a million things to her. Things he wasn't going to say because there was absolutely no point.

She'd made it clear enough she wasn't interested.

Remy led the way to the stairs, sweeping the hall with his weapon at the ready. The hotel wasn't under rebel control, but that wasn't the point.

His other teammates had fanned out to locate the rest of the people on the list, and they were meeting downstairs. Five individuals in all, six now with Paul, the not-quite-a-Marine bodyguard.

Remy went into the stairwell, swept it for intruders, and then signaled Paul and Christina to follow. At least Paul waited for Christina to go first, putting her between the two of them. Remy didn't like the guy, mostly because he hadn't taken as good of care of Christina as he should have. Asshole should have had her out of here two hours ago at a minimum.

But if he had, you wouldn't have her now. You wouldn't know she was safe.

True.

Maybe it would have been better for Remy if she'd already been gone though.

Because, goddamn, he'd been pissed since the second she opened the door, looking all sweet and pretty in her summery dress with the hijab over her hair. He'd had a strong need to kiss her, and that hadn't helped his temper in the least.

He knew where he stood with Christina Girard-Scott. One night in her arms, and he was history. He thought he'd glimpsed heaven with her, and then she'd refused to answer his calls.

Just as well since he'd probably been wrong anyway. She was just another woman, though admittedly she wasn't his usual type. He didn't typically go for the Junior League sort.

Or maybe he was just pissed because she'd given him a dose of his own medicine. Yeah, he'd had one-night stands and he'd failed to call the woman the next day—or ever—but he'd never called and been ignored. That was a new one.

At first he'd thought she was busy. Took him about three days to realize she was ignoring him on purpose.

He'd been unable to ask Matt Girard about his sister. Unable to ask anyone. All he could do was leave messages.

Messages she never returned. He'd gotten the hint after two weeks, but he'd called periodically for the next couple of months. Just in case she finally answered and explained what the fuck was going on—which she never had.

They entered the foyer of the hotel. There were a few people around, but not many. Everyone was busy fleeing the city, which didn't bode particularly well for the SEALs and their charges.

They'd been tasked with putting these people on a plane, but that had changed in the past couple of hours between order and execution. There was no way through to the airport now. People were leaving by car and truck, fleeing north. Some would go east to the port city of Akhira. It was the most direct way to the sea but also the riskiest with the fighting so close. The rebels could cut the route if they overran the road at any point.

The SEALs couldn't call in an air rescue because every helicopter was currently being used elsewhere. Not to mention the sky was particularly dangerous at the moment since the rebels had a supply of shoulder-fired missile launchers. They would most definitely aim them at a Blackhawk appearing on the skyline, and that was a nightmare nobody needed.

The only way out was the way everyone was going—motor vehicle.

Viking was waiting for them when they arrived in the foyer. "We'll go seven to a vehicle. You've got Cowboy, Camel, and Money— Jesus, that sounds like a bad joke."

Viking shook his head and Remy couldn't help but grin. Cody "Cowboy" McCormick thought riding bulls on his off time was fun. Alex "Camel" Kamarov had the misfortune to have a name that lent itself to a name like Camel. And Cash "Money" McQuaid was self-explanatory.

"Akhira is the closest, but we're heading for Merak,"

Viking continued. “It’s more stable, and the commercial airport is still operational.”

Merak was a port city near the northern border of Qu’rim. On a good day, it was six hours north. On a day like today? God only knew.

“Copy that. It’s farther from the fighting and less likely to be cut off. Don’t think we have much choice really.”

Viking looked grim. “Not especially, no.” His gaze slipped over Paul and Christina standing nearby. “She okay?”

Of course Viking knew who she was because he’d been at those same gatherings where Remy had met and talked to Christina.

“Seems to be.”

“Are you?”

Remy’s gaze snapped to his team leader. “Why wouldn’t I be?”

Viking’s expression didn’t change. “No reason. If you want me to take her, I can do that. Trade you a pudgy banker.”

Remy snorted. “Fuck no. You keep the banker.”

Viking tipped his head toward Paul. “The bodyguard, huh?”

“Not much of one. He knew the airport was in danger two hours ago and did nothing.”

“To be fair,” Viking said, “I don’t think there was much he could have done about that. You want him to wander into a hot zone with her?”

“No, but he could have been on the road to Merak by now.”

“Again, would you be satisfied if he’d done that? We wouldn’t know where she was—and Girard would be having a shit fit back at HQ if that were the case."

"Yeah, fine, point that out."

Viking grinned. "Cheer up, you crazy Cajun motherfucker. We've got the girl and we're on the way in five."

Christina recognized some of the SEALs. She'd met them at Matt's or at Buddy's Bar. They looked different like this. Meaner. So big and broad—and armed to the teeth. Not the kind of guys you'd want to fuck around with, that's for sure.

They went outside and started to climb into two light brown vans that sat in the circular driveway of the hotel—she didn't know if they were armored, but she hoped so. They didn't look military grade, but she suspected that was done on purpose. Once inside, she knew why no one could bring a suitcase. If they had, there'd be no room left inside for people. She had her briefcase and her purse, which was all she needed. Her computer was small and fit in the briefcase.

The van wasn't dinky, but it wasn't huge either. The inside was stripped down, with steel floors and bench seats along the sides. At least there were seat belts. There was also equipment stowed at the rear, which severely cut down on the amount of room available. Ammo, she imagined, looking at the boxes.

And didn't that thought just make her shiver? She hoped they wouldn't need to break out the ammo.

Once they were all inside—four SEALs, Christina and Paul, and a pretty woman with big boobs—Remy sank onto the seat beside Christina instead of across from her. His side pressed against hers from shoulder to knee.

Christina shrank from the contact, not because it was horrible but because of the things it did to her insides. Yes he was armored, and yes he smelled like sweat and sand combined, but it didn't seem to matter. Her body was on red alert.

"Let's roll," he said, and the SEAL behind the wheel pressed the gas. She'd seen him playing pool with Remy. Cody? Cowboy? Something like that. The other one in the passenger seat was the one with the Russian name. And sitting across from them, beside the redhead with boobs, was Cash McQuaid. Hard to forget a name like that.

Or a face. Cash grinned at her and then winked. "Having fun yet, little sister?"

"Loads, thanks. So did Matt send you guys to get us?"

"Not Richie," Remy interjected. "Seems as if a State Department evac notice didn't get your attention. You five—six," he added after a glance at Paul, "just thought you'd hang out by the pool and sip margaritas all day."

"I had a flight out tomorrow," Christina said, wanting to wipe the superior smirk from his face.

"Yeah, well that's not happening, is it? You shouldn't have come in the first place. Think I might have mentioned that a few months ago. And I'll damn sure bet your brother mentioned it."

Cash's gaze moved between them with interest. They hadn't been a thing long enough for any of the guys to know about it, but it must seem as if they knew a little too much about each other right this moment. Though, on the other hand, she might have said a little too much during a girls' night out once. If Ivy had told her husband, would Viking tell the others? Surely not.

"I have a bodyguard."

Remy snorted. "No offense, *cher*, but I'm thinking Paul here is ill-equipped to deal with insurgents."

"I've had training," Paul said. "I'm licensed."

"Sorry, buddy, but downtown Baq in a few hours isn't quite the same as nailing a weapons test in a controlled environment."

"Think what you want, asshole, but I could nail your ass in one shot."

"Can't shoot what you can't see, Paul. And trust me, if I was hunting you, you wouldn't see me."

Cash was gripping his weapon and looking about as mean as a scorpion. "Dude, I don't know where you got that chip, but you need to chill the fuck out," he said to Paul. "Save the pissing contest for another time."

"Whatever. Fucking SEALs. Always think you're the best at everything, don't you?"

"Where'd you put that duct tape, Money?" Remy asked. "I'm thinking this guy needs to shut his face before I get pissed."

Christina reached out and put her hand on Remy's arm. It was like touching a hot iron in a way. She wanted nothing more than to jerk her hand away, but she kept it there while her heart hammered harder than before.

"Look, the situation is what it is," she said. "I came to meet with Sheikh Fahd. I was leaving tomorrow even if he hadn't signed the papers. It's not Paul's fault we didn't go today."

Remy whirled on her. God, he was intimidating. He hadn't been so intimidating in her bedroom. Well, not true—he had, but in a completely different way.

"You shouldn't be here, Christina. At *fucking* all. And you damn well know it. You've known it the whole time. But you came anyway, and you put yourself and this man in danger by doing so. Now you've put us all in danger as we work to get your asses out of here."

Her blood was boiling, and yet guilt pricked her too. Maybe she shouldn't be here, but what about these other people? Was she the only person they were here for?

"There are six civilians in this group. You would have been here whether I was here or not," she said tightly.

"*You* have a connection these people don't. And don't think the Freedom Force wouldn't figure that out if you were still in the city when the rebels took it. They'd march every single American—every foreigner—into a prison camp and start figuring out how to exploit the goods. Don't you watch the fucking news?"

Fear gripped her. Yes, she'd watched the news. Yes, she'd seen the hostages and the beheadings. Everyone had. And yet it wasn't here. Not in Baq. Not even close to Baq—though, geographically speaking, it was a lot closer to Baq than to the US.

She noticed he hadn't confirmed what she'd said—that they'd still be here even if she wasn't. She swallowed. "I'm here now, Remy. You have me. It's going to be fine."

He only glowered.

CHAPTER ELEVEN

THE RIDE WAS monotonous. At some point Christina fell asleep. She didn't intend to, but she must have dozed off on Remy's shoulder.

She dreamed. Not of the desert. Not of sand and heat and danger. But of liquid heat, pleasure, veils. Freaking veils, like this was a tale out of *One Thousand and One Nights*.

She pictured veils and Remy. His masculine face contorted in pleasure as she sank onto his cock again and again. His face as he came, the beautiful lines and furrowed brow. The intensity.

She woke with a start, hot and achy and disappointed. Because it wasn't real. Because she smelled gas fumes, heat, horror. The desperation that people emanated because they were afraid.

She hadn't forgotten where she was. She knew precisely what was happening. She looked across the aisle, her gaze landing on the redhead. The woman stared back at her, her eyes wide and afraid. Her mascara was smeared and her hair frizzed from the humidity. She looked wild. Afraid.

"Where are we?" Christina asked of no one in particular.

Cash spared her a glance. "On the road to Merak."

That wasn't necessarily complete information, but she wasn't going to press him. Just then an explosion sounded in the distance and the redhead gasped.

Paul jerked from his dozing and blinked. And Remy… wait, where was Remy?

Christina's heart tumbled as she snapped upright, searching the vehicle. And then she nearly wilted as she realized he was sitting with his back to the two men up front, talking to them over his shoulder. He'd moved to the floor, his gun cradled in his lap, his head turned as he spoke.

"It's behind us," Cash said. "In the city. It just sounds closer than it is. We're safe."

The woman beside him didn't seem appeased.

"What's your name?" Christina asked.

Remy turned his head at the sound of her voice this time, but she didn't make eye contact with him. She was focused on the woman.

"Penny," the woman said softly.

Christina leaned forward and reached across the aisle. "Hi, Penny. I'm Christina."

Penny shook her offered hand with a moist one.

"Look, I know this is scary," Christina said. "But these guys are the best there is. Believe me."

"You know them?"

As if that was in doubt after her conversation with

Remy earlier, but maybe Penny hadn't been paying attention.

"Yes. I know them all. Fantastic guys to have at your back in a fight."

Penny's eyes widened even more, if that was possible, and Christina regretted mentioning fights.

"Or in general," she added. "They'll get us out of here safely."

Penny twisted her hands together. "I didn't want to be here at all, but my boss—Mr. Davis—said it was safe. I have a six-year-old at home."

Her voice broke then, and Christina couldn't help what she did next. She crossed the aisle and sank onto the seat beside Penny. Then she put her arms around the other woman's shoulders.

"You'll get back to your child. Isn't that right, Cash?"

The handsome SEAL next to Penny nodded. "That's right, ma'am. We'll get you home. It might be loud and scary sometimes, but we know what we're doing. Promise."

Penny's smile was shaky. "Thank you."

Christina could feel the other woman trembling. "It's okay, sweetie. You'd be crazy not to be scared."

Penny sniffed. "You aren't."

Christina blinked. "I am. But I trust these guys."

Her gaze tangled with Remy's. His dark eyes were intense, glittering, his sexy, sensual mouth set in a hard line. She didn't know how long their gazes locked—it seemed like forever, but then the van lurched to a stop and her heart sped up again.

She heard a window power down and then voices. Remy turned and got involved in the conversation. A few moments later, he got to his feet.

"Stopping for a few minutes, kids," he said, shifting his weapon before opening the van door and jumping down into the night.

A second later he was back.

"Traffic's at a standstill. No idea what the holdup is, but we're stuck for a while. Everybody out for a few minutes. Stretch your legs while you can, but stay near the vans."

Christina got to her feet with the others, her bones creaking from so long in one position. When she stepped down from the van, Remy was there, his hands spanning her waist as he lifted her and set her on the sand. He let her go as if she'd burned him. She stumbled sideways but recovered.

He helped Penny down as well, so Christina couldn't say he'd stayed to help her specifically. Yet her body had responded to his touch, the same as it always did. Her nipples tightened and her core ached. Ridiculous, considering where they were. What was happening.

She trudged a few steps in the sand, then stopped and stared back in the direction they'd come. The city of Baq was a beacon in the night. But not for the reason it should be. The skyline glowed. She knew instinctively the glow came from fires, not from city lights.

She wrapped her arms around herself and shivered. Qu'rim might be a desert nation, but the desert was cold at night, and she hadn't packed a jacket. You didn't need a jacket when you never ventured out into the night. She'd had a wrap for chilly meeting rooms, but it was still in her bag in the hotel. She hadn't thought to grab it.

She stared at the road behind them. Then she turned

and looked at the road ahead. It was literally jammed with traffic in both directions as people fled the capital. And that traffic was at a complete standstill. She didn't know if that was good or bad, but people seemed to take it for granted that they weren't going any farther tonight. They were setting up camp at the side of the road, starting cooking fires, lingering around vehicles that weren't moving.

She turned back to the van and searched for Remy's dark form. He looked just like the other SEALs, but there was something about the way he moved—or maybe it was the way she responded to him—that meant she knew which one was him.

He helped Penny take a few steps on shaky legs, then Paul jumped from the van and Cash followed. The others climbed from the van in front of theirs. The SEALs didn't relax, however. They were alert, watchful, hands on weapons as they surveyed the area.

She didn't know what they were waiting for, but she shivered again at the chill in the air and the intensity of the situation.

Viking—she knew the big blond SEAL from Matt and Evie's house, Buddy's, and also it was hard not to associate him with a Viking once you heard his team name—came over to her.

"How you doing, Ms. Girard?" he asked, his voice so serious and formal.

"I'm great, thanks. You?"

He grinned then, and she felt a little wave of relief flood her that he could be so friendly during a—what? Siege? Refugee crisis?

"Considering we got all of you out of Baq, fantastic."

She smiled. "Bullshit. You're an adrenaline junkie.

Like my brother. All of you are. This stuff trips your trigger."

His grin got bigger. "A bit." And then he sobered. "But seriously, the most important thing is getting you out of here and on a plane back to the States. Which we will do, don't worry."

"I'm not worried," she said.

"Good." His gaze strayed over her head, and then he touched his helmet as if he were tipping his cap before turning and walking away.

She felt Remy's approach rather than heard it. When she turned, he was there, looking gruff and unapproachable.

"Don't stray," he ordered. "We don't know what's out there yet."

Her throat ached as she looked at him standing there. He was tall and tough. Strong. She felt safe when he was near. And yet she'd run away six months ago and kept running until he'd stopped calling her.

For a moment, she regretted that more than she could say. But then she remembered the utter devastation she'd felt at Ben's betrayal and knew she'd done the right thing. Men lied. They cheated. She knew it better than most.

She also knew that you could never tell who would hurt you. How could she explain it to him though?

"I'm not straying. And I'm not stupid, contrary to what you might think."

"Never said that."

"Didn't you?"

His jaw flexed. "Not directly, no."

He'd implied it during his tirade in the van earlier though. He knew it as well as she did.

"As if Cash couldn't figure out what you meant when you went off on me. He's not stupid either."

"You may not be stupid, Christina—but you did something pretty oblivious when you came to Qu'rim."

"It was a meeting. In and out and done."

"But it didn't work out that way, did it?"

She sighed and rubbed a hand up and down her forearm. "Look, I get that you're pissed at me. And I get why…" She bit the inside of her lip. And then she decided to go for it. "I really am sorry for… for everything."

His face hardened, his eyes glittering hot. He knew what she meant, and he wasn't buying it. "You aren't, babe. If you were, you would have answered your phone any one of the hundred times I called you. You're only sorry that we're here, like this, and you feel uncomfortable. I get it—and you got nothing to worry about. I'm not hung up on you. I'm not harboring hurt feelings or crushing on you like a lovesick teenager. It was never about that—it was about how good it felt with you and how I wanted more of the same before we called it quits. But I'm over it now, so don't worry your pretty head that I'm nursing a broken heart, okay? It's awkward, but we'll get through it. Once we hit Merak and put you on a plane, you never have to see me again."

For some reason, that thought didn't give her the comfort it once would. Or had it ever? Honestly, since the morning he'd left her place and she'd felt so utterly devastated by everything that had happened between them, there'd been no comfort in avoiding him. She'd pretended it was for the best, but seeing him again only ripped the bandage off the wound.

"I was scared," she said, her throat tight.

His expression didn't change, but she thought maybe he softened a little. Maybe.

"Running away never fixed anything for anybody, *cher*. I think you know that as well as I do."

Before she could speak, several of the SEALs materialized out of the darkness. "Got a big problem up there," someone said. "Tractor-trailer jackknifed on the bridge over a wadi. Nobody's going anywhere on this road tonight."

CHAPTER TWELVE

THE SOUND OF babies crying woke Evie from sleep. Blearily, she pushed upright, but her husband spoke in the darkness.

"I'll get them, Evie. You sleep."

"I can do it," she said.

"No, *cher*. You were up all last night. Let me take care of them… and you."

"M'kay," she said sleepily, sagging back into the mattress and thanking God that Matt was home to help out. He worked a lot and was gone a lot, but he'd been home for a few weeks now, and that made her happy.

Sometime later, Evie jerked awake. The house was quiet. She turned to Matt's side of the bed, but he wasn't there. She pushed the covers back and slipped into her robe before padding down the hall and into the twins' room. Her boys were sleeping and Matt wasn't there, so she pulled the door shut and crept down the stairs.

She found Matt in the darkened kitchen. He was sitting at the table, laptop open, the blue light bathing his face. She knew what he was doing—or she suspected, anyway.

"Honey," she said, and his head snapped up. His eyes were bloodshot, but she knew he could get by on little to no sleep. It's what a Special Operator did. What her badass husband did.

She knew more than she should about his job, but it had taken time to learn these things. He hadn't told her, but he hadn't needed to. She'd figured it out. Well, most of it, she thought. He'd tell her if he could, but that was the nature of the military—some things were secret and had to stay that way.

She knew he was an operator—not operative, like in the movies, but operator. That was the correct term. And she knew he went to war zones and did things there that were necessary to the safety of the nation.

And she knew that, right now, he was dying inside because Christina was over there and he wasn't. She suspected that Colonel Mendez had sent someone, but she was grateful that someone wasn't Matt. Not right now. Not when she needed him here.

"You should be asleep."

She walked over to the table and pulled out a chair. "I woke up. You weren't there."

He shoved a hand through his hair and leaned back in his seat. "Couldn't sleep. Christian and Alex went down quickly, so I decided to look at the news. Qu'rim is in bad shape right now."

She reached for him and gripped his hand. "She'll be okay, Matt. I know she will."

"She shouldn't be there. Fucking old man and the business."

Evie's heart pinched like it always did when she thought of Matt and his father. She knew more than she'd ever known when they were growing up. She knew how mentally abusive his father had been and how much Matt still despised him. She also knew that his father wasn't the same man he used to be, just like they weren't the same people they'd been as kids. People evolved. It was simply the nature of life, which was much more complex than platitudes would have you believe.

Good men could become evil. Evil men could become good.

But she was on Matt's side first and foremost. Always.

"I don't think anyone forced your sister to go, honey. Christina's been… not quite the same since what happened with Ben."

Matt curled his fingers into a fist. She didn't think he knew he'd done it. "Motherfucker," he growled. "He didn't deserve her."

"No, he definitely didn't. But it happened, and Chris has been running ever since. I don't think your father had much to do with her decision to go to Qu'rim."

"No, but he didn't stop her either."

Evie squeezed his hand. "Do you really think anyone could stop her from doing whatever she wanted to do? Christina is fierce, Matt. Fiercer than any of us realized. She's a dynamo, and she won't take no for an answer. Just like someone else I know."

He blinked. "You mean me?"

She couldn't help but smile. "Of course I mean you. Fierce, proud Girards. You don't quit. If your father had told her not to go, she'd have cussed him out and gone anyway."

His smile was soft and weary at once. "Yeah, maybe. But damn, did she have to go to Qu'rim now of all fucking times? If she'd told me what she'd planned, I'd have stopped her."

"Which is probably why she didn't tell you. Look, I know you can't discuss it, but I'm going to guess that she's in good hands over there. If I know Mendez, and I think I know a little about him after everything that's happened, he's sending in the cavalry. If they're anything like you, she's going to be just fine."

He tugged her hand until she had to sit in his lap. Which she did not mind at all. Matt was big and solid, and she loved how protected she felt when he held her. How loved.

His hands roamed over her hips, up her sides. He didn't touch her breasts, and she sighed.

"You can touch me, Matt. It's okay."

"You haven't been getting enough rest."

"Then make me come and I'll fall asleep so fast your head will spin."

She felt the response happening beneath her as he grew hard at a rapid rate. "Evie, Jesus, I want that. But the twins take so much out of you. You need to take care of yourself first. I'll be fine."

She wanted to bop him over the head. Since she'd had the babies two months ago, he hadn't tried to have sex with her even once. At first she'd been pretty grateful for that. Now she was growing frustrated.

She cupped his head in her hands and forced him to look at her. “Look, this *is* taking care of myself. Because if you don’t get back to providing me with sex on a regular basis, I’m going to be forced to buy a vibrator and replace your fine ass with a piece of rubber or latex or whatever they’re made out of. I need you, Matt. Unless you’re too upset about Christina, in which case I understand. But when she gets back home safely, I’m going to expect some performances in the bedroom or there will be dire consequences.”

He was gaping at her, but his cock hadn’t grown soft. If anything, it was harder now. “What kind of dire consequences?”

“I already mentioned Tank.”

“Tank?”

“What I’m going to name my vibrator. It’s going to be the biggest, hardest, best thing in the catalog—”

He dragged her down and took her mouth with his. That was the end of the conversation—and the beginning of several orgasms that left her weak in the knees and very, very satisfied.

Christina couldn’t get comfortable in the van. After the SEALs had returned with news of the roadblock, they’d decided it was time to leave by a different route. But one of the vans wouldn’t start, so they’d gotten to work on the engine while the civilians climbed back into the vans to wait. Christina dozed as the minutes stretched by, waking with a start at the sound of explosions in the distance. She didn't know how far they'd gotten from Baq, but it wasn't far enough because the RPGs and gunfire still sounded so close.

Christina pushed herself up from where she'd tried to sack out on a bench seat and yawned. The interior of the van was dark and stifling. Across from her, Penny snored softly. On the floor, Paul stretched out on his back, eyes closed, arms crossed over his chest, totally quiet. He reminded her of a vampire, quite honestly.

Her eyes were gritty and there seemed to be sand in everything, even inside. She brushed it off as best she could and then stumbled carefully on numb legs toward the door. She needed air, and she unfortunately needed to pee.

The two SEALs on guard turned around as she emerged.

"You need to stay inside, Christina."

It was Remy's voice. She didn't know if that was a good thing or a bad thing, really. Someone else she could talk to dispassionately. But Remy? Jeez, it was all she could do to form complete sentences at this point.

"I have to pee. And don't tell me I can't, because I'll pee in the van—which probably isn't a good thing for any of us."

She took a step—and then gasped as she got a look at the skyline behind the convoy of stopped vehicles. She'd known it was on fire earlier, but it seemed to have spread. The entire sky glowed.

Remy's expression was grim. His hands rested on the weapon slung over his chest. He looked as if there was nothing much going on, but she suspected he could change in a heartbeat if the situation required it.

"How did it happen so fast?" she breathed. "They weren't supposed to be able to take the capital." That's what all the news reports had been saying for days. Clearly, they were wrong. Tragically, horribly wrong.

"Priorities change, *cher*. Someone somewhere decided they no longer cared if Baq resisted or fell."

She turned to him, her heart throbbing. "You mean America stopped caring, don't you?"

"It's an unpopular war. We aren't the only ones who want out."

She gazed at the long line of vehicles, her throat tight. It was a mess. A humanitarian crisis. "Where will they all go?"

"Anywhere they can. They'll spill over the borders, some won't get out at all, and some will die in the fighting."

Nearby, a baby started to cry. That was the worst part of all—that children were caught up in this. Whole families were fleeing the only lives they'd ever known, desperate to get away from the conflict between the government and rebels.

"Who's going to win?"

"Hard to say. The king still has the advantage monetarily. And he has a disciplined army. But the rebels fight like they have nothing to lose—they fight dirty and hard, and that's not easy to overcome."

She tried to process that.

"What happens if the traffic doesn't start to move soon?"

"That's not our problem, *cher*." He motioned toward the other side of the convoy. "You have to pee or what?"

"Yes." She hated the idea of these people being stuck here with a war behind them. But what could nine SEALs do? Nothing at all, unfortunately.

"Then do it in the shadow of the vehicles. I'll keep watch."

"Um…"

"What?"

"Paper? Is that possible?"

He reached into the van and handed her a glob of what turned out to be tissue. Christina picked her way around the side of the van and found a spot. When she was done, she went to where Remy stood guard with his back to her. He turned at her approach, his gaze slipping over her for a second.

"Thanks," she said, her skin heating with the intensity of that look.

He waited for her to walk past him before he followed. She stopped and spun around before she reached the van door. He frowned.

"Can I just stay out here for a little while? I can't sleep, Penny's snoring, and the explosions don't help."

He pulled in a breath before snorting it out again. She was certain he would tell her no.

"Twenty minutes, Christina. And you don't move outside the perimeter we've set up."

Which was all of about ten feet, but whatever. It was still freedom. "Okay."

She ran her hands up and down her arms, shivering.

Remy frowned. "You're cold."

It was partly adrenaline, partly the night air, but she nodded. "A little bit."

"Then you should definitely get back inside."

"I was cold in there too."

He went over to the van and pulled out his pack. Then he rifled through it and handed her a shirt. The camouflage material was warm, and she wrapped it around her body, hugging herself. The tail was almost to her knees. If she had a belt, she could make a dress.

When she looked up, Remy was watching her with a hard expression. Her heart skipped a beat at the possessive look in his eyes. Fire kindled in her belly at that look. She remembered what it was like to be possessed by him—again and again, until she was languid and spent and so satisfied she could barely lift her head off the pillow.

Why had she put an end to that again?

Because he's a man. Because you don't want to get hurt. Because getting hurt is inevitable.

"You look at me like I kicked your puppy," he growled, and her heart pinched tight.

"I'm sorry."

"Fucking hell, stop with the apologies. I get that you feel guilty. I get that you don't know what to say to me. Just pretend like it never happened, all right?"

"All right." Her throat ached and her eyes stung, but dammit, that's what she'd wanted him to say, wasn't it? Pretend like nothing ever happened. It was a one-night stand, over and done with. Time to act normal.

A shout split the night, making her jump like a frightened rabbit. Remy caught her as she careened into him. His arms around her were steady. The gun at his chest felt awkward between them, its cool metal bulk unforgiving against her midsection.

She was in the process of taking a step backward, trying to put distance between them, when a bright light arced into the sky. A second later, a deafening kaboom shattered the air and kicked her in the chest.

CHAPTER THIRTEEN

AS THE SHOCK of the explosion rolled over the convoy, Remy shoved Christina behind him as if he could somehow protect her from a second blast. People screamed. The air was heavy with the scents of metal, fuel, and charred flesh.

Remy flipped down the NVG visor attached to his helmet and scanned the darkness. Shapes ran across his field of vision, the flames from the detonation licking the vehicles about a quarter mile or so back.

His team sprang into action the moment the blast happened, every man either scouting the perimeter, protecting the civilians in their custody, or guarding their position from enemy fire.

"Goddammit," Viking said into Remy's earpiece. "Get down there and see what's happening. We're going to have to abandon this van and cram into one. It's looking like the only choice."

Remy acknowledged the order, pushing Christina into

Cowboy's arms before hurrying down the line toward the blast site with Money and Camel. They wouldn't get too close, but they needed to assess the situation before they bugged out.

Remy's stomach churned with disgust and anger the closer they got. People were in shock, huddling together, screaming, crying. There were disembodied limbs on the ground, bodies twisted into unidentifiable lumps, and the strong odor of bleach.

He exchanged a look with his teammates. This blast wasn't military grade but very likely triacetone triperoxide, aka TATP, manufactured by an extremist group. The components were easy to acquire, and the process wasn't too difficult.

That meant the fires were coming from the exploded gas tanks of the vehicles and not from the TATP itself, which produced a lot of gas rather than flame when it detonated. It was also highly volatile, which meant a small amount could inflict heavy damage.

Sonofabitch.

He hated the pain and fear he saw on people's faces, but there was nothing he could do about it—and that was a sick fucking feeling to have. It brought up every rotten ghost in his past, every skeleton he couldn't bury. He'd joined up to help protect his nation, but sometimes that meant making hard choices. Like now when the SEALs had to get the hell out of here instead of helping the injured.

"Report." It was Viking's voice in his ear.

"TATP. A lot of dead and wounded."

"Fuck," Viking said. "Are there any medical personnel?"

Remy scanned the area, focusing on the men and women who ran back and forth between the victims, stooping down and then yelling for aid. Presently someone appeared with a medical kit.

"There appear to be some medics on scene." No idea where they'd come from, but since the city was emptying out, the chances of them being in the convoy were as good as any. They couldn't save anyone in need of surgery—no one could—but they could save those who could still be helped.

"Thank God," Viking muttered.

Suddenly Remy spotted a man with a rifle silhouetted against the fires before he ducked behind a vehicle a few yards back. It could be nothing, but in this situation it didn't pay to take a chance.

"Gunman at six o'clock," he barked to his guys. They dropped as one unit into the sand. "See anything, Camel?"

Alex Kamarov was their sniper. Camel could take down target after target for hours without missing a beat. All the SEALs were expert marksman, but Camel was the one who could take the difficult shots and make them work every time.

Camel had his eye to his scope. "Nothing."

At that moment, a bullet whizzed over their heads before the sound of the shot cracked into the night.

"Son of a bitch," Remy said into the mic. "We're taking fire."

Just what they fucking needed with the carnage all around them. These people had been through enough tonight, and now this too.

"I can go around," Camel said. "Twenty yards to the left and I'll have a clear shot. But you two need to keep his attention."

"Yeah, go on, we got it," Remy said.

"Don't lift your head for more than a split second," Camel warned. "If he's any good, you won't have time to wonder if he's going to shoot."

"Yes, dear," Money drawled.

Camel slunk away into the night while Remy kept his gaze on the vehicle where the gunman had gone. He couldn't see any legs, which meant the guy was either hiding behind the tire or not there anymore.

Still, if they were going to give Camel a chance, he had to raise his head. He lifted up and then ducked back down. Another bullet whizzed overhead. This dude had definitely tagged them as a target.

Money popped up this time and another bullet sounded in the night. And then a second bullet sounded, only this one came from the left.

"Mission accomplished," Camel said coolly in their ears.

"Thank fuck," Viking replied. "Get your asses back here. We're leaving ASAP."

The three of them humped it back to the group. Cowboy and Viking were waiting outside the vans, both of which were now running. Remy breathed a sigh of relief. They could have all crammed into—and on top of—one van, but it would have been rough going.

"We're going to split into two groups again. If we have to go our separate ways, we can." Viking eyed him. "What do you think about our gunman?"

Remy shrugged. "Opportunist. If there was anyone looking for us, they'd have sent more than one guy. I think he saw us in our gear, identified us as Americans, and decided to take the shot."

"Agreed," Camel said. "I saw no one else in the scope, no other activity or signs of an enemy."

"It's possible that's who got blown up," Remy added. "If a group of tangos were transporting TATP, it could have exploded and killed everyone—except this guy who might have been out taking a piss."

"That's likely," Viking said. "That shit is seriously unstable."

Cowboy took out a map and Viking ran his finger along a route. Of course they had GPS, but they still did things old-school too. You never knew when you'd be out of range of a satellite, or when everything would go to hell and you had to know how to navigate and survive without aid.

"We'll head for Akhira. It's our best choice now. If we can get there, we'll hitch a ride with one of the patrol boats. They can get us to a Navy ship, and we can helo these people out from there."

With traffic at a standstill on the road to Merak, and with the chaos ensuing across Qu'rim, there really was no single best way to go. They were all risky. But Akhira was closest, and speed was of the essence. The rebels hadn't cut off Akhira yet, though it was a possibility. Merak was safer, but the only bridge across the wadi was blocked. There wasn't another crossing for a good fifty miles in either direction.

"Same groups as before?" Remy asked, suddenly unable to bear the thought of Christina in a different van. What if they had to split up? He wouldn't know where she was or what was happening to her. He shouldn't care, but he did. Damn her.

Hell, even now he wondered how she was faring after the explosion. She'd launched herself into his arms when someone screamed right before the bomb went off. And then she'd clung tightly to him as the convoy erupted.

He'd felt her fear, but he hadn't been able to comfort her because he'd had to go to work.

Viking gave him a look. "I'm splitting the women up."

"All right." He wasn't going to argue if Viking took Christina into his group. But he wouldn't like it either.

"Christina Girard is with you," Viking said. "I'll take Penny. You get the bodyguard and Donovan Taylor. He's a lawyer working for a foreign gun manufacturer, by the way. Three guesses what he's here for."

"Every war needs guns," Remy said flatly, though he was relieved he still had Christina in his van.

"Yeah, no doubt." Viking took a step back. "All right, let's get rolling."

She was still wearing his shirt. Remy ducked into the van and found Christina huddled on a seat, her arms wrapped around herself. She looked up as he entered the interior, her gray eyes wild—but then she seemed to calm somewhat as their gazes clashed.

He didn't know what that meant, but it kicked him hard in the chest. Did she trust him? Or was she scared for him and just relieved he'd returned? He didn't know and he couldn't ask.

She looked so out of place here. She was elegant and petite, a gorgeous butterfly that didn't belong in the dust and squalor of this place. He wanted to go over and take her in his arms, but that wasn't going to happen either. Not out here. Not in front of all these people. Maybe never again considering the fact she'd been the one to walk away six months ago.

He'd told her he was over her. And he was, goddammit. He'd never been hung up on her in the first place—yet he'd liked her. A lot. She had a way of turning his protective instincts on high. He wanted to fix things for her. Take care of her.

But she didn't want that from him. She'd made that clear when she'd ignored him after their single night together. She'd gotten what she wanted, and then she'd bounced out of his life.

"Where are we going?" she asked as the van lurched into motion.

"Somewhere we can get all of you out of here," he replied.

"And where is that?" Donovan Taylor demanded. "I think we have a right to know."

"Actually, you don't," Remy said coolly. "You just need to hope we get where we're going as quickly as possible."

"What happened out there?" Christina asked. "Was anyone hurt?"

Remy exchanged a look with Money. The other man arched an eyebrow as if to say, *What the fuck, go ahead.*

"It's a war zone. Yeah, people were hurt," Remy replied.

"They need guns to defend themselves," Taylor said.

"Because guns work really well against bombs, especially when you don't know there's one nearby," Money drawled. Dude had a way of going straight for the throat that Remy loved.

Taylor's jaw tightened. Well, fuck him. Asshole had an agenda anyway.

"Look, it happened," Remy cut in before Taylor could speak and piss everyone off more than he already had. "Qu'rim is being torn apart by extremists, rebels, and their own government. We need to get the fuck out of here before we get torn apart along with it. Everyone can save their opinions of the war, the causes, and how to stop it for back home at the neighborhood bar, all right? Ain't nobody here got time to listen to it."

Silence fell for a few moments. It was too good to last.

"This fucking blows," Taylor said. "I've got business with the Qu'rimi government and yet I'm out here, screwing around in the desert with a bunch of commandos who don't know whether to jerk off or take a piss."

Remy made a mental note that he needed to figure a way to get back at Viking for saddling him with this jerk. "We can drop you off," he growled. "I'd be happy to open the door and let you exit. You just say the word."

Money put his hand on the door latch. "Slides open sweet as you please. Not a bit of trouble, asshole, you wanna go."

Taylor thrust out his jaw and kept his mouth shut. Wise move, though Remy wasn't sure he'd keep it shut. Probably he was working up another insult.

"Are we in danger?" Christina asked suddenly, her

sweet voice cutting into the tension like a hot knife through an ice cream cake.

Remy's gaze slid from the lawyer to her. She looked a bit pale, a bit tense—but she also looked like a woman intent on defusing a situation before it went nuclear. Not that it would go nuclear. Remy was annoyed, but he was also a professional. As much as he might like to kick that little fucker's ass out of the van, he wasn't going to do it. And he wasn't letting Money do it either.

"You aren't in any more danger than you ever were," he said, deliberately misunderstanding her definition of *we*.

Christina's gaze didn't falter. "Will they—the rebels—be looking for Americans to capture?"

"Honey, someone around here is always looking for Americans to capture. It's the nature of the war."

She darted her tongue out to lick her lips, and his balls tightened. Not precisely the reaction he expected. He leaned his bulk against the van wall and let his gaze drink her in even as her cheeks grew red and her eyes dropped away for a second.

"I'm not going to let that happen, Christina. Promise."

Gray eyes snapped to his again. He could see the question in them. Did he mean he wasn't going to let her get captured—or that he wasn't going to allow the attraction he still felt for her to flare to life again?

He hardened his expression, sending her a message. *Both, baby. Both.*

CHAPTER FOURTEEN

CHRISTINA DIDN'T EXPECT to sleep, not after the frightening explosion, the screams and smells, and the deadly calm of the SEALs as they dealt with things too horrifying to have to deal with. But, somehow, she did fall asleep as the van rocked back and forth across the sand, moving toward some destination she didn't know.

When she awakened, the van had stopped. Her heart shot into her throat and she bolted upright. She had a bench seat to herself, apparently—and she was still wrapped in Remy's shirt.

She was also alone. She rocketed to her feet, swaying as she moved too fast and the blood in her head rushed to the floor. She shot an arm out to steady herself against the metal wall.

The door opened and a head peered in. "You're awake."

Remy. Oh dear Jesus...

"I am. Where is everyone?" Her heart pounded like

she'd just run a marathon and her head was still swimmy, but she managed not to fall onto her butt and alert him that she was having a weak moment.

"We've had a change of plans. Safe house. They've gone inside."

Well, at least that wasn't as bad as it could have been. Christina swallowed and took her hand off the wall. She didn't feel shaky, so she moved toward Remy and the door. He stood back and then reached out to help her down. She meant to tell him she could do it herself, but his hands closed around her waist and then he lifted her with ease and set her on the sand.

She was still reeling from the contact when his hands fell away from her body, and disappointment flooded her. It took her a moment to gather her thoughts and calm her racing heart. She was standing in a courtyard of some type, and there was a house. A wall ringed the house and grounds. The other van sat nearby. There were two other cars as well. Lights flickered inside the house.

She took it all in, her mind churning. "What kind of safe house?"

Remy's teeth flashed in what she thought might be a grin, except it was too dark to really know. "Best you don't ask that question, *cher*. Friendlies though."

She cocked her head. "Are you sure?"

"Reasonably. You'll see. These guys are mercenaries. American and foreign, but not terrorists."

"Why did you leave me in the van?"

"I didn't leave you. Everyone just now went inside, and I came to wake you."

"Oh… Where are we, Remy?"

"Still in Qu'rim."

A current of worry slid through her. "This wasn't part of the plan, was it? Stopping here, I mean."

He shrugged. "The plan is fluid, babe. It has to be."

"Something must be happening where you were taking us, or we wouldn't have stopped."

His eyes were unreadable. They were too dark. "Something *is* happening. Qu'rim is in the midst of a civil war, and those fuckers are unpredictable as hell. But then you were told that before you chose to come here."

"You can't miss an opportunity to let me know what you think, can you?" He pissed her off sometimes, and yet what could she really say? Qu'rim had been in the midst of a civil war for a couple of years now. It was mostly business as usual in spite of that.

Until the rebels took Baq. That was the game changer, unfortunately.

"You're in danger because you didn't think Matt or I knew what we were talking about. You had to do it your way, Christina, and to hell with what we told you."

Okay, that stung. And it wasn't true. It wasn't that she hadn't listened, but hell, if she never went to any of the countries where there was instability, Girard Oil wouldn't get anything done.

And yet she could have tried to get Sheikh Fahd onto her territory. Or at least to Dubai. But he'd been so difficult to pin down that when he'd finally agreed to meet with her, she hadn't wasted a moment trying to negotiate another location.

"You have a job to do, Remy. I have one too. I'm here because I was doing it."

He made a sound that she was certain was meant to be derisive. Whatever.

"Inside, princess. We clearly aren't going to agree, and the sun'll be up soon."

She walked in front of him to the door that was really just a dark blanket over an opening. Remy pushed it aside, his arm brushing against her head, and she ducked inside.

The accommodations were basic, to say the least. The floor was nothing more than packed dirt, and there were stairs against one wall. The odor of sweat and exertion hung heavy in the air.

She recognized all the SEALs, but there were a couple of other guys too. They were also dressed in desert camouflage and had weapons strapped to their sides. She couldn't tell their nationality by looking at them, but they didn't appear to be Middle Eastern.

The SEALs and their charges were tearing into packages, pulling out food while the other guys talked. Not quite what she'd expected. Her stomach rumbled as if on cue, and Remy thrust a package into her hand. It was a little bigger than a brick and wrapped in tan plastic.

"Dinner," he said. "Follow the instructions. After that we'll sort out where to put everyone for now."

She looked at what she held. The package said MRE in big brown letters. Beneath that it said MEAL, READY TO EAT. It also had information on where it was packed and what it contained—in this case, penne with vegetable sausage crumbles in a spicy tomato sauce.

At the top of the package, she was told that it was held closed by a peelable seal. She glanced at Remy, but he'd already turned away. She started to peel the plastic open as she went over and sat down with Penny and her boss, a banker named Robert. Nobody spoke. The SEALs talked in a low hum with the guys whose place this must be, but the six people they were evacuating did not. Some ate quickly, eyes darting around the dimly lit room as if they couldn't believe they were here. Others kept their gazes on the ground or the food.

"How are you doing, Penny?" Christina asked when she couldn't bear the silence any longer. Which was odd for her considering she was an introvert and always had been.

The woman looked up, startled eyes wide as she gulped down the bite of food she'd taken. "Okay… I… I just want to go home," she finished softly, her eyes turning instantly shiny as tears gathered.

"We all do, lady," Donovan Taylor grumbled.

"Don't speak to her that way," Robert said.

"What way? I just said what we're all thinking. Jesus."

Penny's tears spilled over, and Christina wished like hell she'd kept her mouth shut.

"It's okay, Robert," Penny said, putting her hand on his arm. "I'm emotional and I know it."

"Nothing wrong with that," Robert answered, his voice sounding a little choked up on her behalf.

Christina glanced at his wedding ring. Penny didn't look like the sort of woman who'd be attracted to Robert, but money had a way of making a woman go blind when it came to sex appeal. Or a man, she supposed, considering what Ben's orientation had been and how he'd hidden it for the sake of her money and whatever political cachet he'd decided she had.

"I think we're all emotional," Christina said firmly, meeting Donovan's gaze and daring him to contradict her. He didn't say a word. "Instead of dinner meetings in fine restaurants with expensive wine lists and crystal glasses, we're running for our lives with a group of military commandos. And now we're camping out in a"—she paused as she glanced around the dirt-filled room—"hovel, eating prepackaged food with plastic sporks. It's a bit of a change in circumstances. We won't even discuss the bomb earlier, or the many lives that were no doubt lost due to it."

They went silent after that, eating their meals and avoiding eye contact with each other. Christina had no idea what would happen next, but she doubted it included a shower or a soft bed. She'd get around to asking someone, but right now every muscle in her body ached from the cramped ride in the van, and she didn't feel like moving.

Eventually the floor started to rumble. It was soft at first, a mere vibration, but then it grew more noticeable and everyone stilled, sporks arrested in the act of shoveling food into mouths.

Penny made a sound that turned out to be a sob. Robert put an arm around her and pulled her close. Christina shifted to look at the SEALs. That's when a chill slipped down her spine.

They were all on their feet, weapons held at the ready. She hadn't heard them move. The other men had unholstered their sidearms. All of them looked at the front of the building, listening as the rumble grew louder and louder.

Nobody said anything. A series of head jerks and meaningful looks passed among the men. Several of them disappeared through the door. Remy was one of the ones who stayed behind this time, and Christina's heart pounded. When he'd taken off after the bomb exploded, he'd scared the hell out of her. But he'd come back, and she'd been able to breathe again.

He met her gaze now. Then he quirked an eyebrow and gave her half a smile. Her heart wanted to melt. Might have melted if she weren't sitting on a dirt floor in a Middle Eastern country and waiting for enemy fighters to come blasting through the door any minute.

Hard to melt when you were terrified.

The rumbling grew louder, the walls and floor vibrated—and then it stopped. Everything stopped. A few seconds later, there was a shout. It seemed as if everyone had stopped breathing, as if the air grew heavy with silence and anticipation.

But then there was a laugh from somewhere outside, and relief made Christina sag against the wall and let out a breath. If they were laughing, it couldn't be bad.

Soon the flap to the door opened and the SEALs came inside. So did a group of other men. One stopped and surveyed them all sitting on the floor. He was tall and handsome in a way that drew the eye, with dark hair cropped close and several days' worth of growth on his face. He was also clearly the man in charge of the men this house belonged to, because they all deferred to him.

He turned to the SEALs after he'd looked over the six civilians on the floor.

"Does Mendez know you're here, kids?"

"He's aware," Viking said evenly.

The man raked a hand over his head. Then he laughed. "Goddamn, isn't this a kick? HOT and Black's Bandits together again. Let the good times roll, boys."

CHAPTER FIFTEEN

THE SAFE HOUSE they'd stopped at turned out to be larger and more complex than Christina had first realized. There was an upstairs, and there was a series of buildings connected to the one they'd sat down to eat in. She now found herself in a dingy room in one of those buildings with a sleeping bag and a window that showed a slice of star-studded sky.

Penny was supposed to be in here with her, but she'd refused to leave Robert's side since the incident earlier, confirming what Christina suspected. That particular boss-secretary arrangement was definitely more than friendly. How Penny had ended up in the van with her and Paul in the first place, Christina had no idea. She wasn't being parted from Robert now for anything.

Christina had retreated to the small room she'd been given and sat in the dark, staring out the window and trying to calm her mind enough to sleep for a couple more hours. But sleep was elusive now that the sky was starting to pinken at the edges.

It wasn't just that, of course. It was this night. Remy. Everything that seeing him again churned up inside. Regret and emptiness swirled within her, refusing to leave her alone. She felt empty because of what she'd given up, and she regretted it too.

Except what had she given up? A fling? No way would they still be together if the affair had played its course. He'd have grown tired of her. Men grew tired of things. She knew that better than anyone.

He'd have especially grown tired of her considering how boring her life generally was. *This* was his life—war zones. Fighting. Surviving. Protecting. A few months of hanging around with her, discovering that what she really liked were quiet nights at home with a book and a glass of wine, sometimes a movie, would have bored him to absolute tears. A man like Remy needed more than that.

A sound in the corridor brought her head up. She waited, her heart speeding up. When there was nothing else, she stood and crept over to the entry. There was no door. Just an opening into the room. The others were in rooms nearby, but she felt like one of them would have made more noise if they were up and walking around.

Christina stood very still, breathing as quietly as possible. Listening.

"Who's there?" she finally said, her voice soft, her pulse skipping as she told herself that an enemy wouldn't sneak into the building and silently move through it. No, an enemy would enter in a blaze of gunfire or breaching explosives.

"Why are you still awake?" came the reply. *Remy.*

Her heart soared, and her cheeks ached with the effort

to hold back the smile that wanted to break out. Why would she want to smile now? In this place?

But she did.

"Why are you?" she asked, because she couldn't help but be sassy with him. She'd never been sassy with a man in her life, but this one—oh, this one made her a better version of herself somehow. A braver, sassier, take-charge version that she liked and that scared her at the same time.

What if he didn't like that version of her? What if no one did? She'd been raised to be ladylike, demure, a debutante from head to toe. Firmness had to be cloaked in politeness, not put on display like a challenge.

And yet she enjoyed challenging Remy. Got a charge from it.

A second later, Remy appeared in the door, his bulk taking up the entire frame. She had an insane urge to fling herself at him and kiss him, but she didn't let herself act on it. She knew the urge came from this place. This situation.

And the fact a bomb had exploded earlier and he'd left her while he raced toward it.

She wanted to wrap her arms around him and tell him how glad she was that he was okay.

But he was armed and armored, his body like a cactus of metal and leather. He wore a sidearm strapped to his thigh, and though he'd removed the rifle from across his chest, he still looked badass and untouchable.

Not that it had stopped her earlier when someone had screamed back in the middle of the convoy. She still remembered what it had been like to press herself to him, even if she had been mostly squeezed against his rifle.

"Because it's my job," he said in a low voice.

"Surely you get to sleep sometimes," she replied.

"I do. And I did."

"That's good… I was worried for you when you took off back there." She didn't say where, but she didn't have to. He knew.

"Again, it's my job. I had to see what was going on. For your safety, and the safety of my team."

For the first time, she realized what her brother must go through. She'd had no idea how bad it could be out here. He'd always insisted his job was routine, that the bad stuff didn't happen near where he was—but it was a lie.

No wonder Matt had been so pissed at her for coming to Qu'rim. Well, she was pissed right back, especially now that he had two babies to care for. Did Evie know it was a lie?

Then again, after what Evie had gone through when she'd returned to Rochambeau and her sister had been kidnapped, she had to know the truth. Because Matt had helped her through it all, and the two of them had faced criminal enforcers together in the bayou.

Christina still remembered the shiner Matt had sported at her wedding two days afterward.

"I've never heard a bomb go off before," she said. "I've heard shotgun blasts, of course. But I never felt those like a kick to the whole body. It was terrifying… How do you stand it? How do you not lose your shit when it happens?"

"Training, *cher*. Lots of training. My body knows what to do even before my brain figures it out. Is it foolproof? Of course not. But so far, I do what I know how to do and I'm still here at the end of the day."

Christina swallowed the lump that formed in her throat. "You would have never told me any of this if we'd kept dating, would you?"

"Probably not, no. What good would it have done?"

What good would it have done? She didn't know. Couldn't say. But she knew if they had been together, she would have wanted to know. It seemed wrong not to understand what happened to someone if he was important to you.

"We did everything backward, didn't we?" She didn't expect him to answer, but he did.

"If you remember, you're the one who dictated the pace." He blew out a breath and shook his head. "But I didn't say no when I should have. Should have stuck to my guns and walked away from you instead of going along with your crazy plan to get back in the saddle."

"It didn't seem crazy at the time. And it made a difference, Remy."

"Oh yeah? How's that? All I remember is that it made you run."

She clasped her hands into a knot to keep from reaching out to him. "I ran because I was scared of how intense it was with you. You made me hope, and I couldn't afford hope. But you also made me aware of myself, and you made me realize that Ben's problems were his and not mine."

"All that in only one night?"

"You're mocking me." Not that she blamed him really.

"Not trying to. I just don't see it the same as you. What I see is that you were determined to get back at him, even if it was just in your head—and you did it. You evened the score. You were done, because if your ex had hurt you, then I might hurt you too if you stuck around long enough."

My God, how his words cut to the bone. Because they were accurate. Because she had been afraid to get hurt again. Convinced there was nothing between them and wouldn't be, at least not on his part. If she took his calls, if she kept going out with him, she'd be the one who got hurt. Not him.

She turned and went over to the window. The sky was growing lighter now, and she could make out their surroundings a little better. They were on the second floor in one of the buildings attached to the main structure, which was surrounded by a solid concrete wall—or maybe it was mud brick. In the distance, there seemed to be a clustering of buildings. A village?

"If I'd taken your calls," she said, not looking at him, "whatever we had going on would have ended by now. You'd have moved on."

"Are you fucking kidding me?" he growled, and she turned to see he'd come into the room. His eyes flashed in his handsome face, his brows drawing low.

He had a couple of days' worth of beard, and he was still the sexiest thing she'd ever seen, even with the dirt of the desert and remnants of greasepaint streaking his face.

"You don't know that, Christina. You don't know a goddamn thing about me other than what you decided for yourself without ever giving me a shot."

She swallowed as she watched him standing there, looking furious and sexy all at once. Her heart ached with memories of their night together, and she knew she'd imbued it with far more importance than she should have.

This was why she had to be careful. Her stupid, lonely heart. The heart that had only ever wanted someone to love her. She'd been so lonely growing up. She wasn't like Matt. After their mother died and their father went off the rails, she hadn't had anyone to be close to—her father's succession of stripper wives had been out of the question, of course. None of them had been very motherly anyway—except for Misty Lee, but she'd come along after Christina was out of the house.

Matt had always had Evie. Christina had only had Granny, who'd been a wonderful woman but obviously not someone her own age. Not someone who understood all the things a girl went through as she grew up—or at least not all the things a girl of Christina's generation went through.

When Granny was growing up, things were different. She'd tried, but her solution to loneliness was a good book and some ice cream. Both very good things for the soul, but not always the most nourishing when it was human comfort Christina had needed.

She sucked in a breath and willed herself not to cry. But dammit, she was here in the middle of a foreign desert, and she had no idea if or when she'd make it home again. The one person she could be close to, at least for a little while, was standing right in front of her.

And she kept screwing the whole thing up.

"I want to ask you something," she said.

"All right, ask." She heard the frustration in his voice. And the patience, even though she probably didn't deserve any.

She took a deep breath. "Will you hold me, Remy?"

CHAPTER SIXTEEN

REMY BLINKED. AND then he squinted at her in the pale predawn glow. Was she serious? Had she really just asked him to *hold* her?

But she was standing there with her hands clasped together, her pretty hair loose and flowing down her back—she'd removed the hijab—and her gaze fixed on him. She was so small. Wispy, as if she might float away on a good breeze. She'd always been thin, but it had hit him about an hour ago that the vague thing bothering him about her being in his arms earlier was just how much lighter she felt. More frail. Not that she *was* frail, but she felt it.

And that made him angry, because here she was in fucking Qu'rim of all places. A place where frailty would not be rewarded, where the slightest weakness could mean the difference between surviving and dying.

Christina was not the sort of woman to be stuck in a war zone. And she *was* stuck, as they all were, while they waited for intel to give them a better way out. Thankfully,

Ian Black had a safe house here and they were able to use it. But it wasn't ideal. Nothing about this situation was ideal.

"It's okay if you don't want to," she said, her voice sounding tight with control. "I shouldn't have asked."

"Jesus," he said before crossing the distance in a single stride and tugging her gently against him. She shuddered as her arms went around his body. And then she squeezed him tight.

"You aren't wearing the body armor. I thought you still were."

Fucking hell. He threaded his fingers into her hair, cupped the back of her head, and held her against his chest. "No," he said thickly. "Took it off earlier. We're in a safe zone, at least for a while."

She hugged him tighter. "I can feel *you* now. You instead of prickly armor and ammunition."

He warred with himself. Part of him wanted to push her away, put an end to this touchy-feely shit. And part of him wanted to wrap both arms around her and pull her in so close she never wanted to leave him.

"What are you trying to do to me?" he growled, and she pushed back until she could tilt her head back and gaze up at him with those liquid eyes of hers.

He remembered the feeling of drowning in those eyes. They were like clear pools of rainwater. Gray-green sometimes, gray-blue at others. He wanted to dive into them and stay there.

"I'm lonely," she said, "and scared. I thought if you held me, I might not feel so alone."

He pressed her head to his chest and stared sightlessly at the wall. Her fingers curled into the back of his shirt and she trembled.

He hated that she shook. Hated it. It made him want to slay dragons for her. And yet he knew that even if she was scared, she wasn't helpless. Not like that woman Penny. That one was terrified of her own shadow and unable to hide it.

Christina wouldn't let that shit show. Not if she could help it. So brave.

Just like Roxie. He closed his eyes as his sister's face rolled through his mind. Poor, brave Roxie, who'd thought she could fight her own battles when what she really needed was backup. The kind of backup that would have sent her motherfucking boyfriend running for cover and begging for mercy.

"You don't have to be scared," Remy said, still holding her with one arm only while the other dangled at his side because he didn't trust himself. "We'll get you home safely."

"I know you will."

Her hands splayed on his back and then curled into his shirt again. Damn, it felt good to be touched by her. Too good. He wouldn't get hard over such a simple touch, but if he let himself think of all the other ways she'd touched him, he definitely would.

"You've certainly picked a helluva time to ask me to hold you, *cher*. If you'd answered my calls, I'd have held you all you wanted."

"I know. I… I was stupid. But you scared me. Everything about you, about the situation, scared me."

She took a tiny step backward, put her hands on his cheeks. He vaguely thought he should put an end to this here and now, but he kinda didn't want to.

Okay, he really didn't want to. He'd told her he wasn't hung up on her, and he wasn't, but she'd definitely made an impact.

"You're pretty much the most interesting woman I've never dated, you know that?"

She laughed, but it was more of a sad sound than anything. "Thanks. I think. Wow, this is weird, isn't it?"

Her hands slipped to his shoulders, but she made no move to step away. And he made no move to push her away either.

"Yep, definitely weird. We had to come all the way to Qu'rim to have a conversation we could have had six months ago."

"If I'd picked up the phone," she finished for him.

"Pretty much."

"I'm sorry, Remy. Really." She shook her head. He could still smell the vague scent of the shampoo she'd used the last time she'd washed her hair. "My head wasn't screwed on right, and I couldn't handle getting involved with anyone just then. And to be fair, I did mention that."

"Yeah, you did." He was the one who'd wanted more from her, and he'd been pissed that he didn't get it. But how fair was that when she'd set the limits in the first place? He'd known what they were, but he'd thought he could change that. Intended to change it.

But of course he hadn't, because Christina was stronger and fiercer than she looked. She wasn't about to be steamrolled by anyone. Even if she did tremble in his arms tonight.

"So you threw yourself into work," he said, trying to have a normal conversation even while the subtext ran in his head that he wanted her naked and beneath him. So pretty. So sweet. So hot when she got worked up.

Stop.

She let her hands slide down his arms, then slipped them around his waist again. Fucking hell, she was going to kill him before this was through. She pressed her cheek to his chest.

"I did. I traveled a lot, made a lot of pitches, and brought in millions of dollars in new business. Job wise, it's been good."

"You've lost weight."

She stilled, her breath hitching for a second before she let it out again and kept breathing normally. "A little. It's hard to eat on a normal schedule when flying all over the place. Time zones really screw with a body."

"Tell me about it."

Without thinking, he put both his arms around her. Then he wanted to drop one, but it was too late. *Hell.*

So he held her in both arms, loosely, and let her drive the conversation. Partly because he was trying not to respond to her being in his arms, especially when she kept holding him so tight. Like he was a lifeline.

"You don't feel like you've lost any weight," she said, her hands roving over his back. "I'd say you feel as solid as ever."

It was suddenly too much for him. He grasped her arms, gently, and unwrapped them from his body. Then he took a step back, away from her. She didn't try to hug him again. She crossed her arms and hugged herself instead.

And that made him feel like an asshole. *Jesus.*

"I'm sorry," she said in a small voice. "I didn't mean to make you uncomfortable."

"Christina." He stopped, swallowed. Because he

couldn't think of how to say it. How to tell her he didn't mean to hurt her but that she had to stop. For both their sakes. He shook his head and barreled on. "I'm a man, not a saint. When you touch me like that, even if in your mind it's harmless—well, it's not. I can't do it. Because I want more. I know how sweet you taste, so it's not easy to stand here and pretend we're buddies. If you want someone to hug you, I'm not the guy. I can't be the guy. I will always want more from you. So make of that what you will. If you need to talk to someone because you're scared, I'll sit on the other side of the room and you can talk until you feel better. If you just need another body in the room, I can do that too—but I'll be on the other side of it. It's the best I can do."

CHAPTER SEVENTEEN

CHRISTINA'S THROAT WAS dry. Oh, she knew, didn't she, what she'd been doing? She knew she'd been baiting the lion. Touching him because he was here and she missed him. Yes, dammit, she missed him. Stupid, crazy heart. Missing a man she barely knew just because he'd made her feel so damned special at a time when she'd desperately needed it.

"I..." She hugged herself tighter. She'd been so alone the past few months. And she'd hated it. But what about the fear? She hadn't been wrong to fear him. Fear what he could do to her battered heart.

But her heart was stronger now. She was stronger. Could she handle him? Handle being with him again?

"What?" His voice was compelling. Demanding.

And she knew she was going to plunge. Maybe it was the situation. Maybe it was temporary insanity. Didn't matter. She was still plunging off the cliff.

"I want more too. More of you."

He was silent. Still. She'd expected him to come to her, take her in his arms. Or hold out his arms and welcome her into them.

He did neither of those things.

"Fuck," he said. "Fuck."

Embarrassment prickled her skin. Heat rose to the surface, washing her in too much warmth. She was still wearing his shirt, the abaya, and her clothes. It was too much now.

But she couldn't strip it off. If she did, he'd know she was humiliated.

"Forget I said it," she said in a rush.

He blew out a breath. "Dammit, Christina—which is it? You want more or you want me to forget you said it? And how's any of this supposed to make me believe that you know what you want, that you aren't just reacting to what happened today? Being so close to a bombing—that's pretty intense shit. Makes people do things they might later regret."

"I don't regret you. I never regretted you. I regretted I wasn't ready—maybe I'm ready now."

"And this is precisely the kind of shit that makes me think you aren't." He held up a hand, silencing anything she might have said in response. "It's bullshit, babe. You don't know what you want, and I'm not getting sucked in by those pretty eyes this time."

He pivoted and walked out the door. Christina's feet were glued to the floor. She wanted to follow him, call out, demand he come back. But she did none of those things. She sucked in deep breaths—angry, hurt, sad—and told herself she deserved every bit of what he'd said. She deserved him walking out on her, the way she'd walked out on him.

This wasn't love, but it still managed to hurt a whole damn lot.

Remy strode down the hall, down the stairs, and shoved his way outside. He was pissed—at both her *and* at himself. At her for jerking his chain and at himself for, well, walking away when she wanted to reestablish relations with him.

He snorted. *Reestablish relations*. As if they were a fucking country at war like Qu'rim. As if they had to sit their diplomats down at a table and work out a solution.

No, the solution would have been to sweep her up and take her mouth in a hard kiss. And then the solution would have been to shove her jeans down and robes up, free his cock, and sink deep within the heaven that lay between her legs.

Jesus, he was an asshole for even thinking such a thing. And he was pretty much a red-blooded man for thinking it too.

He stopped and shoved a hand through his hair. Then he turned and looked at the door he'd just walked through. He could go back. He could still kiss her. Still push those jeans down…

"Lose something, Cage?"

He whirled, cursing softly as he spotted Camel leaning against the wall, one leg bent at the knee, foot against the cement.

"My motherfucking mind," he said, shaking his head.

"Oh yeah? Surprised to hear you still had any of it left. Thought we'd all lost our minds when we signed up for BUD/S."

"Eh, you love it and you know it."

"Yeah." Camel straightened, stretching his arms skyward. "Be glad when we're out of this one. Hate seeing Christina Girard in this mess."

Something very like jealousy pricked Remy's soul. "She knew better than to come here and she did it anyway. It's her own fault."

Camel blinked. "Maybe so… but I still hate it. Girard's a good guy. Must be driving him crazy that his sister's out here and he can't help."

"That's what we're here for."

"Still, if she were my sister…" He cleared his throat. "Kinda glad she's not though. She's a hot one, isn't she? If you like them with their noses in the air."

Something ugly was beginning to stir inside Remy's gut. "You think she's stuck-up?"

Camel scratched his cheek. "She's nice enough, I guess. But she doesn't say much, does she? Sits there looking at you as if she's better than you—not saying she thinks that, but she looks like she does. Snooty, as my mother says." He shrugged. "Still, I'd like to get into her panties. Wouldn't say no if she asked."

Remy's head was pounding by now. He wanted to punch Camel's lights out, but he also knew it was just normal guy talk. Camel had no way of knowing that Christina was Remy's.

Jesus… she was *his.*

He felt like he'd been zapped by a lightning bolt. Nothing worked for a long moment as he stood there processing everything. Christina was his. He wasn't finished with her. He had no idea where this was going or if he was about to commit a huge mistake, but he wasn't finished yet. He was about to dive out of an airplane and pray there was a parachute attached to his back.

"Dude, you okay?"

Remy snapped his gaze to Camel's. "Yeah, fine." He glared. "Christina isn't going to ask you to get into her panties. And you aren't trying, got that?"

Camel held up both hands. "Easy, brother."

"Woman's a lady," he growled. "Not a skank you met in a bar. Just because she doesn't say much doesn't make her stuck-up. It just means she doesn't have a lot to say. Or maybe she's an introvert, you ever think of that? Not everyone's comfortable around strangers."

"Whoa, man, all right." Camel's eyes were wide as he regarded Remy. As if he couldn't believe the ferocity in Remy's voice.

Yeah, Remy knew he sounded crazy right about now, but he couldn't help it. He was in the grip of something. And it wasn't just about Christina. Roxie had been quiet. Sweet and tender, with wells that ran deep. She'd fallen for the wrong man because he'd known how to get behind the walls she'd built—something Remy blamed himself for because Eric had been his friend. Eric learned what he needed to know about Roxie, and then he'd gone in and manipulated her. He'd used her insecurity against her, kept her by his side even when she surely knew she needed to go.

That's what abusers did. Remy knew that now. He

wished he'd known it then. Jesus, what he wouldn't give to go back in time and beat the hell out of that son of a bitch before he ever got his hooks into Roxie.

"Look," Camel was saying, "no insult intended, okay? She's Matt's sister. She's family. You know I'll do whatever it takes to take care of family."

Remy's pulse pounded. "Yeah, I know it. Look, I got-ta go back inside. Need to get my armor."

He turned and went through the door, up the stairs he'd pounded down, retracing his steps. When he got to the opening to Christina's room, he stopped just inside it. Her head came up, her eyes widening.

"Remy? Did something happen? What's wrong?" She got to her feet, looking pale and frightened.

He cursed himself for scaring her.

"Nothing's wrong." Except that everything was. She shouldn't be here, and he shouldn't want her the way he did.

"Why did you come back?"

He strode over to where she stood, but he didn't touch her. He held her gaze for a long moment, watching as her pupils dilated. Her gaze slipped to his mouth, and he knew she was thinking the kinds of things he always thought when he was with her. Bodies entwining, naked skin, so much heat and need, wet tongues—and an even wetter pussy taking him deep.

They were combustible, he and Christina. No idea why, but they were. Desire was never far behind when he was near her.

"Because I had to," he said.

She reached out carefully and palmed his cheek. "I missed you," she said. "It's crazy, because I hardly know you. But I really missed you."

He put his hand over hers, then ran his fingers up her arm, cupped the back of her head.

"I missed you too."

And then he did what he'd been dying to do from the moment she'd opened her hotel door. He dragged her into his arms and kissed the daylights out of her.

CHAPTER EIGHTEEN

HOW JOY COULD suffuse a soul when danger was all around, Christina didn't know. She only knew it did. Remy kissed her hard, his tongue sliding against hers, demanding she give him everything.

She cupped his jaw in both hands. He had several days' worth of scruff that scraped over her chin and upper lip, and she didn't much care. It felt far too wonderful to kiss him. Presently he gentled the kiss—and then he pulled back, breaking the contact.

For a brief moment, she thought he might be about to leave her there and take off again, but he ran a thumb over her lower lip, pressing it until she moaned.

"This is not the place," he said gruffly.

"I don't care. We're alone, and I need you."

He took her by the wrists, gently, when she tried to wrap her arms around him and pull herself closer. It was a stark contrast to the way he'd pushed her away earlier. This time he was tender, regretful.

"Not doing this here, Christina. I need you in a bed, not on a sandy sleeping bag in a room with no door."

It made sense, and yet it worried her too. She didn't know what had changed his mind, but she knew he could change it back again with little warning.

"A bed could be a long way off," she whispered, her heart aching. Her body ached too, but that was because it hadn't gotten what it wanted—him, deep inside her, taking her to heaven and back.

"It's a chance we have to take."

She hated that he wasn't going to give in to what they both needed, but she knew he was right not to. It was still early, the sky still pink at the edges, but the light was growing stronger by the minute. There were sounds outside in the courtyard—including a rooster, oddly enough—but nothing much inside yet. Though there soon would be as people woke and wanted breakfast. No telling who would wander past the room then.

He led her over to the sleeping bag and sank down on it in a sitting position, pulling her with him. Then he leaned against the wall and tucked her against his side with his arm curled around her. She snuggled against him, hardly believing this was happening and yet so damned glad for it too.

She put her arm over him, around his waist, and just lay there breathing him in. "I'm glad you came back, Remy."

"Me too, *cher*."

They didn't speak for a long moment.

"It seems awkward to ask...," she began. "But what have you been up to the past six months?"

He snorted. "Yeah, just a bit awkward. Let's see...

went on about five missions, took a couple of weeks off and went snorkeling in the Keys, ate some donuts, worked out, visited my mother…"

She waited for what he didn't say—that he'd had a few dates. But of course he wasn't going to tell her that. And yet she wanted to know. Desperately.

"Did you, um, go out with anyone?"

He hesitated. "A couple of times, yeah."

A sharp pain stabbed her in the heart. "I guess I have no right to feel any kind of anger over that. But I do." Why was she always so damned honest with him? No wonder she'd run away—he made her spill her guts simply by being who he was.

"No, you don't have a right to be angry."

Her eyes stung. He traced a finger over her cheek, tucked her hair behind an ear.

"I didn't take any of them home, Christina. I haven't been with anyone since you."

Her heart thudded as she pushed herself away from him so she could see into his eyes. He was gazing at her evenly, and she knew he wasn't lying. Or maybe her confused and crazy heart just wanted to believe he was being honest. She was no authority on when a man might be dishonest, after all.

Oh God, this *was why he was dangerous…*

"Is that really true?" she croaked.

"Yeah, it's true. I get why you'd think otherwise, but quite honestly, there hasn't been a lot of time—missions take a chunk out of the days and weeks, and we've been on several. Not to mention I spent a lot of time waiting for you to answer the damn phone."

"You are almost too good to be true, Remy

Marchand."

"Tell me about it." He grinned, and she laughed because she couldn't help it.

"Seriously, in six months you could have gotten an entire stadium full of women to take off their panties for you."

His expression sobered. "Yeah, well, the older I get, the less interested I am in casual sex with strangers. I want to like the person I'm with. I want to know her and be interested in who she is outside the bedroom."

Whoa damn, her heart was really flipping in her chest now. "Like I said, too good to be true."

"What about you? Any dates? Any dudes whose asses I need to kick?"

She laughed. "No dates. No dudes. Unless you count my ex-husband, who recently decided he might have made a mistake and wants to try again."

His eyes nearly bugged out. "What the fuck? Seriously?"

"Yep, seriously." She hadn't been able to believe it herself, but she knew Ben wasn't exactly regretful or missing her. He missed the life he'd had with her, the respectable one where he was on his way to a political career. He'd blown that when he'd had butt sex in a public bathroom, but for some reason he now believed he could get it all back if only she'd forgive him and pick up where they'd left off. If she didn't know better, she'd say he was cracked in the head.

"So what did he do, text you his regrets and ask for another chance?" He sounded as disbelieving as she felt.

"I blocked him a long time ago, so no. He came to my place."

Remy's arm tightened around her. "He fucking came to your house?"

"Yes." She'd been so surprised to see him through the peephole that she'd opened the door and gaped. Ben had looked like a whipped puppy. He'd asked to come inside. Against her better judgment, she'd let him.

"And?"

Christina blew out a breath. Why had she even mentioned Ben? Because she could feel the tension in Remy's body now, and it was harshing the mellow she felt from curling up against him.

"He came inside, said his piece, and I asked him to leave."

His fingers went under her chin, tipping her head up so she had to look at him. "You let him inside your place? What happened when you said no to him?"

She shrugged. "He was pissed, but he went." She put a hand on his wrist, stroked his skin. "It's nothing. He hoped I'd be lonely or desperate enough to try again, I guess. But I'm not—and I'm not ever going to be. That ship has sailed."

He continued studying her, searching her gaze. He seemed… disturbed on some level. She wasn't sure why.

"You're sure he didn't threaten you?"

Christina blinked. "Threaten me? No. I mean he wasn't happy that I wouldn't consider getting back together, but he didn't threaten me. He was angry, of course. He thinks that if we get back together, we can spin his infidelity and he can still have the political career he wants. He thinks he can be elected governor of Louisiana with my family name to help him—and then he thinks he's got a shot at the presidency someday."

Ben had rambled a bit about legacy and destiny, but he hadn't been back since she'd told him to get lost. The entire encounter had made her uncomfortable, but Ben wasn't dangerous. Just narcissistic as hell.

"If he shows up again, you are *not* letting him in—and you're calling me. Got it?"

She wanted to huff and tell him she was a grown woman and could take care of herself. But she liked the way he took control and told her what she needed to do. Not about everything—God no—but about Ben? Yes, she liked it. It made her feel special. Protected.

And if that wasn't politically correct, then she didn't care. Sometimes it was sexy when a man took charge. It was also sexy when he knew how to give up control too.

"And if you aren't in town?" she said, lifting an eyebrow. Knowing it would get a rise out of him.

He gritted his teeth before he answered. "You'll call Matt. Or Mendez. Don't think the colonel wouldn't do something about it."

She thought of Colonel Mendez and suppressed a shiver. Yes, that man was untouchable. Hard, cold, and lethal. She didn't really know him, but that was her impression based on the few times she'd been around him. Matt idolized him, so that was a good sign in her opinion.

"But if Ben ever tries anything, Christina—you call the police. Don't wait, don't call one of us first. Don't even think that he's harmless or it's all a misunderstanding. Call someone."

He said it so fiercely that she knew it was important to him. What she didn't know was why. "Don't worry, Remy. I'm not stupid. I'll call someone if he comes around again—and if he crosses a line, I'll call the police."

He nodded, but he still looked fierce. "Good."

She put a hand on his cheek and stroked his whiskers. She couldn't help but touch him now that she seemed to have the right again. She wanted to touch him in so many places, but that wasn't happening just yet.

"Can you tell me why it worries you that Ben came to see me?"

She didn't think Remy was concerned she would actually get back with Ben. If he was, then he didn't know her at all. But his fierceness and protectiveness seemed to indicate that he feared for her safety.

But Ben wasn't violent and never had been. The fear, if that's what it was, was groundless.

Remy leaned his head back against the wall and closed his eyes. She thought he might not answer, but he breathed a sigh and rolled his head back and forth on the wall.

"I had a twin sister," he said in a low voice. "Roxie. She was sweet, gentle—and she had a boyfriend. My best friend, in fact."

He opened his eyes and she nearly gasped. The pain she saw there was stark, deep. She found his hand and squeezed it. He squeezed back. She knew this wasn't going anywhere good. He talked about his sister in the past tense, for one thing. Then again, maybe she was wrong, maybe everything was okay—

"He was an abuser. A sneaky, quiet, subversive one. I never saw it happening. Had no idea. I don't think anyone in our family did." He sucked in a breath. "Roxie tried to leave him. He begged her to come back. But I think she was determined for once. So he waited for her one night and shot her on the steps of my parents' house when she came outside."

"Oh Remy." Her heart pounded.

"She died six days later. He's in Angola for life."

She put her hands on his cheeks and pressed her mouth to his. She didn't expect it to help at all, but she wanted him to know she cared. He dragged her into his lap and kissed her back, his mouth firm and demanding on hers. He'd said this wasn't the place, and yet she could feel his control slipping, his body hardening…

"Cage? You in there? Oh shit—"

Christina sprang back at the same time Remy set her away from him. Cash McQuaid stood in the door, his back to them, hands on hips.

"You found me," Remy growled. "What is it?"

"Uh, nothing much. Viking wants you. Incoming from Mendez. Fifteen minutes."

CHAPTER NINETEEN

"THE ROAD TO Akhira's been cut off," Mendez said on the screen.

The SEALs didn't grumble or complain. After all, the only easy day was yesterday. But Akhira being inaccessible sure did put a crimp in the plan.

Ian Black frowned. The dude hadn't even asked if he could remain for this briefing—but Mendez hadn't asked him to leave either. "Your boys are welcome here as long as you need, but I can't stay longer than another day. Got a war to fight."

Remy didn't much know what Ian Black and his crew did, but he figured it wasn't all good. Or legal. Hell, he didn't really know. Come to think of it, he didn't know a fucking thing.

Such as why he'd told Christina about Roxie. He never told anyone about his sister. It was too painful, and it usually caused him to spiral into a pit of guilt and regret when he talked about it. He wanted to fix it. Wanted to bring Roxie back. Wanted to see what was coming and stop it before it happened.

Too late.

"We'll find a way around, sir," Viking said. "Akhira is still our best option at this point. Merak is too far now, and the convoy route is unstable."

"Agreed. Form a plan." Mendez looked at his wrist. "Two hours. I'll want to hear it then."

"Yes, sir."

The screen went blank, and Viking ran a hand through his hair. It had gotten somewhat long lately and stood on end.

"Black, you got a way out of here?" he asked. Because that was the first option. The best option, and they all knew it. Including the man to whom the question was directed.

Ian Black sat on the edge of the desk, one leg dangling, arms crossed, as he contemplated Viking. "I'm not HOT, dude. That's your deal. I've got shit to do that doesn't involve you."

"Fucking hell," Remy said, suddenly unable to stand Black's attitude or the sense of tomcats circling. There was too much at stake here. "You aren't HOT, but you're on our side. And while you may not like us for some reason, you can't have anything against those civilians. They're the ones who need to get out of here. Help *them*, for fuck's sake."

Black had turned to look at him. The man's eyes narrowed as he studied Remy. He reminded Remy of the colonel in some ways—cool, dangerous, lethal. But younger. Mid to late thirties, probably. A man who'd seen a lot in his life, and not all of it good. Former CIA. Disavowed, apparently, which was interesting considering they were here with him and Mendez didn't seem to mind.

"I get paid to do what I do. You got money? Because if I stay here and help you whiny bitches out, then I'm losing business elsewhere. You're going to have to make it worth my time."

"We'll all suck your dick," Remy said. "How's that, motherfucker?"

Because he was pissed now. This asshole knew things. He was just being a prick about it because he had a chip on his shoulder where HOT was concerned. Remy didn't know why that was or what it was about, but he fucking knew he wasn't going to let some asshole like this put Christina in danger for another minute.

Black's eyes narrowed even more. And then the jerk laughed. Fucking laughed.

"Man, you boys have a way of sweet-talking me even while you yank my chain. I've got a meeting to be at, and I'm not missing it. But I can grease some palms, get you through to Akhira. Thing is, you're going to owe me more than a blow job. You ready for that, stud?"

"I'll get on my hands and knees if it helps," Remy drawled.

Black snorted. "Not my type. But you just remember —" He turned to look at them all. "Remember who got you out of this scrape. I'll expect to collect someday."

"Long as it isn't illegal or contrary to orders," Viking said.

"Can't guarantee that," Black replied. "But you'll just have to make up your mind when the time comes, won't you?"

Remy didn't like the way that sounded, but fucking hell, if the dude managed to get Christina through to safety, Remy'd do just about anything Black wanted. He'd lost Roxie, but he wasn't losing Christina. Not when he could do something about it.

"Help us get the civilians to safety," Viking said. "We'll listen when you're ready to talk. Best we can do."

"I'll make some calls," Black replied. "You can chill until the sun goes down."

Alex "Ghost" Bishop sat across the table from Mendez, studying the HOT commander. They were in the war room, a secure room that was separated by soundproof glass from the command center. They could see into the command center and view the giant screens, which pinpointed all the HOT operators' locations. Men and women with headsets sat in front of the screens, tapping away on keyboards and talking into microphones.

It was a slick operation and one that Alex was proud to be a part of. He'd spent nearly his entire career in Special Ops and he loved the challenge. But HOT was the pinnacle. He'd been here before, but now he was here as the deputy commander.

A duty which he did not take lightly. After all, Mendez wouldn't have picked him if he'd been the type to take it lightly.

Just then, Mendez ended the call with the SEALs in Qu'rim and slid his chair back from the console.

"Always a goddamn clusterfuck," he said. "Ian fucking Black."

"You don't like him." It was an observation based on the evidence at hand. So when Mendez blinked and then laughed, Alex was confused.

"If you tell anyone I said so, I'll deny it—but he's fucking brilliant. And probably more of a patriot than you or me. Black believes it so hard and so deep that he's rearranged his entire life to serve."

That was an interesting piece of information. Alex tapped his fingers on the desk. "Isn't he disavowed?"

Alex had read the files when Mendez sent them to him. Ian Black, former CIA operative with the Middle Eastern bureau. Spoke Arabic, Chinese, French, and Farsi. Disavowed under classified circumstances. Fled the country and went to work as a mercenary. He'd built his own organization, routinely called Black's Bandits by outsiders. They typically worked for the highest bidder—and they didn't care who that was or what side they were on.

Hardly a patriot. Then again, if Mendez said so, that was mighty fucking intriguing. And Mendez wasn't the type to say anything lightly, which meant there had to be a grain of truth.

Either that or the colonel was losing his marbles. And Alex didn't believe for two seconds that Mendez was losing it.

"Oh hell yeah, he's disavowed. Try as I might, I can't find out *why* either." Mendez leaned forward, his dark eyes glittering in the low light in the war room. "You shouldn't always believe everything you hear though. Shit happens at these levels—"

He shook his head and didn't finish the thought.

Alex frowned. "It's in his official record. Something must have happened."

Mendez laughed then. "It damn sure is. Look, Alex—you're going to inherit this job someday. Never take what you're told at face value. Always question, always probe. And make up your own mind. You always have to obey the law—but question the circumstances anyway. Use your gut and your instinct."

"Yes, sir." He nodded at the console as he processed everything Mendez was saying. "You trust Black to help them?"

"I don't trust him as far as I can throw him. But I trust his ability. If it suits his purposes, he'll cooperate." Mendez got to his feet. "Two hours from now, we'll know the answer. No sense hanging around and speculating. Let's get back to business. Qu'rim isn't the only crisis we have."

That was certainly the truth. Alex glanced at the command center through the glass. The dots were all over the map, and they were active. The world was a volatile place, but HOT wasn't giving an inch of ground to the bad guys.

Not one fucking inch, which was why Alex loved this place more than any other.

It would be hours before they could travel, assuming Ian Black gave them the go-ahead. Viking was communicating with HQ to tell them the status of the plan. There was a backup plan, of course. That plan was to head northeast across the desert and avoid civilization while they made for Merak. It was farther and more dangerous because of the desert crossing, but it was a possibility if Black couldn't deliver.

Money made eye contact with Remy as they walked out of the room. He knew his teammate was curious, but he didn't really want to talk about Christina. Still, he had to say something. He couldn't have Money thinking he was taking advantage of her—or, worse, that she was some kind of SEAL groupie.

Because those definitely existed. They'd all run into groupies—and bedded a few too.

"It's not what you think," Remy said as they walked outside and into the shaded courtyard. The sun wasn't high in the sky yet, but already it was growing warm. The temperatures would top one hundred degrees later in the day.

"Looked a lot like what I think," Money said. "And I'm certain her brother will pound your ass into the ground if he finds out, so you'd better be careful."

Remy sighed. Yeah, the fact he'd had Christina on his lap, his mouth plastered to hers, didn't look like it was nothing.

"I care about her, okay? There's history—and while I'm sure Girard would pound me into the ground if he knew about it, I'd rather he didn't just yet."

Money shrugged. "No skin in the game, brother. He won't hear it from me."

"Appreciate that." Remy turned to gaze in the direction of the building where he'd left Christina. "We've got things to work out before that happens."

"Looks like it's working just fine."

"Yeah, well, trust me, *that's* not one of our problems. It's everything else that is," he grumbled.

"Women, man. Can't live with 'em. Can't live with 'em." Money laughed as if he'd made the best joke in the world.

And, hell, maybe it was true. Remy didn't know what he wanted out of Christina, but the thought of living with her didn't actually terrify him. Not that he'd ever lived with a woman. Stayed with a few for short periods of time, a few days to a week or two, but never a live-in situation with clothes in the closet and a spot on the couch.

Maybe that wasn't something he was prepared to do with her either, but he wanted the time and space to figure that out. Didn't need Matt Girard coming down on him just yet.

Though, to be fair, if the situation were reversed and it had been some guy sneaking around with Roxie… Well, fuck, he'd have gone ballistic on the dude. Except for Eric, dammit. The one fucker he should have gone ballistic on. But when Roxie called him up and told him she was dating Eric, he'd been equal parts stunned and pleased—because he'd thought Eric was normal.

They'd spent hours together, hunting gators and deer, fishing, getting into normal adolescent scrapes. Those had been some good times.

"I'd appreciate it if you don't tell the others," Remy added. "I'd like to do that on my own time."

Money sighed. "Dude, I get it—but we're out here on a mission, she's our responsibility, and that could affect your thinking. You need to tell them before we move out tonight."

Remy pushed a hand through his hair. "Yeah, all right."

Because Money was right. Because the possibility existed, however small, that his decision-making could be compromised if something happened that put Christina in direct danger. And his teammates needed to know that. He turned around and went back inside to find Viking.

The big blond SEAL looked up as Remy approached. "What's up, Cage?"

Remy thrust out a leg and crossed his arms over his chest. "Christina Girard. We had a thing about six months ago. It didn't last, but that was her doing. She's not a groupie."

Viking raised an eyebrow. "I see. Anything else?"

"Nope."

Viking nodded. "All right. And Cage?"

"Yeah?"

"I already knew you had a thing for her."

Remy blinked. "How the fuck did you know that?" He'd been so careful—and, hell, he didn't have a *thing* for her. He liked her. Wanted to fuck her some more. Wanted to know what else there could be between them.

That was not a *thing*.

Or was it?

"Dude, women talk. Don't you know that by now?"

It took him a minute to figure out what Viking was saying. "You mean Ivy?"

"Yeah, Ivy."

Viking's wife was one hot DEA agent. She was also freaking smart. And, apparently, somehow friends with Christina. Which he hadn't known. Or suspected.

Though maybe he should have. Whenever the guys got together with Alpha Squad, the women ended up over in their own corner, talking and laughing and no doubt plotting mayhem. That's where Christina would have gotten to know Ivy.

"What do you know?" he asked his team leader.

Viking shrugged. "Not a lot. There was a one-night stand after which she avoided you. I've been wondering how pissed off you were and how you were going to handle having to deal with her again."

"Goddamn." That was more than he'd ever told anybody—while Christina was apparently telling Ivy.

And who the hell else? All the women? Evie Girard?

Fuck...

"Welcome to my world, bro. Ivy's spy network is far greater than mine. No telling what she knows."

Remy shook his head. "Well, hell. Why didn't you say something before?"

He remembered the way Viking had looked at him when they'd found out Christina was in Qu'rim. He'd wondered then what that look meant. Now he knew.

"Hey, I've had my own woman troubles in the past. Ivy and I married, divorced, and married again. Who am I to judge? Besides, you're too professional to let it interfere with the job. And if it did in some way, you'd be the first to say something about it. So I'm not worried—unless I need to be. Do I?"

Remy was surprised at the catch in his throat. "No. And thanks. Appreciate your confidence."

"Never in doubt, you crazy Cajun motherfucker."

Remy grinned. *"Motier foux*—half-crazy."

Viking snorted and waved a hand. "Yeah, whatever. So is it over for good? Or is there still a chance?"

Remy shrugged. "Don't know. Might be a chance. Not entirely sure I want to take it though."

"Always take the chance," Viking said, his expression serious. "If you don't, you'll never know what you missed. Life doesn't often hand us a second chance. I say grab on with both hands and don't let go when it does."

CHAPTER TWENTY

THE DAY WAS strange. It was hot, the air seemed heavy with impending danger, and yet it was also dull and quiet. Christina sat in the common room of the safe house, hair twisted on top of her head and held in place with a banana clip she'd thankfully found in her purse. She'd shed the abaya and hijab, and right now she was wishing she'd worn a dress instead of jeans. Or that she'd stuffed a dress into her purse when she'd been grabbing things from the hotel.

The best she could do was take off the button-down shirt she'd put on over a tank top and hope that was enough to get through the day since the jeans had to stay on.

Unfortunately, it was hot in the house in spite of the swamp cooler that beat out a pitiful tune as it worked to do a job far beyond its capability. The air coming from it was rusty and vaguely cool. This was the only building that had any kind of AC, so they'd all gathered here to wait.

Penny and Robert sat across from each other. Today they looked like a boss and secretary trying to keep their affair secret. They didn't look at each other, and they barely spoke. Yet Christina watched Robert's eyes cut toward Penny from time to time. And then Penny would glance at him and a look would pass between them.

Robert didn't look too good in this heat. He was overweight by a good thirty pounds, much of it in his belly. His face was red as he mopped his forehead every once in a while with a rag he'd picked up somewhere. Now that Christina had gotten a good look at him, she could better understand the attraction. Sure, he could stand to lose some weight and looked like a heart attack was right around the corner, but he also had a handsome face and thick dark hair with only a hint of silver at the temples.

Not to mention the way he'd leapt to Penny's defense last night. A man willing to fight for your honor was always sexy.

Christina looked at the other occupants of the room. Donovan Taylor had been writing in a notebook for quite some time. Paul the bodyguard sat with his head against the wall and his eyes closed. The sixth person in their group was an amateur filmmaker who was not pleased to have been dragged from the Abu Bashar Hotel on the eve of the fall of Baq. He had his camera, a small thing that fit in one hand, but the SEALs had taken his battery away.

He looked forlorn, but really, what did he expect? That an active duty group of Special Operators—oh she was proud of herself for knowing what those terms meant—would allow him to film a secret mission? Not likely.

Next she looked at the SEALs who were in the room.

There were six of them, the other three presumably working on something or other designed to help them leave this place later. She studied them each in turn—Alex Kamarov, Cash McQuaid, Corey Vance, Zack Anderson, Cody McCormick—before finally coming to the one she really wanted to study, Remy Marchand.

Remy was looking back at her, his blue eyes filled with heat, and her heart flipped. She hadn't gotten to talk to him again after he'd left her a couple of hours ago. She hadn't gotten to say anything else about his sister. She wanted to hug him tight and tell him how sorry she was for his loss.

My God, to lose his twin that way. Shot by her boyfriend on the steps of her parents' house. Tragic and unfair.

Her eyes stung as she thought of it. His eyebrows lowered, and she knew that her discomfort must show on her face. So she thought instead about how much she'd liked kissing him and how wonderful it would have been if he'd stripped her clothes off and buried himself inside her.

His gaze sparked, and she knew that some of what she was thinking now must be showing on her face. Well, good. He didn't need to see her sadness over his sister.

She thought about breaking the eye contact, but of course she didn't do it. Sure, she felt a blush rising to her cheeks, but she did what she always did with Remy—she faced him boldly and told him without words precisely what she wanted.

She darted her tongue out to lick her lower lip. *Who was this woman?* It was such a naughty, ridiculous thing to do. She almost felt foolish, but then he stiffened slightly, his gaze narrowing to slits while his expression grew fierce.

A second later he was on his feet, striding toward her. She would have squeaked at the look on his face, but the truth was that he mesmerized her. And excited her. Her skin tingled, her heart pounded, and her body tightened.

He stopped beside her and held his hand out. "Need to talk to you, Miz Girard."

Christina's throat was drier than the desert outside these walls. Sweat trickled down the inside of her bra, and she felt like she'd never get the sand out of her clothes. But she gave him her best debutante smile and put her hand in his.

"Why of course," she said, faltering at the last second and not saying his name the way she wanted. It seemed too intimate, especially in front of all these people. Too personal, as if she couldn't say his name without letting everyone know how thoroughly he confused and aroused her.

He helped her up and then escorted her out of the room. She knew the SEALs were probably looking at them with interest. Maybe they knew. Maybe they didn't.

Remy held her hand as he led her away from the common room. The building was mostly abandoned, with empty rooms and wide-open windows that let hot air sweep in. But it was surprisingly cool in some parts of the house due to the angle of windows and the strength of the wind blowing through them.

Remy stopped in the hallway when they'd gone a distance and turned to face her. He put a palm to her cheek and then cupped her head with his big hand. When he crushed his mouth down on hers, she didn't protest. No, she stood on tiptoe and grabbed his shirt in her fists.

His tongue was hot against hers. His lips were heaven. Oh God, she could kiss him forever like this. Who cared if the day was sweltering and dirty?

He pressed her against the wall and put a knee between her legs. Then he moved it, and the friction of her sex against that hard knee sent a lightning bolt of pleasure streaking through her.

"You're a bad girl," he whispered in her ear. "So bad."

"Do you want to spank me, Remy?" she whispered back, her pulse hammering as adrenaline and desire raced through her system like fire through a parched field.

He laughed, a broken, beautiful sound of thwarted need. "Yeah, I do. And then I want to lick you and make it all better."

She pulled him closer, but he resisted. Still his knee applied pressure right where she wanted it.

"I didn't bring you out here for this," he said. "Swear I didn't."

"I don't care if you did." She gasped as she pressed herself against him. She tried to pull his head down for another kiss, but he wouldn't budge. She took a deep breath and then pushed against his chest until he took a step back.

He gripped her head gently and made her look up at him. "What's wrong, baby?"

"Not without you," she said simply. She couldn't read everything on his face, but she knew her answer surprised him.

"Okay," he told her. Then he sucked in a breath. "I honestly didn't bring you out here for a quick fuck. I wanted to kiss you, and then I wanted to talk to you without everyone listening in."

"Well, that's a disappointment, Remy Marchand." Her voice was flat and he laughed.

"Can't figure you out, sexy lady, that's for sure."

She sighed and ran her palms up the front of his shirt. "I'm sorry about your sister, Remy. I know that can't be easy to talk about, but I appreciate your sharing it with me."

He looked angry and sad at the same time. "I'd give anything to change it, but I can't. Why didn't I see what he was? I grew up with him, hunted and fished and hung out. And I never saw it. If I had…"

"Oh, honey," she said, lifting up so she could kiss him again. Just a soft, sweet kiss. He didn't try to make it into anything more. "It's not your fault. It's never anyone's fault but the asshole who's so fucked up he does something like that. You do know that, right?"

He closed his eyes for a moment, opened them again. "I try to remember it, but I'm still pissed I didn't figure it out before it was too late."

She stroked his jaw. "I understand."

"And you understand why you can't trust your ex? Why you don't really know what he's capable of?"

She didn't think Ben was capable of that kind of violence, especially where she was concerned—but she understood Remy's fear, and she wasn't about to tell him different. "Yes, I understand. And I won't let him inside my house again. I promise."

He dropped his gaze down her body, lingering on her breasts. She knew what he saw through the thin material of her tank. Her nipples were still aroused from his kiss, still tight and thrusting against her shirt.

"Damn, what I wouldn't give for an uninterrupted

hour with you." He cleared his throat and fixed his eyes on hers again. "It could be dangerous tonight, Christina. You need to know that. Things will probably happen fast once we get to Akhira. Until then, I need you to stay safe. Do what you're told, stay down, don't draw attention to yourself if we're stopped."

His words made her shiver. "Okay… Do you think we'll be stopped?"

"It's possible. But you'll be safe, baby. I won't let anything happen to you. None of us will."

She thought that maybe there were some things he really couldn't promise, but then she thought of his regret over his sister and knew she couldn't say anything to the contrary.

"I know you won't, Remy. I trust you."

And she did. She knew he would do everything in his power to protect her. In that, he reminded her of Matt. Her brother had spent their childhood standing between her and their father. Being the one to take Beau Girard's scorn, his moods and temper tantrums. His drunken rages. She'd never once taken a blow from her father. She'd had to bear angry words on occasion, but that was nothing in the scheme of things. Thanks to Matt, she'd been safe. And after Matt left for West Point, Granny had taken over, bless her.

When Christina got home—if she got home—she was telling him how much she appreciated that.

Remy tipped her chin up with a fist and studied her. "When we get home, I'm coming to your place the first chance I get. You are letting me in. No running away, Christina. If you intend to run, then you need to tell me now and stop pretending like you want more."

She swallowed the knot in her throat. Part of her still wanted to run—because what did she have that would keep him interested for more than a few weeks? And what would she do when he was done with her? It would hurt, dammit.

But she felt so alive when they were together. "I do want more."

"So you'll be there when this is over, right? No ignoring my calls or flying away on business trips."

"I'll be there—but my job involves travel so I might have to go. That doesn't mean I won't be back."

"Good."

"Is that all you wanted?"

His gaze slipped down over her again. "No, but it's all I'm getting right now. Except you can tell me when you and Ivy Erikson became friends."

Oh dear. Apparently wine and girls' night didn't always go together. Or they did go together, but then the wine made her say things she ordinarily wouldn't—and her friends repeated those revelations to their lovers and husbands.

"Dane knew about us, didn't he?"

He nodded. "Found that out earlier when I went to tell him myself. I had to because Cash-Money caught us and my team needs to know that your presence could compromise my decisions. Turns out Viking already knew."

She only focused on one part of that statement. "My presence could compromise your decisions?"

"Yes. Because I'm involved with you. Because, if it came down to it, who would I save?"

Her heart thumped. "You'd save me."

"At what cost? That's why my team needs to know."

"Hopefully it won't come down to that."

"Hopefully. Now who else did you tell besides Ivy?"

"Um, all of them?" Her cheeks heated as his eyebrows went up. "What? Women talk. We discuss the men in our lives. Or the ones we've kicked out of our lives but sometimes wish we hadn't. Stuff like that."

And since she'd never really had close girlfriends growing up, she cherished the friendships she'd made with these women. Sure, Evie had been the one to bring her into the circle, but everyone was welcoming and supportive. She'd spilled the beans, and yes, she'd felt somewhat better afterward.

"You mean your sister-in-law knows? Holy shit."

"Don't worry, she won't tell Matt. Oh, she'd tell him if you'd been the one to dump me and I was hurt—but she wasn't about to tell him all the things I told her. You're safe."

He growled. "Safe? Do you think I couldn't kick your brother's ass if I had to?"

She almost giggled at the macho posturing. "I'm sure you could. Or maybe it'd be like that silly thing where two superheroes fight—didn't they make a movie? Bat Dude versus Super Guy or something?"

"You're being funny, aren't you?"

She grinned. "Trying. Is it working?"

"Jesus, you're cute. Yeah, it's working. At least until we get back home and your brother comes at me with a roundhouse kick."

She patted him. "He won't. I swear."

Though, to be perfectly honest, she didn't really know that. Maybe she needed to talk to Evie first thing and make sure Matt still didn't know. And then maybe she was going to have to tell him herself. Eventually. If it worked out.

"Cage," a voice called, and she whipped her head around to see Viking standing at the other end of the passage, looking all big and bad and ready to kill something. He made her shiver, but not in the way Remy did. Still, he was married to Ivy, and Ivy was one cool—and badass—chick.

"Yeah, boss man?"

"Got some intel to discuss. When you get a chance."

Remy hadn't pushed her away like she was a guilty secret. That warmed her.

"Be right there." Then he leaned down and kissed her, a quick peck on the lips. "You're mine, baby girl. *Mine.*"

CHAPTER TWENTY-ONE

"TONIGHT. TWO A.M.," Viking said.

Remy stood in a room with his team leader and Ian Black while Viking delivered the news of their departure. He shot a look at Black. The dude simply arched an eyebrow.

"It is what it is, fellas," he said with a shrug. "I can't get you through in broad daylight. That's more money than I'm willing to part with—not to mention the probability the bastards would take the money and shoot you anyway. Tonight there will be less likelihood of getting caught. I'll travel with you as far as Zamor, but then I've got to peel off and head south. Best I can do."

Remy sucked in a breath and blew it out again. "Then I guess that's what we have to do."

Viking nodded. "Pretty much my thoughts as well. I'll inform Mendez."

"Give the colonel my love," Black said as he walked away.

Viking shook his head. "Don't know what the deal is with those two, but I'd love to be a fly on the wall for a few hours."

Remy felt considerably less amused by the whole thing. "Maybe they've had a lovers' spat."

Viking snorted. "Maybe Black swings that way, but I've seen the way Mendez looks at women. Dude's not gay. You ever in the room when that Samantha Spencer from the CIA comes around? They pretty much undress each other with their eyes the whole time."

"Nope, haven't seen that. But Miz Spencer is hotter than fuck, that's for sure."

"She's probably twenty years older than you, bro."

"And?" Because if he weren't so tangled up with Christina, he'd be interested in a woman like Samantha Spencer if she gave him a chance.

Viking laughed. "Yeah, and what, right? No kidding, I'd tap that too if I were single." He lifted an eyebrow. "Speaking of single, what's happening with you and Christina? Looked pretty intense."

Remy shrugged. "Just taking your advice, man. Grabbing on with both hands." And wondering if she was going to slip through his fingers again.

"Yeah, well take some more advice. It'll probably get worse before it gets better, so don't be too quick to let go."

Christina slept badly. Every little noise in the building seemed to wake her. She lay there, straining to hear movement, hoping Remy would come to her. Penny had retired with Robert, same as last night. The other three guys bedded down in a different room, and Christina was on her own. Once more huddled in her sleeping bag, staring at the moon out the window when she woke, and wondering where Remy was.

She didn't know what time it was. Her phone was dead, and she didn't wear a watch. After waking for what had to be the twentieth time that night, she decided to get up and look out the window. As she pushed herself upright, she heard soft footfalls in the corridor. She sank back down, held her breath, and waited.

The shape in her doorway was big, male. And she knew instinctively it was Remy.

"Hi," she said softly.

"Why are you awake?"

She laughed. "Didn't you ask me that a few hours ago while standing in that very same spot?"

He made a sound that might have been a snort. Or maybe it was a chuckle. "Yeah, I did."

She sat up and put her arms around her knees. "I can't sleep," she said. "I tried."

He came into the room and stood above her with hands on hips. "It's midnight. Still a couple of hours before we need to be up. Will you sleep better if I'm here?"

She wouldn't sleep at all, but she wasn't going to tell him that. "Maybe."

He let out a breath and then settled beside her, sitting back against the wall. She wasted no time in snuggling into him, her nose against his chest, his hand on her head, holding her lightly against him.

"I was hoping you'd come sooner," she admitted.

"Too many things to do, *cher*. I came as soon as I could manage it."

"Did you sleep?"

"I sleep every chance I get. We all do. It's in fits and starts, but that's how it goes out here."

"What made you want to do this for a living?"

And now that she knew what it was he did, she was wondering about her brother. Except that she figured she knew what had made Matt choose this life. He'd always had so much energy. Unless he was challenged in some way, he'd implode. He'd been on the way as a teenager, but then he'd gone to West Point and everything changed.

"My parents aren't wealthy, Christina. College wasn't an option—unless I went to one of the academies. So I got into Annapolis."

"But why become a SEAL? You could have gone to sea as a ship's officer."

She felt him shrug. "Didn't seem right. This did. I needed the challenge, especially after Roxie's death."

Or he'd wanted to suffer. She knew how hard SEAL training was. Hell, they'd made movies about it. Had he entered that training as a way of punishing himself for not saving his sister?

She didn't know him well enough to make that judgment with one hundred percent accuracy, but she suspected she might be onto something.

"And now? Do you wish you'd chosen a different path?"

"No." He said it without hesitation. "No, this is the right one. I won't always be an operator, not as an officer.

I'm here to learn how to command SEALs."

She thought of Matt, and again, she wasn't sure Remy wasn't lying to himself. Matt was an officer. Matt still went into the field. Often. But he was Army, not Navy, so maybe it was different.

"I'm going to admit I don't understand anything about the military. For instance, why do we have SEALs, Green Berets, Delta Force, and all that other stuff? Why not just one group of badasses who do top secret stuff?"

He laughed. "Each branch of service has its own Special Operators. You have to do it that way. SEALs are meant to work in maritime operations, but we do more than that these days."

"Such as this. There's no ocean under our feet right now."

"You never know, *cher*. It's a big ocean, and it's not that far away."

"I take it you're at home in the water?"

"I'd have to be, or I wouldn't be a SEAL. I've spent months—maybe years if I added it all up—of my life in the water."

"Well, right this minute I'm pretty glad you're a SEAL. I'd hate to be here alone."

"You wouldn't be here alone. You'd have SEALs to help you. Just not me."

She tilted her face up and met his gaze. "No, I'd still be alone. I like being alone… usually. You kind of ruin that for me when you're around."

His eyes sparked in the moonlight shafting into the room. "You say the damnedest things, Christina."

"Not typically," she said. And that was the problem. She just couldn't stop herself with him. "I'm usually quiet and reserved. You bring out a side of me that I find both alarming and refreshing."

He snorted. "Baby, you've always been *you.* For some reason, you've never minded being you with me. I think because you didn't care what I thought from the very beginning."

He might be right. When she'd first met him, she'd been reeling from Ben's betrayal and unwilling to even consider having a relationship with another man. But she'd been powerfully attracted to Remy, and she'd wanted him like she'd want a steak or a chocolate bar.

He'd been a craving, and you knew once you fed the craving it would go away, so therefore you said whatever it took to get what you wanted.

Lord have mercy.

"And for the record," he said. "I like who you are. Keep saying the damnedest things. I enjoy it."

Warmth flowed over her like a hot shower on a cool day. He made her feel good. She wanted more of that. But what if she didn't get it?

"What if we don't get out of here? What if something goes wrong tonight?"

He squeezed her tight. "We're getting out of here. It's what I do, what my team does. We haven't lost anyone yet. We won't start tonight."

"Kiss me, Remy. Make me believe it."

"Honey, if I kiss you, I'm afraid I won't stop with a kiss."

"And what makes you think I want you to stop there?"

"We can't, baby."

"Why not?"

"Fuck," he whispered. And then he kissed her.

His mouth on hers was sweet and hard, warm and demanding. He tilted her face up and took what he wanted, his tongue sliding into her mouth and tangling with her own. Christina clung to him, her hands clutched in his shirt, her heart beating fast and hard as he devastated her mouth with his own.

Oh, she'd never expected to be this kind of woman. The kind who craved a man so desperately she'd do anything to have him. Sex had always been pleasant, but not earth-shattering. Not until Remy.

He was a revelation to her. A need beyond any she'd ever had before.

"This isn't the place," he said, breaking the kiss to trail his mouth down her throat. "Too exposed, too shitty. You deserve so much better, baby. So much better."

"You're all I need right now, Remy. I don't care where we are."

And she meant that. Really, truly meant it. She slipped her hand down his washboard abdomen and over the raging hard-on pressing against his camouflage pants. His hips rose of their own accord, his cock thrusting against her palm.

"Jesus," he hissed. "Don't do that, baby."

"I want to," she said. "I want to make you come."

"You're killing me, Christina."

"Then do what I want and you don't have to suffer."

He laughed, but it was a strangled sound. "You're more formidable than any battle I've ever been in."

"Free the beast, Remy. Slide it into me and give me what I want."

He snorted. "The beast, huh?"

She rubbed her palm along the ridge of that massive erection. “Oh yes, definitely a beast.”

He sighed. “Can’t slide it into you, honey. No condom.”

Her heart thumped at what she was about to say. “You can. I have an implant. And, in spite of Ben, I’m clean. We hadn’t had sex in months before he did his, um, thing—and I’ve been checked out.”

“And there’s the deathblow,” he muttered. “The chance to come inside you without anything between us. Damn, girl, you know how to fight dirty.”

“Whatever it takes, Remy—except for lies. I’m not lying about being clean.”

He kissed her. “I believe you. And even though you didn’t ask, I’m clean too. I don’t go in without the raincoat. Ever.”

She threw a leg over him and climbed onto his lap until she could ride the ridge of his hard-on. “Do you think you might this time?”

His hands were on her hips, holding her down as he shifted and sent a sizzle of electricity rocketing through her core.

He didn’t say anything for a long moment. Then he lifted a hand and unclipped her hair. It tumbled in a damp mass around her shoulders.

“Yeah,” he said softly. “I think I might.”

CHAPTER TWENTY-TWO

SHE WASN'T GOING to give him a chance to change his mind. Christina gripped his jaw and kissed him, taking what he offered like she was a marauding invader. This was so not her—and yet, with Remy, it *was* her.

She thought she was in control until the moment he gripped her hips and shifted so she was on her back and he was on top of her, between her legs, looming over her like the mountain of muscle he was.

She loved his strength. Loved that he made her feel so safe even in the middle of a war zone.

"I hate that I can't do everything I want to you," he said. "Everything you deserve."

"It's enough, Remy. For now it's enough."

And it truly was. Because she couldn't help but think that if something went wrong later, she would regret not having done this one more time. Even if it was fast and furious. Even if they couldn't linger or explore.

"To tell you the truth," she said, "I've never had

quick, dirty, desperate sex like this."

His fingers went to the button of her jeans. He flicked them open effortlessly. "Well, maybe it won't be that quick," he murmured. "But it will be desperate, no doubt."

She thought he would shove her jeans off, unbutton his fly, and slip inside her. She was mistaken. He stripped her as much as possible with others so close by—shirt open, bra shoved up, sucking her nipples while she clutched his shoulders and bit her lip so she wouldn't moan, and then he removed her jeans and panties in one go. He sat up and unholstered his sidearm before unbuttoning his pants and freeing his cock.

When he sat there with his hand wrapped around his erection and his hot gaze on her, she wanted to moan. Then she wanted to lick him until he lost his mind.

She thought he might strip, but he didn't. He hovered over her, kissing her again while she wrapped her legs around his hips and tried to bring him closer. Then she felt him. The blunt head of his cock eased inside her, stretching muscles that hadn't been used since the last time he'd been inside her.

"Remy," she gasped as he sank deeper. He was hot and smooth and big, a blunt instrument for her pleasure.

"Shh, baby," he said, gripping her hands in his and lifting them over her head. "Goddamn, you feel amazing. So amazing."

"So do you."

"Tell me if it's too much, okay?" He pressed forward, filling her so full that she felt she might split in two.

But it wasn't too much. It was perfect. Sensitive tissues that hadn't been used in so long sparked to life, sending waves of pleasure cascading through her. And this was only the beginning. How had she run away from this man for so long? Why? Was she crazy?

"It's not too much," she gasped. "Too good."

He shifted his hips, pulling a little way out and then sliding forward again. "True dat, *cher*."

"Oh, Remy—" She couldn't stop the moan that escaped her when he moved again. But he put his mouth on hers and captured it before anyone heard them.

His clothing scraped against her flesh, but it was erotic this way. He was her big bad warrior, dressed for battle, and she was his prize. He rocked into her harder now, faster, and she thrust her hips up to him, wanting more.

Her body caught fire as the base of his cock bumped against her clitoris again and again. She gripped him hard with her legs, lifted herself to meet him, angling just right, just perfect—and oh hell, she was coming, her body splintering as white-hot pleasure sizzled into her nerve endings. Her scalp tingled. Her toes. Her arms and legs.

And she was moaning into his mouth, sucking his tongue, dying for every drop of bliss he gave her. He was so beautiful, so amazing—and oh my God, she never wanted this to end.

But it did. Remy let go of one of her hands, gripped her ass, and ground into her until she felt a hot stream of semen pumping into her body. He tore his mouth from hers and groaned, his lips pressed against her neck.

It was such a sexy sound. Especially since she'd been the one to cause it. She sighed as his whiskers abraded her skin, as his tongue slipped out and licked her. A second later he bit her shoulder lightly, and she shuddered anew.

"You feel so good, Christina. I want to stay here all night, but that's not possible."

She gripped him harder when he tried to move away. A hand slid down her naked side.

"Don't make this any harder, baby. We got to be ready to go when the time comes."

"I'm ready to go again," she whispered, and he chuckled. Then he flexed his muscles and she realized he was still hard inside her. All that coming hadn't done a damn thing to deflate the beast.

"Me too. And I promise you, soon as I can, I'm coming to your house and keeping you in bed for at least twenty-four hours."

That was a thought that both scared her and excited her. But it was definitely too late to change her mind now. She'd let him back into her life, and she had to ride out the storm and see where it went.

She just hoped there was some little piece of her left when the storm was over.

They left the vans behind and took the big truck that Ian Black had. The SEALs kept the ammunition and left everything else. They wouldn't need it where they were going. The journey to the coast was about two hours if they were lucky. Once they reached the outskirts of Akhira, they'd change vehicles again and head for the port. Another SEAL squad would meet them there. They'd pile on board a waiting vessel and head for the aircraft carrier that sat a few miles offshore.

Only four people fit in the front seat of the truck. The rest were in the back, sitting up against the sides of the truck bed. Remy could have been up front as the second-in-command, but he'd wanted to be here. Near Christina.

Viking didn't give him a hard time about it. He'd simply nodded and said, "Understood."

So Remy was near Christina but not touching her. She leaned against the rear of the cab where he'd made sure to put her, her eyes bright and cheeks flushed. Once in a while she caught his gaze, and her skin flushed brighter.

She fascinated him. Completely and utterly. He'd known when he was buried inside her that there was something between them. Something real and wonderful. Something terrifying.

Because he'd never been attached to a woman before. Not like this. He'd never spent his waking hours thinking of her, remembering what it was like to possess her, and planning everything he was going to do when he got to be inside her again.

The taste he'd had of her a couple of hours ago hadn't been enough. Yeah, it had been pretty spectacular having her wrapped around him, her warm, wet pussy gripping him as he sank into her over and over. There was a time when he'd never expected to do that again with her.

And maybe he shouldn't have done it now, in the middle of all this shit, but he wasn't sorry for it. He was, however, worried that she was going to pull another disappearing act on him. He got that she was fearful of committing, but he wanted a chance to prove to her that he was worth taking a chance on.

Holy fuck, that was a new thought.

But, yeah, he wanted her to take a chance. And he

wanted to commit to her even if they had to take baby steps.

He shoved a hand through his hair and leaned his head back, closing his eyes. Jesus, where had that come from? Commitment? Him?

Yeah, him.

He'd spent his entire life chasing pussy and having meaningless relationships. It had been fun while it lasted, but he was over it now. He wanted to spend time with one person, wanted to know her completely. Wanted to make her happy.

Christina was that person. From the first moment he'd met her, she'd been different. Beautiful and fuckable, sure. But it was more than that. She'd stood toe-to-toe with him from the first. She hadn't tried to impress him, hadn't tried to be something she wasn't. She'd stood face-to-face with him and told him she wanted a one-night stand.

He'd been the one who asked for more, the one who'd tried to put the brakes on. But she'd had none of it. She'd gotten what she wanted and then she'd kicked him to the curb.

Hell, maybe he was fascinated because of that. Or maybe it was just her.

Her sweet scent, her glossy brown hair, her gray eyes, her elegance and brains and humor. Didn't hurt that she tasted like heaven to him, though that was only a small part of it.

The truck rocked back and forth as it moved through the sand, lulling him into a doze. It wasn't his turn to be on point, but he still fought it at first. But the lack of sleep over the past few days caught up with him. He didn't sleep deeply, and he didn't dream. Or at least he didn't think he dreamed.

Until he heard horses. They were galloping, their hoofbeats pounding in rhythm against the sand. There were shouts, war cries—

And he jerked awake, his eyes gritty and unfocused, his heart racing as he automatically reached for his rifle.

The shouting was real. The horses were real. He moved until he was in front of Christina, blocking her as much as he could. The other SEALs were also holding their rifles, crouching in defensive positions, and waiting for the order to fire.

The truck's engine whined, but it was no match for the horses in this terrain.

"Don't shoot," Viking said in their ears. "For God's sake, don't shoot them. Black says he can handle this."

A rifle shot sounded in the night as one of the attackers aimed into the air and pulled the trigger.

Remy touched his mic. "Are you certain about that? They don't fucking sound friendly to me."

"He says they're pirates basically. They want money. Ideals don't matter to them."

The truck slowly rolled to a stop even while Remy ground his teeth together and hoped like hell Black was right. Because if the motherfucker was wrong, this was going to go bad very fast. As they came to a halt surrounding the truck, Remy counted twenty armed and mounted men. They wore dark robes and head scarves that covered everything but their eyes.

They did not look friendly. But they also didn't raise their rifles.

Ian Black stepped out of the truck. He was dressed in camouflage, but he wore a head scarf similar to the pirates'. Except his wasn't fastened over his eyes. One of the men dismounted and walked over to meet him. They clasped hands and then spoke in Arabic for a few moments while the leader gestured at the truck from time to time.

Ian shook his head, spread his arms, and said a few things that Remy couldn't quite hear. The other man folded his arms over his chest and looked like he wasn't planning to budge. Finally Ian shrugged. The two clasped hands again.

The man went back to his horse and swung up into the saddle in a movement as graceful as it was quick. Ian strode back over to the truck and stopped where everyone could hear him.

"They're going to escort us through their territory."

"What's the price?" Remy asked. Because it clearly hadn't been an easy agreement to come to.

"You aren't going to like it," Ian said.

"Tell us anyway," Cowboy growled.

Black raised an eyebrow. "They want the ammunition… and the women."

"That is not fucking happening," Remy snapped. "And you damn well know it."

"Yeah, well, you tell them that right now and see how far you get. You want your precious cargo to get out of here? Then you fucking play along until you can't play anymore. Unless you have a better idea," he finished, eyes flashing.

Unfortunately, he didn't. But he knew he'd die before he handed Christina over. No way. Fucking *no way*.

"I don't," he said. "But you'd better hope to God that you do when the time comes."

CHAPTER TWENTY-THREE

THE MOOD IN the truck had shifted as they drove through the night. Not that it had been a party atmosphere before the mounted men arrived, but it definitely was subdued now. Christina let her gaze slip over each SEAL and knew there was no way they were letting those men have her or Penny.

She glanced at Remy again and found him watching her. He still looked pissed, but she knew it wasn't at her. He'd been pissed at Ian Black and the situation. He'd told her after he sat back down that he'd shoot every motherfucker out there before they touched a hair on her head, so she didn't need to worry.

She wasn't worried, except that she really didn't want anyone to get shot either. And especially not because of her.

Penny had been somewhat harder to console, but Robert was doing a good job of it. Any pretense not to be lovers was gone. They didn't try to hide anything anymore as they huddled together, Penny in Robert's arms.

Poor Mrs. Robert, Christina thought.

Then she turned her gaze to the men riding alongside the truck, and her heart thudded at the idea of being traded to them—but that was *not* going to happen. The SEALs were the ones with the superior firepower when you compared their weapons with the rifles these men carried. There was really no contest.

But Ian Black had a point about them. They were useful on this journey, clearly, because whenever they encountered military checkpoints on the road, the other men didn't even try to interfere with their party's progress. They simply watched as twenty horses and a truck full of Americans eased by.

She didn't know how long they drove, but eventually they came to a stop. The sun hadn't yet risen, but the sky was pink at the edges and the desert terrain was beginning to stand out against the darkness. The air smelled faintly of salt.

She turned her head and realized why. They were on a ridge. Below them, spread out in either direction, was a city. Beyond that was a dark, inky mass that she could only assume was the sea.

Ian Black stepped down from the truck. The headlights from another vehicle shone toward them as it came up the road in the opposite direction. No one seemed alarmed about that, so she didn't panic over it.

The men on horseback milled about. One of them—the leader, she presumed—yelled something at Black. He turned and strode over to where the man still sat his horse.

She glanced nervously at Remy. His face was set in stone, unreadable. But he gripped his weapon and looked ready to defend their territory with his life.

And didn't that thought just make her shiver? She didn't want Remy defending anything with his life. She wanted him alive and well and able to keep his promise about coming to her house and not letting her out of bed for twenty-four hours.

Black and the leader argued—or at least it sounded like arguing from here. And then the turbaned man drew a sidearm and pointed it at Black's head. Christina gasped at the sudden violence.

"Fucking hell," Remy muttered. "Now what, ass-hole?"

He did something next that shocked her to the core. He stood up in the bed, took aim with his rifle, and yelled —in Arabic? The leader seemed to understand, because he turned his head and gazed at Remy.

When the man spoke, she had no idea what the reply was. But Remy did because he answered, the gun never wavering. The laser dot on the man's forehead told her what he was targeting. And then the dot flickered and she realized it was the conjunction of several dots as all the SEALs took aim.

The dots split again, shining upon multiple heads. But it wasn't enough, because there were twenty horsemen, nine SEALs, and Ian Black. Those weren't good odds, which everyone had to know.

In the next instant, a shot rang out, the sound coming toward them.

Remy yelled at her to get down, and she dropped to her side, flattening herself as much as she could while bullets flew and the air smelled sharp and flinty. The gunfire was deafening. The truck lurched into gear, men shouted,

Penny screamed—so did a couple of the men, though not the SEALs—and the bullets kept ricocheting through the air.

Christina's heart hammered and her ears ached. The truck picked up speed, but it wasn't quite enough. Cash McQuaid grunted and dropped his rifle. Blood seeped in a dark stain over the fabric of his desert uniform, but he unholstered his sidearm and kept firing.

She wasn't certain when the gunfire stopped, but it did. One minute it was there and the next it wasn't. The SEALs didn't leave their defensive positions, however. She dared to ease up and peek over the side of the truck. The other vehicle that had been approaching them earlier was a Land Rover, and now it raced down a parallel road, heading toward the interior of Qu'rim.

Behind them, there was nothing. Or so she thought. The closer she looked, she realized the lumps on the road were bodies. The horses had bolted.

Hot tears sprang into her eyes at the horror of what just happened. Men had died. And Cash was hurt, which she remembered right about the time Alex Kamarov grabbed him and cut his sleeve open.

Blood streaked his arm and there was a neat hole…

Oh dear God. Christina put her hand to her mouth and turned her head, retching, trying hard not to be sick. This wasn't her thing, wasn't anything she could get used to.

Remy put an arm around her and dragged her against him. "He's okay, *cher*. It's fine. Camel and Cowboy are gonna field dress the wound and cover it up again."

She buried her face against his shoulder because she could—and because it felt so good. Comforting. Yes, he smelled of sweat and guns and sand, but she didn't care.

"Those men," she said and couldn't finish the sentence.

"They shot first, honey."

"Ian Black?"

"He's alive. He disarmed the guy with the weapon and then used it on him. The Land Rover was here for Black. He's off to wherever he was headed, probably without a fucking scrape."

"And us?"

Remy squeezed her. "Almost out of here. Just a few more miles to go."

She pushed away from him and searched his face. She didn't know how many days' growth of a beard he sported, but it was sexy nonetheless.

"You're okay, right?"

"I'm not hit."

"But you have been before?"

He sighed, his dark gaze sparking. "I've never been hit bad, no. Nicked once."

Christina shivered, both at the thought of him being shot and at the scene she'd just witnessed. She'd grown up in the South, her father and brother went deer and gator hunting, and so did practically every boy she ever knew in school. Some of the girls too.

But men? She'd never seen men shot before, and that was a new, sickening sensation for her. Those men might have had families—wives, children, brothers, sisters. She tried to remember they'd wanted to take her and Penny and they'd fought over that right. No one had forced them to fire their weapons or start the battle.

Tears pressed hard against her eyelids. She hated this place. Hated that she'd ever come here. People could be so horrible. Right now, Baq was probably burning. What had happened to those people in the convoy they'd left behind? What about the ones who'd died when the bomb went off?

Remy rubbed a hand up and down her arm, as if he sensed what she was thinking.

"It's gonna be all right, *cher*. Not long now."

She couldn't shake the feeling that it would get worse before it ever got better.

It wasn't over yet. Remy knew it, but he wasn't about to tell Christina and confirm her fears. The nomads weren't a threat anymore, true. The next threat lay in front of them. The sun would be up in a few more minutes, and they were nowhere near the coast. They could see it, but they couldn't reach it just yet.

And they had to reach it. That's where the boat was. Where their path to freedom lay. Choppers couldn't land anymore because of the threat of RPGs. The airport in Baq was controlled by the rebels. That left Akhira and the sea.

But to get to the sea, they had a long stretch of road to drive along first. A dangerous, hot, dusty road that ran straight through the middle of contested territory. They'd hoped to be into Akhira by daybreak, not rolling toward it with several miles left to go.

But Ian Black had insisted they leave the safe house at two a.m. Not a moment sooner or later, because that's the point from which he calculated his contacts would be in place.

Remy tapped his mic. “Any word on the road?”

“We’re half an hour late. The contacts could be gone,” Viking replied.

Indeed, they’d been supposed to meet Ian Black’s contacts a few miles from here where they would be waiting with a refrigerated truck that could get the SEALs and their cargo to safety. The truck was supposed to be heading into Akhira for a produce pickup. The drivers went to the docks and loaded perishable cargo before turning around and driving back into the interior.

If they dropped off a load of SEALs while there, so what?

But first the SEALs had to get to the rendezvous point. Remy locked gazes with Money. The dude probably wasn’t comfortable, but he was stable now that Camel had dressed the wound and shot him up with some painkillers. He shrugged with the shoulder on his good arm as if to say, “What you gonna do?”

What, indeed.

The sun kept climbing upward, its light spilling across the golden sand and illuminating the desert as it made the journey toward the horizon. Another couple of minutes, and it would spill light over everything in its path.

The truck sped down the embankment road, heading for the flat desert. When they hit the bottom, whoever was driving put his foot hard against the pedal because they picked up speed quickly.

Nobody said anything. Not that they could be heard over the wind anyway.

Christina had shifted herself away from him and sat

with her back to the cab, her knees up, her arms clamped around them. He wanted to draw her into the circle of his arm again, but he needed both hands free in case they encountered more trouble.

He glanced at her from time to time, trying to figure out what she was thinking. Her eyes had that faraway look of someone desperately trying to be anywhere but where they were. He got it. The violence back there had been pretty raw and sudden. He doubted she'd ever seen men shot before. Watching people die wasn't an easy thing, even if they meant you harm.

"Ten minutes," Viking said. "Any longer and our ride is gone."

"Copy," Remy said.

When the truck started to slow a few minutes later, Remy turned and peered around the cab. Sure enough, a refrigerated truck sat by the side of the road, waiting. The men inside threw the doors open and jumped down as they approached. One went around and swung open the cargo doors.

The truck rocked to a stop, and the SEALs jumped down first, helping the civilians to the ground before ushering them toward the back of the semi. Remy was reluctant to leave Christina's side, but he turned her over to Camel with a glance and went to join Viking, who stood with two of the men who'd been waiting for them. The third was climbing into the truck they'd arrived in. So he could get rid of it, presumably.

"We good to go?" Remy asked of nobody in particular.

Viking nodded at the two men. "They said there's a roadblock leading into Akhira. It's a government checkpoint. They haven't had any trouble getting through lately, but the king's troops are on edge after yesterday."

No fucking kidding there. They still had to be reeling from losing the seat of government to a bunch of terrorists and rebels. And while the Qu'rimi government was technically an American ally, that didn't mean getting through a checkpoint would be as easy as flashing a passport and saying howdy, y'all.

"Anything happen in Akhira the past few days?" Remy asked the two men.

The SEALs hadn't been briefed on any activity, but that didn't mean people who lived there wouldn't know a bit more about the day-to-day status of their city.

"Nothing," the first man said. "But the city is on edge. The rebels have supporters here. It is not a good time to be in Qu'rim."

No, it definitely wasn't.

"We should go," Viking said, squinting into the distance. The sun was fully up now, golden light spilling across their faces with the promise of heat to come and chasing away the lingering shadows beneath the dunes.

There was no more hiding in plain sight now.

"How long to the port?"

"Half hour," the man said. "We go as fast as we can."

CHAPTER TWENTY-FOUR

IT WAS COLD inside the truck. Christina shivered and huddled against Remy. He slipped his arm securely around her shoulders as he held her against his body. A couple of the SEALs looked at them with interest in the dim light from a lantern someone had turned on, but no one said anything. It was clearly not a secret anymore that there was something going on between them.

"What happens now?" she whispered to him.

"We're hitching a ride to the port. From there, it's a boat to a carrier at sea. Then we'll have you on a helicopter to the nearest airport. From there, military transport to Germany."

She blinked. "Germany?"

That seemed like the long way around, but he sounded confident.

"Standard procedure. You'll be flown to Ramstein Air Base and checked out at the Landstuhl military hospital. They'll send you home as soon as possible."

Her heart thumped. "Where will you be?"

His eyes glittered. "I won't be there, Christina. I'll have to meet you back home."

Disappointment flooded her. And, yes, even a touch of fear. They'd been together for what, two days now? It wasn't long, but a lot had happened—and he made her feel safe. She had no idea how she'd feel once he was no longer with her.

"I'll be waiting for you."

He looked down at her, studying her. "You sure about that?"

She knew where the question came from. And a part of her still wanted to run. But mostly she didn't. She was all in now, whatever happened.

"Yes, I'm sure."

"That's good, baby," he said for her ears only. "Because we have a lot of catching up to do."

She shivered anew, but not because she was cold. "I can't wait."

He squeezed her to him, his eyes hot and possessive, but he didn't make a move to kiss her like she wished he would. Then again, maybe it was best he didn't. They weren't exactly alone, were they?

The truck rumbled along at speed for about fifteen minutes, then it slowed. Christina didn't miss the way the SEALs looked at each other or the way their grips tightened on their weapons.

But the truck didn't stop, merely swung into a turn and kept rolling. A few minutes later, however, they did stop.

This time the SEALs looked intense.

"Everyone stay quiet," Viking said. "This is most likely a checkpoint. They're going to open the truck and look inside. You need to stay absolutely silent, got it?"

He wasn't talking to his SEALs, of course. The civilians all nodded. Penny turned her head into Robert's chest and buried her face as tears rolled down her cheeks and her body started to shake.

Christina was done feeling sorry for the woman. For heaven's sake, if she wailed while the doors were open, they'd be compromised. And Christina might just choke her for it.

"I'm serious as fuck," Viking said. "You have got to stay quiet. I'm shutting off the lantern now, but we'll turn it back on as soon as they're gone."

The light winked out. There was banging on the back of the truck, and then the doors creaked open and daylight streamed inside.

She could hear men talking in Arabic, but she didn't know what they were saying. She watched Remy's face in the shaft of light coming over the boxes. If it was something bad, she knew he'd understand.

Everyone was quiet, even Penny, though Robert pretty much had her face smushed against his chest in an effort to keep her from sobbing aloud. Robert looked a bit desperate, and Christina knew it wasn't an easy task.

Maybe Mrs. Robert was looking better to him now. Maybe Mrs. Robert was sensible and not flighty. On the other hand, Robert got what he deserved for banging his secretary on a business trip.

Eventually the doors shut again, and they were plunged into darkness. Someone breathed a sigh of relief. The truck's engine began to rumble, and they started forward. The lantern came back on, bathing the group in cool light.

Penny's sobs became audible then. Christina wanted to pinch her. And then she wanted to tell her to grow up and stop being helpless.

Nothing irritated her more than a helpless woman. A woman who needed rescuing and couldn't lift a finger to help herself was a menace. If this were a survival course, which in a way it was, Penny wouldn't make it if she had to fend for herself.

Then again, what did Christina know about survival? Not much, even if she did like to watch Bear Grylls on television from time to time. But she knew she wouldn't lie down and cry like Penny. She'd fight to the bitter end if she had to.

The rest of the ride seemed to take forever. The truck slowed, sped up, stopped, started again, turned, and repeated the whole cycle numerous times. Finally they came to a halt, and the rumble of the engine ceased. Viking switched off the lantern.

The rear doors banged and then swung open. This time a man called out. Viking answered, but Christina's eyes were on Remy. He didn't look worried, which was a good thing.

"Let's go," Viking said.

The SEALs went first, jumping from the trailer and turning to help the civilians. Christina's legs felt stiff when she hit the pavement. They were a combination of cold and cramped, and she shook each one in turn to wake it up.

Remy stayed close by her side, his gaze darting over their surroundings.

They were in a warehouse. Oil and the salty smell of water and fish battled for supremacy in the air, which meant they were at the port. Christina let out a breath. They'd made it this far, but she didn't think she'd truly relax until she was on an American ship in the Gulf and Qu'rim was far behind.

The driver of the truck came over to talk to Viking and Remy. They shook hands with him, and then he was climbing into the cab and starting the engine again. With a wave, he backed out of the warehouse and the truck rumbled down the street.

"All right, kids," Viking said. "We're about to make a run for it. As soon as I give the signal, you will each be escorted out of this warehouse and onto the dock by your own personal SEAL. Do not stop. Do not pass Go. Do not collect two hundred dollars. You stop when your SEAL tells you to stop. Not a moment before. You do what you're told, without question, and everything's going to be fine. Any questions before we go?"

No one said anything. Not even Donovan Taylor, the loudmouthed attorney. The amateur filmmaker looked about as disgusted as he had from the first. Paul and Robert had blank looks. Penny's puffy, tear-streaked face was pale.

"Then we're off to see the wizard," Viking said cheerfully. "Homestretch, people. Almost there."

Remy's hand wrapped around hers. A second later, they were on the move. They trotted toward a door at one end of the warehouse rather than the opening the truck had gone through. When they were all there, two of the SEALs went through with guns at the ready. Then someone whistled, and Remy urged her forward again.

The pier was across the street. Christina jogged beside Remy, darting her gaze over the area as they moved along the pavement. It seemed empty, but that didn't mean they were safe yet.

A large boat sat beside the pier, its red hull stained with rust. But they ran past the boat, feet slapping the wooden pier, equipment squeaking and banging with every step. At the end of the pier, a black—or was it gray?—armored boat appeared. It slowly motored up to the pier, and her heart skipped at the sight. Was it here for them? Or here to stop them?

The boat flipped around, and Christina could see men in black assault suits, holding weapons, lining the deck. The SEALs didn't break pace but kept running toward the boat, which was all the answer she needed for whose side they were on. When the SEALs got to the boat, the men onboard reached out to help pull the civilians up.

It took Christina a moment to understand that they were also SEALs, and relief rolled through her. One of the newly arrived SEALs reached for her then, but she shrank away, unwilling to let go of Remy. She clutched his hand, but he wrested free and gripped her shoulders, his gaze fierce.

"No, baby, you have to go now."

"You're coming with us, right?"

Three of the men from his squad were on the boat now. Why wasn't he?

His mouth was a flat, hard line. "There's not enough room, honey. Next boat."

Christina's body shook with fear and fury. "You didn't tell me it was going to be like this."

He cupped her cheeks. “I told you I wouldn’t be with you. I told you I’d see you at home.”

“Cage,” one of the SEALs growled. “We gotta go.”

“I know it,” he snapped. And then he kissed her, a rough, hard, quick kiss before she felt herself being swept up bodily and tossed into another man’s waiting arms.

Christina cried out, but Remy and five of his SEALs were already running back down the pier. The SEAL holding her gripped her tightly as she squirmed. The boat began to speed away from the pier just as a truck rocketed into view between the warehouse they’d just come from and the dock. The men in the truck definitely weren’t American—they wore head scarves and khakis—and they poured from the truck with weapons pointed at the SEALs on the pier.

“No,” Christina yelled. “You have to help them!”

She couldn’t see Remy and his men anymore, but she knew there was nothing they could put between them and the men who’d just arrived except water. They were loaded down with gear and not prepared to swim. How would they escape?

She listened for gunshots, but she heard nothing.

“This is the job, Miz Girard,” a voice said in her ear. “Let him do it.”

She sucked in a breath, fighting to hold in tears. What was happening back there? Where was Remy?

“Put me down, Cody,” she growled, finally realizing who held her tight.

He set her on the deck, steadying her as the boat bobbed across the waves. She slumped onto a bench because she had no choice, because she couldn’t stand in the rocking boat any longer. She searched the dock for some sign of Remy, but he was long out of sight.

When she gazed up at Cody, he was blurry. He smiled anyway.

"You haven't seen the last of Cage, don't worry."

CHAPTER TWENTY-FIVE

CHRISTINA HELD ON to that thought for hours. *You haven't seen the last of Cage.*

She held on to it as the assault boat that picked her and the others up sped across the water and the coastline of Qu'rim receded. She held on to it as they approached a ship that was so huge it made her heart hammer, and as that tiny assault boat drew up alongside and a door opened in the hull.

She and the others were helped onto a ramp and ushered inside the gray behemoth floating in the Persian Gulf. The last glimpse she had of a SEAL was Viking's face as he shot her a quick grin before the door shut.

She held on to the thought of seeing Remy while she was shown to a briefing room, and then while she boarded a helicopter and watched the deck of the carrier—stacked with airplanes and the men tending to them—get smaller and smaller as the copter winged its way toward shore again.

Only this time they were taken to a stable ally country where there was a US base. They boarded a military plane and took off again. A few hours later, they were in Germany and being taken by hospital bus up the winding hill to the American military hospital that perched high above the city of Landstuhl.

Christina held on to the thought of Remy while she was checked for injuries, while she showered and slipped into the hospital scrubs they'd provided her, and while she ate her first meal that didn't come out of a plastic pouch in days.

She plugged her phone in to charge, and then she fell asleep. When she woke, it was dark. Penny was in the room with her, and Christina could hear the other woman whimpering in her sleep.

She checked her phone, found it fully charged, and hesitated only a moment before turning it on. Naturally there were messages from her brother. And several from Ben, which was a surprise since she'd blocked him. He must have gotten a new phone number. She blocked that one too, and she erased the messages without listening to any but the first. It was typical Ben—self-involved, wheedling, and even a bit desperate, which wasn't typical at all.

Most importantly, however, there was nothing from Remy, and that made her heart sink. She couldn't get over the thought of him on that dock, his hands on her shoulders, telling her he couldn't go with her right now, that she had to go alone and he'd see her later.

Twenty-four hours ago she'd lain beneath him in a dusty safe house and felt the power of his body moving inside hers. She wanted that again, and soon. But what if she never got it? What if something had happened to him?

A cold knot of fear congealed in her belly. It didn't bear thinking about. She *couldn't* think about it. To lose Remy now… Oh God.

Trembling, she scrolled to her contacts and hit the button to dial Matt before she could change her mind. He answered on the first ring.

"Chrissy?"

Her eyes filled with tears. "Hi, Mattie."

"Jesus Christ." He was silent for a long moment, and her heart skipped a beat. "It's good to hear your voice, *ma petite*."

"Yours too."

"How you holding up?"

She swallowed. "I'm fine." She wasn't fine, not really. Her heart hurt. There was a hole in it that didn't want to close.

"I got the word hours ago that you'd been picked up. But I know it's not easy out there, honey. I know you've seen things…" He cleared his throat. "You can talk to me, Chris. If you need to."

She felt the corners of her mouth turning up. Yeah, it hadn't been a picnic out there, and she would never forget the horror of that bomb exploding so near—but the love she heard in his voice warmed her. Thank God for big brothers.

A little piece of her ached hard at the thought of Remy's twin sister and what had happened to her. Poor Remy.

"I know that," she said, grateful for him. She couldn't talk about it right now, but one day she would. And she knew he'd be there for her if she needed him. "But Mattie, the SEALs…they didn't all board the boat with us. Do you know—?"

She couldn't finish the question. A knot clogged her throat.

"Can't talk about operations, Chrissy."

"I don't want to know about operations… I just want to know if, um, everyone made it out okay."

"I've not heard differently. Believe me, I would have if we lost someone. I'd say they're all alive."

Her heart pounded as she latched on to that single ray of hope. "That's good. They're nice guys. I wouldn't want any of them to get hurt because… because of me," she finished softly.

"Nobody's getting hurt because of you, sweetie. The job is dangerous, yes, but it's not because of you. It's because there are bad people in this world and they do bad things."

The lump in her throat ached and her eyes stung. "I'm mad at you, by the way."

He snorted. "Me? What'd I do?"

"This thing the SEALs did—it's what you do too. You risk your life, Mattie. And you never told me."

His voice was soft when he spoke. "Don't worry about me. I'm fine."

"It's dangerous." She thought of the mercenaries on horseback, the bombing of the convoy, the way Baq had burned in the night.

"It is. But it's what I do. What we all do. Someone has to, Chrissy. Why not me?"

She had a million answers for him, but she knew that not one of them would persuade him. Or maybe one would. "Christian and Alex need you."

"They need a safe and secure world even more, don't you think?" He sighed, and she could picture him running his fingers through his hair in frustration. "Evie and I will meet you at the airport tomorrow, okay? We'll talk more then."

"Okay… But Mattie, if you hear anything different about the SEALs, you'll let me know, right?"

She could almost hear the gears grinding in his head. "If it's important to you. Care to tell me what this is really about?"

"Nothing. I just need to know."

She thought he swore softly, but she wasn't sure. "I know you, Christina Caroline Girard—and I know when you're hiding something. But yeah, I'll let you know. Now get some rest before tomorrow comes."

Evie had just put the twins down and headed to the kitchen to whip up a new cake recipe when Matt walked in, a puzzled frown on his face.

It made her heart skip a beat. "Everything okay?"

His piercing gaze met hers. He was so handsome he made her heart flip in her chest and her stomach squeeze tight. How she could love this one man her whole life was a mystery in a way, but she honestly had. Since she was about eleven years old, she'd known he was her everything. It had taken him far too long to realize she was his too, but he finally had.

"Christina just called. She's fine."

"Yes, you mentioned she was fine earlier when you got the report from Mendez. But what's putting that frown on your face, Matt? Does she sound upset? Was Mendez unaware of something that happened?"

He shook his head. "No, she sounds all right—but she's worried about the SEALs who rescued her. If I had to guess, I'd say one of them in particular."

Butterflies swirled in Evie's stomach. She didn't keep things from Matt, especially if they were important, but some things were still private. Especially when it was something personal that Christina had told her. Matt did not need to know everything his sister did.

"And if it is?" Evie asked, quirking an eyebrow.

Matt's gaze met hers. And then his brow knitted. "You know something, don't you?"

Evie flipped her stand mixer upright and started to measure flour. "I might."

He came over and turned her to face him, tipping her chin up with a finger. His eyes were a mixture of thunderous and curious—and hot. Mmmm.

"Evie."

He said it sternly, and her insides melted just a little. Not in a bad way but in an oh-my-God-that-sexy-voice-of-his way.

"It's not my place to tell you these things about your sister, Matt. But yes, there's one in particular. Though she hasn't actually been seeing him lately so I don't know what's going on. Not really."

He trapped her with an arm on either side of her body, wedging her against the counter. She tipped her head up and stared at him. His eyes focused on her mouth, his jaw going slack for a second.

"You aren't going to tell me, are you?"

"Not planning on it, no. Unless you mean to torture it out of me?"

His gaze sharpened. "Torture you how?"

She put her hands on his chest. "Oh, you know." Her fingers walked up his pecs and over his shoulders. "In the best way possible."

His hands went to her waist, pulled her against a burgeoning erection.

"I've got just the thing for you, baby."

"Yes, you definitely do," she practically purred.

A look of worry flashed through his eyes again, and she felt a little bad for not telling him about Remy Marchand and Christina.

"Is it serious?" he asked. "This thing with the SEAL?"

"I don't think so. I think it was a fling, quite honestly. But if she's worried about him now, well, who knows?"

"Not sure I trust any of those bastards. Not after what she went through with Ben."

"It's not up to us, honey. It's up to her."

"Yeah, I know. But she deserves the best. I don't want her tangled up with someone who's going to hurt her in the end."

Evie put her hand on his cheek. "Again, it's not up to us, Matt. Christina is a big girl, and she can make her own decisions."

"I can't believe you didn't tell me." He didn't sound pissed, which was good.

"If I had a brother, and he confided something personal about his life, something which did not affect me at all, would you feel compelled to tell me, especially if he asked you not to?"

"I would tell you if you asked me directly—but no, otherwise I probably wouldn't."

She studied him. "You would, wouldn't you?" She sighed. "Are you asking me who it is?"

"Yes, I'm asking. But if you don't want to tell me, if it goes against the sister code or something, don't."

"The sister code?"

He shrugged. "You know, like the bro code. Bros before hoes, baby."

Evie snorted. "Did you really just say that? Am I a *ho*?"

He pushed his hips into hers. "I hope so… but only with me."

She laughed. "You crack me up sometimes. Are you sure you want to know? Because so far as I know, she's not seeing him anymore."

"I still want to know."

"It's Remy."

His jaw tightened for a second. "Remy. He's a good guy. Nothing against him. Except, shit, we've been on missions together, played pool and volleyball, worked out. Hell, he's been over here countless times for barbecues—and he made moves on my sister."

"Honey, this isn't the eighteen hundreds. He didn't have to ask your permission to court your sister, you know."

He closed his eyes for a second. "No, he didn't. You're right. Still, I thought he'd have said *something* about it."

Evie stood on tiptoe and kissed him. "Stop right there,

big boy. Not your business. Adults, consenting, all that jazz. Get over it."

"Yeah, yeah. Working on it, okay?"

She slipped her hands down to his belt buckle and started to drag it open. "Why don't you work on me for a while instead? You'll feel better, I promise."

His breath hissed in when she slid inside his fly and pressed her palm to his cock.

"Damn, Evie girl, you sure play dirty."

"Oh honey, I haven't even started to play dirty yet…"

CHAPTER TWENTY-SIX

CHRISTINA TRIED TO get back to life as usual. After she arrived in DC, Matt and Evie picked her up and took her to dinner. They'd left the twins with the nanny they'd hired to help, though Evie kept checking her phone throughout dinner. She apologized, but Christina didn't mind. She got it because she kept checking her phone for word from Remy.

There was nothing, had been nothing since she'd last seen him on the pier. Matt eased her fears somewhat by telling her he'd specifically checked on Viking's SEALs and all were accounted for. They were no longer in Qu'rim, but beyond that he couldn't say.

So she breathed easier, but she still wondered where Remy was and why he wasn't calling her. Maybe he'd decided she wasn't worth the trouble after all. She couldn't blame him if he had. She'd pushed him away six months ago, and then she'd pulled him in over the past couple of days as if she couldn't get enough of him.

Those signals were mixed enough to confuse anyone, though she thought she'd made it clear that she was ready to move forward and see where this thing took them. If he still wanted to. Which, maybe, he did not.

"You're taking the next week off," Matt said, and she jerked her head up, meeting his gaze.

"What?"

Her brother looked intense, as he often did when he was determined. "I spoke to the old man. You're taking a week off. No flying anywhere, no business deals, no Girard Oil."

"I think I can determine my own schedule, Mattie. I don't need your help. Or Dad's either."

Matt reached across the table and squeezed her hand. "You've been through a lot, and you need to process it. Running from what happened out there won't help, trust me."

"Nothing much happened. We rode across the desert in vans. And then th-there was a bomb and people died, but you see that on the news every day." She didn't mention the horsemen, or the fact that her heart hitched when she thought of the convoy and the bomb. She'd never forget the sound of it, or the smell. Bleach and charred flesh. In fact, if she had any bleach in her laundry room, she wasn't opening it ever again.

Matt didn't let her go. Evie wore a soft smile of encouragement.

"It takes time, Chrissy."

"It does," Evie said. "There's so much adrenaline when everything happens, and then it's over and you feel kind of, well, off a little as you start to process everything you saw. The world continues on as before, but you were in danger and you watched people die. That doesn't go away overnight."

Christina stared at her sister-in-law. She hadn't forgotten what a crazy time Evie'd had in Rochambeau with Matt when her sister was kidnapped, but it all seemed so ordinary now that Christina never thought of it. And she'd never thought of what Evie must have felt when she found her ex-partner's body or when the woman driving Christina's father's yacht wrecked it and died. There had been a lot of violence in a short amount of time, and Evie had been through it all.

"So what do I do?" Christina asked. "Sit in my house and think about it for the next week?"

"No, of course not," Evie said. "But you don't need to jump on a plane and head to Houston either. If you go back to Girard Oil tomorrow, you'll be on a plane for who knows where, and you'll say you're just fine. Give it a few days is all we're saying."

Christina shifted her gaze between the two of them. Her heart filled at the love and concern she saw there. She'd been such an introverted child, a loner, and she'd thought at one time she was always destined to be that way. To keep everything to herself, because it was safest. She'd found friends and opened up to them, yet she was always cautious deep down. Always ready to lock the gates and protect herself.

But here she had two people who loved her and always would, no matter what she said or did. It was a comforting thing to know.

She didn't tell them that she hadn't planned on flying anywhere for a while because she was waiting for Remy to show up. Of course she'd planned to do some work though. She hadn't given up on Sheikh Fahd, and she intended to call him and try to close the deal over the phone.

But she could do that from home if it made these two happy. She bowed her head for a moment and worked on containing the emotion welling inside her.

"A few days," she said. "I can do that."

Matt squeezed her hand again and let it go. She could tell he was relieved. "Good."

"Mary is working out so well," Evie said brightly, referring to the new nanny. "Maybe we can plan shopping and lunch one day?"

"I'd like that," Christina replied. And she would. But she'd like it even more if Remy showed up on her doorstep as soon as possible.

Five days.

Christina stood at the window in her bedroom and gazed at the street below. She'd heard nothing at all from Remy, even though she knew he wasn't in Qu'rim anymore. He was safe, but he wasn't calling her.

Okay, so *this* was what it felt like to be ignored. He was giving her a taste of her own medicine. He'd made love to her in a war zone, made her feel safe and special, and now he was done with her. He wasn't going to answer his phone—she'd tried once, but he hadn't picked up and she hadn't been brave enough to try again—and he wasn't going to come and see her.

There was no plan to keep her in bed for twenty-four hours, no plan to call her. And she deserved it, didn't she? This was what she'd done to him. When he'd walked out of her house the morning after they'd first been together, he'd believed he would see her again. That they'd explore the attraction between them more thoroughly, maybe ease into a relationship.

And she'd been too much of a coward to answer his calls. Why hadn't she just picked up the phone and told him it was too much too soon? He would have respected that.

Christina sighed and tugged on her ponytail. She'd been so afraid of what had happened between them that she hadn't trusted herself to tell him no. That was the problem. She'd run for her own protection. She hadn't trusted herself.

Well, she was certainly getting a dose of her own medicine now, wasn't she?

She turned away and went to get dressed. She'd spent the past several days working from home, only going out to the grocery store or the coffee shop. She'd gone shopping with Evie one day, as promised. They'd had a good time at the mall. Evie hadn't pressed her for details of what happened in the desert, and she hadn't offered.

She'd wanted to. She wanted to talk to someone about it, but every time she'd thought about opening her mouth, she couldn't do it. Something held her back.

It was almost the holidays, but the days weren't too cold yet. She put on a pair of dark jeans with heeled boots and a blazer before grabbing her trench coat. Today she was going into the office. She'd only waited five days and not seven, but whatever. She'd spoken to Sheikh Fahd, and he'd finally agreed that selling his oil to Girard Oil was the best way to go. She needed to head into the office and oversee the paperwork.

And she really needed to fly to Houston, but she kept putting that part off. Just a few more days. If Remy didn't show up by then, well, she'd go. And she'd throw herself into work with more enthusiasm than ever before. She'd travel twenty-five days a month instead of fifteen. She'd go around the world making deals and overseeing oil production. She'd be the best motherfucking business development manager in the history of Girard Oil.

She grabbed her purse and keys and whipped open the door. Then she gasped. Ben stood there with his hand raised to knock, though why he didn't just press the doorbell she didn't know.

"What are you doing here?" she asked, grasping the door and holding it tight. As if she was going to have to whip it into his face or something.

He gave her a hangdog look. "You aren't answering your phone."

She closed her eyes for a second. "Yes, but that's because there's nothing to say."

Every time her phone rang, she'd freaked. Then she'd pick it up, see Ben's number, and want to scream. She'd tried to block him, but apparently that wasn't quite as easy to do on a landline as it was on a cell phone.

For the hundredth time, she berated herself for keeping a landline. But, dammit, she'd grown up in the bayou where storms often knocked out cell towers and the only thing that worked was a landline until the towers were fixed. It was a habit to keep it, though it was inconvenient as hell too when the only people who ever called were the ones she didn't want to hear from.

Ben and telemarketers and political candidates. It was enough to drive a person insane.

His eyes flashed with anger, but he quickly banked it. "I need to talk to you, Christina."

She gripped the door like a shield. "About what, Ben? You and me? It's not happening. Not ever again. You lied to me and cheated on me and… and what, you're not gay now? You want me instead of Chardonnay?"

His jaw tightened. "That was a mistake. And I'm not gay. I'm bisexual. I like men and women both. I had a moment of weakness."

She snorted. "I am aware of what the term means. I am also aware that you promised to love, honor, and cherish me—and then you fucked someone else in the most embarrassing way possible."

He looked scandalized. "You don't talk like that, Christina. Not ever. What's gotten into you?"

Her heart hammered hard in her chest, and her skin prickled with heat. She wanted to slap him. And she wanted to scream at him. He was criticizing her use of language? Really? After everything *he'd* done?

"I *do* talk this way, Ben. I'm done pretending to be perfect. I'm not. I cuss and I cry and I get mad and I say things that are rude."

"You never used to."

She sniffed. "Yeah, well I'm learning to be me and not some version of me that makes others happy."

He shook his head sadly and gave her a puppy dog look she would have once fallen for. "I'm sorry for everything, Christina. I made a mistake. I just want you back. I want to start over."

"That's not possible."

His face twisted into a mask of anger. It was so sudden that she took a step backward. And then she gripped the door hard and prepared to slam it in his face.

But he anticipated her, shoving a foot into the opening before she could get the door closed.

"It *is* possible, Christina," he said, the corners of his mouth turning down in a hard frown. "You need me. Nobody else understands you like I do. You're a sad, neurotic mess, the daughter of an alcoholic, the child of a wealthy man who ignored you to screw strippers your whole life. You mean nothing to him. *Nothing*. Together we can show him how wrong he was—I'll run for office again, we'll get it right this time, and you can invite him to the inaugural ball when I am the governor. We'll rub it in his face. We'll laugh so hard."

His eyes gleamed bright, and she stared at him in horror. He really believed what he was saying. Believed he had a chance, not only with her but also in politics. For a moment, she wondered if Ben was out of touch with reality, but then she realized it was just his supreme narcissism coming to the fore. He honestly believed he was capable of anything he put his mind to, even coming back from a huge scandal and winning a gubernatorial race.

"You need to go, Ben," she said as calmly as she could. He wasn't big like Remy, but he was still bigger than she was. Maybe it was just an instinctive reaction after what had happened in Qu'rim, but she felt threatened.

Scared.

For a moment Ben looked as if he would shove his way inside her house. But the tension left his body and he took a step back, brushing off imaginary lint from his custom Brooks Brothers suit. His Italian loafers clicked on her porch as he moved.

He wasn't violent. Never had been. Christina breathed a tiny sigh of relief, though her pulse still fluttered in her throat.

"Fine, I'll go."

"Please don't come back. It's over between us. We're divorced—and there's nothing left to say."

His lips flattened, the corners whitening. "If that's what you want."

She swallowed. Her heart hammered and beads of sweat popped up beneath her sweater. But she nodded firmly. "Yes, that's what I want."

"All right. Then I guess this is good-bye."

Ben turned and went down the steps. He didn't look back as he walked out to the street and got into the silver Mercedes sitting at the curb.

Christina watched him get inside and drive away. She considered staying home and locking the door, not leaving the house at all today. But then she sucked in a breath and gritted her teeth. She wasn't going to let him win. No, that hadn't been pleasant, but she also knew she was still very much affected by what had happened in Qu'rim.

Not every man who got angry was a killer. And not every situation was dangerous.

Still, she waited a few minutes before she stepped out onto the porch where Ben had so recently stood. She closed and locked the door with trembling fingers, cursing her weakness as she did so. Then she walked briskly to her own car and got inside.

It was going to be a good day at the office, dammit. And if Remy hadn't come by the end of the day, well, she'd make plane reservations for her weekly trip to Houston. It was time to get moving with her life again.

CHAPTER TWENTY-SEVEN

GODDAMN, HE WAS tired. But he was also aching to see Christina. Remy grabbed his bag from the overhead compartment and strode off the plane first since he was sitting in the exit row. He'd flown commercial back to the States because sometimes HOT went that way after a mission. The squads weren't tied to military transport when out of the hot zone, which meant they could often get where they were going a lot faster on Delta or American or whoever had a plane going back to DC at that moment.

It was later than he wanted it to be, but that's because he'd been routed through JFK on his way back instead of straight to BWI or Dulles. He strode up the gateway and through the door into the airport. He had to wait at baggage claim for his duffel, but then he was on his way, calling an Uber that greeted him at the curb.

He dozed a bit in the car, but he never fully slept. He was aware of every turn the driver took. When he reached Christina's street, he had the guy drop him at the corner. It was a habit not to let someone take him to his precise destination. He'd have to walk a block or so, but that was a cakewalk compared to the kind of hikes he normally took on the job.

Hikes involving sixty pounds of equipment and weaponry through enemy territory while being fired upon. Yeah, a block carrying a duffel and a backpack was nothing.

He slowed as he rounded the corner near Christina's house. It was a cute cottage on a quiet street. The house was gray with black shutters and a red door, and the porch light was on. Inside, as he well knew, it was frilly and girly, a feminine palace fit for a lady like Christina.

A lady who made him harder than marble with a single hot look and then fucked him with abandon until he exploded in a hot rush. Jesus, what a quickie that had been back in the safe house. Hot and perfect, just like her.

He'd been aching to see her for days, but there had been things to do in Qu'rim, and then there'd been a quick mission into neighboring Acamar to retrieve a couple of military contractors who'd gotten themselves snagged by a militant group. Thankfully that militant group hadn't been the Freedom Force. If it had been, the mission would have been a lot longer and more complicated.

He had no idea if she'd even be at home. He could have called her, but no matter what she'd said back in Qu'rim, she had a reputation of not answering her phone and then running away from him. He wasn't going to give her that chance.

Nope, best to show up and see what happened.

He continued down the street, slowing when a man got out of a silver Mercedes that sat under a streetlamp directly across from Christina's. The man was dressed in a suit and tie, and he seemed to stare at her house. A lamp burned in the living room, and a shadow crossed over the curtain. A flash of heat rolled through him then. She hadn't left—though if she'd let him in was another story.

Remy waited instinctively to see what the other man would do. He was probably someone who lived nearby, but the habits Remy had gained as a SEAL meant he took nothing for granted. The man stood there for another minute or so, fooling with his phone. He wasn't doing anything harmful, even if he did appear to be loitering. But he was loitering in front of a two-story house that could very well be his own.

Remy decided he was finished waiting. He continued down the sidewalk and then turned and went up the steps to Christina's house. He turned to look across the street and check where the man was. But he wasn't there, though the car still sat where he'd left it. Apparently he'd finished whatever he'd been doing and gone inside.

Remy took a deep breath and punched the doorbell. He heard her moving inside, though she was light and barely made a sound. She flipped on the porch light, and then she must have put her eye to the peephole because he heard a gasp.

A second later, the door swung open and Christina stood there looking like a dream come true. She wore yoga pants and a sweatshirt that said Army on it. No doubt a gift from her brother. Remy made a note to buy her one that said Navy.

"Hey, *cher*," he said softly.

She launched herself at him. He caught her, lifting her up to hold her as her legs wrapped around his waist and her mouth fused to his. He backed her against the door-jamb, kissing her with all the pent-up sexual heat and frustration that had been hammering through him for the past few days.

Hell, the past few months, because that brief taste he'd gotten of her in Qu'rim hadn't been nearly enough.

Their tongues caught, tangled, their mouths claiming and branding and worshipping. Remy held her tight, his hands under her ass, his duffel at his feet. He didn't want to put her down for a minute, not until he was deep inside her, but that wasn't happening out on her porch.

"Your neighbors are gonna call the cops, baby," he growled in her ear. "Because I'm going to strip you naked and bury myself inside you in about five seconds. Which means you got four seconds to move this party."

He was right, of course, though she didn't want to let him go. A car door slammed just then, as if reminding them they had an audience. Christina unhooked her legs from his waist and he let her go, but not before sliding her down his body. She couldn't miss the particularly hard bulge below his belt, and her body trembled with the knowledge she would soon get to be up close and personal with that bulge.

She stepped back while he grabbed his duffel and backpack. Her eyes scanned the street out front. A car pulled away from the curb and she stiffened for a moment, unable to tell what it was in the dark other than a light-colored sedan. Was it a Mercedes? Or some other car? Not that other people couldn't have a Mercedes too, but the memory of Ben standing on her porch and glaring at her was too fresh. Would he come back? Would he try again, or had he really taken no for an answer?

She didn't have any more time to think about Ben though, because in the next instant, her door slammed shut and then Remy was tugging her into his arms again. He was so big and strong, and she loved how he enveloped her when he hugged her.

"Not kidding about that five-second thing, *cher*. Unless you have a different plan, or you're really not on board with this."

"Not on board? Are you kidding me? I jumped on you when I opened the door."

"And you can keep jumping, baby. But not until I've had what I want…"

In one smooth move, he lifted the sweatshirt she'd changed into when she got home over her head. Then he unhooked her bra and her breasts spilled free. Well, as much as beestings could spill, she supposed.

It made no sense but she felt suddenly shy. She wanted to put her hands over her breasts, but the way he gazed at them made her think maybe he didn't mind so much that she didn't have a lot to play with in that department.

His fingers went to the waistband of her yoga pants. He shoved those down along with her panties, and then she was standing naked before him, her skin breaking out in goose bumps. Not because she was cold though.

She definitely wasn't cold even though her nipples made it appear otherwise.

"Beautiful." Remy dropped to his knees and spanned her waist with his hands before pulling her forward and sucking one tight nipple into his mouth.

Christina gasped as he tugged. Pleasure so good it hurt spiked from her nipple to her pussy. As if he knew it, he pushed her legs apart so she was standing with her thighs open.

Then he skimmed his fingers down into her wetness, and she gripped his hair, her fingers tightening in the silky locks. He would have to get it cut soon, she knew that, but oh she loved his hair like this. Slightly wild and untamable, like him.

"Remy," she gasped as his fingers skimmed upward again. It was such a light touch, but she craved more.

He sucked her other nipple into his mouth, giving it equal attention. Then he lightly pinched her clit between his thumb and forefinger, and she thought she might come unglued.

He laughed, the evil man.

And then he did something she did not expect. He picked up her left leg and threw it over his shoulder. Then he blazed a hot trail down her abdomen with his mouth. Just when she thought he was going to lick her, he leaned back and parted her with his fingers.

"So wet," he said, looking at the petals of her sex. And, holy cow, she was. Almost embarrassingly so. "Wonder if you taste as good as you look?" he murmured.

And then he gripped her hips and pulled her to him, his tongue sliding into her heat and making her moan.

"Yes," he said, "you definitely do."

Before she could find her equilibrium, he sucked her clit into his mouth and started to fuck her with two fingers.

Her knees went weak as he flicked his tongue back and forth over her clit. He was too good at this to let her explode, however.

He kept her on the edge, licking and sucking at just the right moments and then backing away and blowing cool air on her when she was ready to come.

"Did you miss me?" he asked, and she blinked.

"Are you doing this to torture me?"

He ran his fingers between her folds again, spreading her wide. His chin glistened with her wetness, and her knees nearly buckled as he gazed up at her, his eyes hot and possessive. *Mine. He's mine.*

"You could have had this in your life for months, *cher*. Months of me eating your pussy and making you scream. Yeah, I'm torturing you."

And then he licked her again, his tongue lashing against her clit with perfect rhythm. As her climax built inside her, she threw her head back and rocked her hips against him, riding his face, seeking out all the good stuff that was hers for the taking.

"Don't stop, dammit," she cried when she was close. "Don't you dare stop!"

He didn't. He flicked his tongue against her again and again, his face buried between her legs, her body tightening like a spring until the moment when the tension broke and she cried out in a rough voice, begging him to keep going until the moment when it all became too much, when her body was too sensitive and she thought another touch might make her scream.

He didn't stop, however. Or not for long. He surged up and lifted her until she had her arms wrapped around him and her legs around his waist. Then he turned her until her bare back was against the wall.

"Damn, Christina, that was fucking hot," he said, holding her against the wall with his body while he fumbled with his belt. "I can't wait another minute."

Her body was like rubber, but she managed to hold on while he freed himself. Then he put his hands under her ass and held her while he surged upward into her body, his hard cock stretching and filling her to the brim.

"Remy," she cried.

"Sorry," he muttered. "Shit, I'm sorry."

"No, please." She swallowed. "More. Give me more."

He held her hard and withdrew from her body before slamming in again, sinking even deeper this time, until they both groaned from the contact.

"Holy shit, you are so fucking perfect," he said. "So hot and gorgeous."

"I love your cock, Remy," she said, feeling bold and hot and ready to be wild with him. Ready to let herself go and do all the things she'd never been brave enough to do.

"My cock loves you too, baby," he said, dragging it out and slamming it into her again and again.

The head of his massive cock tugged at her walls as he withdrew and bumped up against all her pleasure zones as he sank into her again. She was stretched wide and loving the feeling of being pinned to a wall and fucked by this gorgeous man.

He pushed harder into her, grinding her down on the root of his penis each time, hitting the pleasurable knot of nerves at the base of her clitoris with every stroke. The wall at her back was solid, but the man at her front was solid too. Warm and hard and so strong it amazed her.

He wasn't tiring from holding her up, wasn't tiring

from using his legs to surge and withdraw again and again.

Sweat broke out on her body, and her heart hammered in her chest. Remy's mouth was on her throat as she tipped her head back and turned it to give him better access.

Just then, she spotted herself in the entryway mirror. And, oh God, how fantastic they looked.

She was utterly naked, wrapped around Remy, and his pants were around his knees. He was still mostly clothed. He was in such control of his movements. His arms corded with muscle as he held her, his hands spreading wide under her ass, his hips pistoning with precision.

He knew what he was doing. This was no uncontrolled coupling. This was precision movement designed to elicit the most pleasure from her body.

She watched in fascination as he fucked her against the wall. It only heightened the pleasure, and she found herself panting and urging him on in terms she'd never used in her life.

He stilled only a moment—and then his eyes met hers in the mirror and a slow smile spread across his face.

"You like to watch the action, baby? Turn you on?"

"Yes… yessss."

He pulled her away from the wall and held her up, putting a little bit of distance between them before he brought her back down on his cock.

"Then watch this. Watch as I disappear inside you."

She watched. And the tension inside her gathered into a hard knot. It was beautiful the way his cock sank into her again and again. He was slick and shiny with her juices. And the word came to her head again: *mine.*

MINE.

"Can't last, baby," he said on a groan before pushing

her against the wall again and surging inside her harder and faster than before. “Come for me, Christina.”

As if she was waiting for him to command her, she splintered apart in that moment, gasping for air as stars exploded behind her eyes. He rocked into her two more times and then groaned as he came deep inside her.

CHAPTER TWENTY-EIGHT

"I DIDN'T THINK you were coming," she said as they lay in her bed together. Even after holding her against the wall for so long, he'd still managed to carry her upstairs to her bed after they'd finished earlier.

It hadn't taken long before he was buried inside her again, rocking into her and making her beg for mercy before she exploded in yet another spectacular orgasm.

Now they lay together, him on his back, her halfway across his chest, the covers thrown back because they were hot even though it was cool outside.

Christina loved touching him. She couldn't get enough of touching him. Even now, her hands roved over hard, hot muscle.

Remy's eyes were hooded, sensual. "Always with you, baby."

She sighed and smacked him playfully. "I wasn't talking about that kind of coming. I meant coming to see me."

"I know. Fun to tease you though." He drew in a breath. "So you thought I'd changed my mind?"

"Yes."

"Told you the job is unpredictable."

Her heart hitched. "But Remy—when those men showed up at the pier. God, I was so scared for you. Cody said you would be fine, and Matt said all the SEALs were accounted for when I called him—but I feared the worst before that."

His fingers skimmed up and down her naked spine. "Just another day at the office, *cher*. Those men weren't prepared for the likes of us. We disarmed them and left them tied in the warehouse. Then we got on the next assault boat."

"But I never saw you before we were taken from the carrier."

"No, you didn't. My team and I had somewhere else to be for a little while. Told you it might be like that."

She sucked in a breath. "Yes, you did. I just wished I'd known you were okay."

"I wanted to get word to you—but there was no way to do it. No time. I knew you'd learn our status from Matt."

"I suffered for hours…" She sighed. "I guess I have no choice but to forgive you. Especially if you give me another orgasm or two tonight."

He laughed. "I can definitely do that, honey. Next time let's try it from behind. In your bathroom where you can watch it all in the mirror."

Christina shivered. "It'd be better with a three-way mirror."

"Then we'll head down to the nearest department

store and snag a dressing room."

"I half believe you'd do it if I said yes."

"Nah, not really. But don't think I'm not going mirror shopping tomorrow. And then I'm fucking you every conceivable way I can think of so you can watch it all. Dirty girl."

Christina's cheeks were hot, but she laughed. "Only dirty with you, Remy."

His eyes sparked. "Oh yeah?"

Her heart pounded, but as usual she'd told him the truth. "Yes, only you."

"You never told a man to fuck you real good before?"

And now her cheeks were seriously hot. But she *had* said that to him, hadn't she? And other things besides. Like how much she loved his cock. The size, the shape, the girth. Oh dear.

"No, I never have. In fact, I don't think I've used the word fuck in bed before. Ever. Ben wasn't a dirty talker—or at least not with me. He did tell Chardonnay to fuck him in the ass, after all, so I guess he didn't mind the dirty words. He just minded them with me."

She thought about Ben being horrified with her for her language earlier today. She almost told Remy about that but then thought it probably wasn't a good thing to keep mentioning her ex-husband while in bed with her current lover.

He'd been so angry the last time she'd told him about Ben showing up that if she said Ben had been here again, Remy would probably do something rash like go and pound her ex into the ground.

She didn't need that. Remy didn't need that. And besides, she didn't want Ben spoiling her good time here tonight. Which he would if she mentioned he'd come to see her again.

"I don't mind them at all, for the record. I especially don't mind them when you want to tell me what to do to you in bed."

She bit her lip and then dropped her chin and rested it on his chest. "So did you consider not coming to see me when you got back? I'd understand if you said you did."

He tipped her chin up with a finger and held her gaze long enough that she started to squirm.

"I came straight here from the airport. I didn't go home. I didn't call anyone or do anything except come to you. I couldn't think of anything but you, Christina."

And didn't that just make her feel tingly all over? Tingly and special and good about herself, as if she were made of awesome.

She hadn't felt like she was made of awesome since, well, ever. And yet it scared her too. What was it about this man that got under her skin and made her feel so spectacular? And what would happen if that went away?

She'd survived Ben's betrayal, but it hadn't been easy. She'd been stunned at first. Then sad, then mad, then numb. And then she'd been determined to build a cocoon around herself, to never feel so vulnerable again.

She'd done a good job of it—and then she'd met Remy and he'd made everything go sideways in the short space of time she'd let him into her life and her bed.

He'd been supposed to be a fling, a hot sexy time with a beautiful man in order to make her feel better, but he'd turned out to be dangerous to the walls she'd built to keep people out.

And here she was letting him back in, knowing that

this time the walls would crumble and she'd be more vulnerable than ever.

He pushed her hair behind her ear. "That bothers you, doesn't it?"

She hesitated. "It doesn't bother me."

"I think it does."

She dropped her gaze for a moment. "All right… It scares me just a little bit."

"Care to tell me why?"

"Because I'm afraid of caring too much about you, and then you'll leave."

"I'm not leaving."

"You don't really know that," she scoffed. "People leave. They get tired of each other and they say, 'I'm done.' Happens every day."

His brows drew down and he looked pissed. "Don't you think we need to take this a day at a time? We haven't even started yet, and you're forecasting the end of this relationship. Can't you just enjoy what's going on here?"

It was a simple enough question, and yet she didn't have an answer. Because it wasn't entirely simple to her. None of this was simple—and he didn't understand.

"Are we having a relationship?" she asked.

He looked angrier than he had a moment ago. "If it's not a relationship, what is it?"

She was very aware of her naked flesh pressed to his. Of the feel of all that hot, smooth skin and hard muscle. Maybe it was kind of ridiculous to discuss whether or not this was a relationship under the circumstances.

Still, she swallowed and refused to look away even though it would have been more comfortable. "We've had sex a few times, Remy. I'm not sure what this is yet."

They looked at each other for a long moment. But she wasn't prepared for what he did next. He sat up, pushing her away from him, and then climbed from the bed. When he started to jerk on his jeans, her stomach clenched tight.

She bolted upright, clutching the sheet to her body. "Where are you going?"

"Home." His eyes flashed as they met hers again. "We did the one-night-stand thing six months ago, Christina. A week ago you told me you wanted more. You implied you were ready to move forward—if that's not true, then I'm going home and this is over."

Her heart skipped at the idea of him walking out. Sure, it would hurt for a little while, but she'd get over it. And then she'd be alone again. Safe, her heart locked up tight and impenetrable.

God, how lonely and sad that sounded.

"I'm trying," she said. "I know this is easy for you, but for me it's more complicated. I haven't even been divorced a year. My ex humiliated me in public and destroyed my trust. I'm afraid. Afraid of feeling too much, afraid of it blowing up in my face—afraid of myself and my judgment."

He'd stopped in the act of closing his jeans. Now abdominal muscles that mere mortals didn't possess flexed as he bent and picked up his shirt. He didn't put it on though, and it dangled from his fingers, forgotten. He was tousled and sexy and her belly tightened. He looked as if he could climb back in bed just as easily as walk out of her life.

"I understand that, baby," he said softly. "But you're going to have to make up your mind about us. We're either moving forward or we're not. And if we're not, I'm outta here. I'm not investing more time in you if it's going nowhere."

She wanted to scream. And she wanted to tug him back to the bed and shut him up with her mouth on his. But he wasn't going to let that happen.

"Why do we have to define this?" she asked, desperation prowling through her veins. "Why can't we just see what happens?"

He shook his head. "You are so messed up you don't even see it, do you? Jesus, Christina—you're forecasting the end of something you refuse to call a relationship, but then you want to see what happens, take it a day at a time, right? That's fucked up because you can't do both. If we take it a day at a time, it's a relationship and we're moving forward."

Her heart throbbed. He was right, of course. She shoved her hands through her hair and pressed them to her skull. And then she took a deep breath. "I don't know what I want, Remy. I can't put a label on this right now—but I know I don't want you to go. Please don't go."

He let out a long sigh. "Then I won't go. But *cher*, this *is* a relationship. We're seeing each other. That sweet body of yours belongs to me. Nobody else but me. Is that a problem for you?"

Relief roared through her.

"No." Because she'd have to be crazy to want another man when she had this one.

He pulled the shirt on and zipped up his pants. It wasn't quite what she thought he'd been planning to do, and she watched him warily, uncertain what was going on.

"Come on, baby," he said as he picked up her panties and tossed them at her. "I'm starved. Let's find an IHOP and tear into some pancakes before the next round."

She blinked. "The next round?"

He shot her a wolfish grin. "You didn't think I was finished with you, did you? All night long, Christina. All night long."

CHAPTER TWENTY-NINE

REMY LIFTED THE weight stack and did eight quick reps before dropping the bar again and blowing out a breath.

"Good job," Cowboy said. "Considering you've skipped the gym for a week…"

Remy snorted as he picked up the towel and wiped his face. "I was busy. And I didn't skip it."

Or not completely, anyway. Christina had a treadmill in her house. She also had a weight bench, but the weights were laughable for someone his size. So he'd settled for lifting her instead.

Rep after rep on his cock. Standing, sitting, standing again. Yeah, not a bad way to go. He'd gone to fatigue—that point at which his muscles burned—so it had to count.

Not that he was mentioning any of that to Cowboy.

"Man, we've hardly seen you."

"We get R & R after a mission. I've been relaxing."

Cowboy snorted. "Relaxing. Riiight. Does it involve

a pretty brunette named Christina Girard?"

Before he could answer, another voice called out, "Yeah, does it?"

Both Remy and Cowboy swung around to see Matt Girard standing there. He was dressed in workout gear, and he sported a frown that would make lesser men tremble.

Remy was not about to tremble, however. Yeah, Christina was the man's sister, which meant that he was concerned for her. Remy got that. If he'd done a better job of protecting Roxie, maybe she'd still be alive today.

Goddammit, stop that. Nothing you could do. She didn't tell you the truth. She didn't tell anyone the truth.

"Hmm, think I heard someone call my name," Cowboy said as he slung his towel over his shoulder and strolled for the door. They all knew it wasn't true as they were the only three in the HOT HQ gym.

Remy mopped the sweat from his face again. Then he met Matt's laser-like stare. So similar to his sister's and yet not. "Yeah, I'm seeing Christina. I care about her."

Matt's jaw flexed. "You could have told me, man. I think you owe me that much."

A flash of anger sizzled through him. "With all due respect, Captain, I don't owe you anything when it comes to my personal life. If I were seeing anyone else, you wouldn't want to know who it is. Just because Christina is your sister doesn't give you the right to know who she sees."

"Motherfucker," Matt grated. And then he shoved a hand through his hair and threw his head back, staring up at the ceiling for a long minute. "Look, I understand the principle here. You're both adults. She doesn't need my permission and neither do you—but dude, her ex fucked her over. He did a real number on her head, and I'm not sure she's ready for another relationship right now—and especially not with someone like you. Like *us*, Remy. It takes a special woman to put up with what we do—and while I know my sister is as special as they come, she's not cut out for our world."

Remy's gut clenched. Hell, he'd wondered about the first part himself. Wondered if he was pushing her too far and too hard. It wasn't like he planned on proposing to her, so why the push to be together, to ride out this sexual wave until it ended?

He'd thought of walking away, of ending it all and moving on—and his chest ached. It was more than physical. There was something about her. About her sweet vulnerability and delicate strength. She attracted him like she was gravity and he an unmoored object. He fell into her because he couldn't help himself.

It was scary as all fuck in a way and comforting in others. He wanted her, needed her. The thought of being without her hurt. He was strong. He'd survive. But he didn't want to. He wanted Christina.

And as far as her not being cut out for their world? She was stronger than Matt thought she was. No, Remy didn't want her ever in danger again, but the way she'd reacted told him she could handle this life. She hadn't fallen apart in Qu'rim at all. She'd weathered the storm and kept her head the entire time. She was small and mighty.

"I know what happened with Ben. I have no intention of hurting her. And as for our world? I think that's her choice—but you should know that she was amazing in Qu'rim. Never once lost her cool—and there was plenty there to fall apart over. She's levelheaded and smart. She can handle more than you think she can."

Matt looked sheepish for a second. "Thanks for being a part of the team that got her out of there. I appreciate it very much."

"You're welcome." They both knew Remy would have done the same for anybody—they all would—but a thank-you was never misplaced for a job well done.

"I'm pretty sure Ben didn't plan to hurt her either," Matt said, his mouth flattening in disapproval. "But then he did. So yeah, it worries me."

Remy had a sudden urge to punch something. Whether he intended to or not, Matt was suggesting that Remy was like Christina's ex-husband. That rankled.

"Dude, I have sisters. I get it." Remy swallowed. "My twin was killed by her boyfriend. I know how it feels to be so fucking helpless it makes you sick, and I know how it feels to wish you could protect her from all harm."

Matt's expression had softened, his eyes widening. "Jesus. I'm so sorry. I had no idea."

Remy blew out a breath. "I don't like to talk about it, but I wanted you to know that I understand. I'm seeing your sister. I care about her. A lot. And I think she cares about me. I don't know where this is going, but I want it to go farther and faster than she does right now. She's cautious. She's smart. She's also broken, and I know every bit of that. I'm careful of her heart because I know it's fragile."

Matt's gaze grew sharp. "Do you love her?"

There was a sharp stab somewhere in the vicinity of Remy's heart. Love? How could he love her when he barely knew her?

"I don't know," he said honestly. "This is still new to us both."

Matt didn't look happy about that. "She deserves the best."

"She does."

"Then I'd appreciate it if you'd figure out real fast whether or not that's going to be you."

Remy wanted to bristle at Matt's tone—but how could he? Remy cared about Christina. But Matt loved her.

"Copy that, brother."

Matt held out his hand. Remy took it. "I'm sorry about your sister. That fucking blows hard, and I know the words aren't enough, but I mean them. I really like you, Remy." He squeezed Remy's hand just a little harder then. "But you hurt Chrissy, and I'm going to be all over your ass like a bad rash."

Remy squeezed back. "Understood, Captain."

Christina put down the phone and frowned. Then she dropped her head into her hands and took deep breaths to quiet her frustration. She'd been home for two weeks now. She'd spent the past seven nights with Remy, tangled up in his arms and lost in a world of intense pleasure.

They'd had no more uncomfortable conversations about relationships or where this was going. It just went. Every day when he called her, she answered her phone, her heart pounding giddily.

They made plans. Those plans usually involved some sort of takeout, her bed, and him. After work, he'd come to her house bearing food. She said she was willing to go to his, but he'd said hers was nicer. Plus he had a roommate. He shared an apartment with Cash McQuaid near the military base.

She liked Cash well enough, but she wasn't going to go over there and stay the night with the other SEAL around. Since they all worked with Matt, it felt wrong to be so blatant about her relationship with Remy.

She smiled to herself. Relationship. There, she'd said it.

They were having one. The thought made her panic just a little bit, but she told herself there was nothing she could do. It was too late. She was in it now.

Which was where the frustration came from. She'd been back for two weeks, and she needed to fly to Houston. Then she needed to get back on the road. There was a company in Brazil she'd targeted for Girard Oil's needs, and she had to go down there and start the negotiations.

Then there was Russia and the interesting maze of Moscow politics to navigate.

Once, she would have loved the challenge and the adventure. Now she just wanted to stay in DC and have a normal everyday life like everyone else.

But since she couldn't put it off any longer, she'd buzzed her secretary and told her to make the arrangements for Houston and Brazil. The negotiations with Sheikh Fahd were finished, and she was still riding high from that triumph. It was time to forge ahead with her plans and acquire more business for the company.

She would tell Remy tonight, though she dreaded it.

How would he react? He knew what she did, and she could no longer put it off just to enjoy long nights with him. She had a job to do the same as he did. And when Uncle Sam came calling, Remy wasn't going to be able to put it off at all. So why should she?

She got through the rest of the afternoon, and then she went out to her car and got inside. The days were getting longer, but it was still growing dark around six at night and so it was dusk when she went outside. The parking lot was lit and guarded, so she wasn't worried about anyone bothering her.

The trip home took around twenty minutes. She parked in the driveway and gathered her purse and brief-case before getting out of the car. Her phone dinged and she dug for it, smiling when she saw the text from Remy.

Pizza and you tonight. Be naked when I get there. 7 pm.

She texted a quick reply as she walked around the car and headed for the door. But she collided with something solid, gasping in surprise as two firm hands reached out to steady her.

Her stomach bottomed out as her eyes met those of the man holding her.

"Ben. What are you doing here?"

He was dressed impeccably in what she knew was a custom-made suit. Anger flashed through her then. He'd bought that suit with *her* money, just like he'd bought the Mercedes with her money. Ben had never had a pot to piss in. He'd seen her as a one-way ticket to fortune and fame as a politician. He was a brilliant lawyer, but he wanted more than a legal career.

His grip on her tightened. "I came to talk to you, Christina."

She wrested free of him and took a step back. "I've told you there's nothing left to say. We're through, Ben. You need to understand that."

"I don't agree with you."

Another wave of anger rolled through her. Dammit, she was so sick of this man trying to steamroll her. That's all he'd ever done in their marriage. Told her what his opinion was and expected her to go along with it.

And she had, idiot that she'd been. Just so she'd feel like she belonged. So she wouldn't *lose* him, because a wife was supposed to keep her husband happy. Gah.

"I don't care if you agree or not. It's over, and I never want to see you again. Now get away from me or I'm calling the cops."

She held her phone up as a threat. But what he did next took her by surprise. He knocked the phone from her fingers and it tumbled into the grass. Then he grabbed her by the hair and jerked her forward.

She started to scream, but the cold barrel of a gun dug into her ribs and shocked her to silence.

"We're talking, you superior little bitch. Like it or not."

CHAPTER THIRTY

REMY STOPPED AND picked up the pizza he'd called in before continuing on to Christina's house. He was a few minutes late, but that's because he'd had to help Cash extract a drunken woman from the hallway outside their apartment. Cash claimed he didn't know her and that she wasn't there for him, but Remy didn't quite believe it.

No doubt she was another of those poor women who'd taken one look at Cash's Hollywood good looks and lost her ever-loving mind. Cash might have slept with her and forgot he'd done it. Or he'd just flirted heavily with the woman at a bar somewhere and then she'd stalked him until she found out where he lived.

Wasn't the first time. Probably wouldn't be the last.

Remy pulled into Christina's driveway, his cock beginning to tingle with interest.

"Yeah, you know what's happening, don't you?" he said and then shook his head. "Jesus, talking to my fucking dick. What's next?"

He grabbed the pizza and shut the door of his truck, clicking the button to lock it before he strode toward her front door and the heaven that awaited him behind it.

He nearly stopped on the sidewalk as he thought of her brother and the worry on his face as he'd asked if Remy loved Christina.

It was too soon for love. Too new and too raw. Not to mention he'd never actually been in love before, so he didn't really know what it was supposed to feel like. Was it this tightening in the chest whenever he thought of Christina? Was it the rush of warmth that filled him when he held her in his arms and they went to sleep curled together?

Was it this need to be near her that made his skin itch and his brain jump until the moment he saw her again?

Maybe it was, or maybe he was just really into her.

He rang the bell. She didn't come, but his phone dinged.

Come inside. I left it unlocked for you.

Remy frowned. He was going to have to talk to her about leaving the door unlocked. Yeah, the neighborhood was nice, but this was fucking Washington DC. You didn't leave the door unlocked in DC, no matter where you lived.

Still, he turned the knob and walked inside, locking the door behind him because that's the way he operated.

Waiting for you in the bedroom, baby. Hurry.

He chuckled, shedding the jacket he wore and tossing it on the couch. The room was still as sweet and girly as ever, but he liked it. It was like walking into a feminine lair filled with roses, lace, and silver tea sets. So ladylike. So Christina.

He didn't know what a Cajun boy like him was supposed to do with a lady like her or why she'd even be interested in him, but he was damn glad she was. Maybe it was because she had Cajun roots herself, or maybe she just liked the tall, dark, and deadly type.

Whatever it was, he wasn't questioning his good fortune at this moment.

He picked up the pizza and started up the stairs to her bedroom. Too bad the damn pizza was going to get cold before they ate it, but getting inside Christina would be so worth it—and it would be the first thing he did. He knew himself well enough now to know there was no way he was walking in there, finding her naked on the bed, and eating a slice of pizza first.

He'd fucked her as often as possible over the past few days, and it hadn't gotten boring or routine yet. She was sweet and hot and sexy, and he loved making her moan. Loved the dirty words she said when she couldn't help herself.

Usually happened when she was on the brink of orgasm or when she wanted him to do something he wasn't doing yet—like licking her sweet pussy until she screamed his name.

He went up the stairs softly because it was a habit and went over to her door. It was shut, which gave him pause. Why shut the door if she was waiting for him? Then again, who knew what Christina was thinking.

He twisted the knob and the door swung open. She lay on the bed, totally naked, her flesh so pale and beautiful. She was wearing the pearls and her legs were spread—

A chill rolled through him as he took in several things simultaneously. First, her arms were behind her back and her legs were tied to the bedposts with what looked like scarves.

She wore a gag, and her cheeks glistened with moisture, her eyes wide and frightened. He dropped the pizza and prepared to fight, cursing because he wasn't armed at that moment.

His weapons were locked away at HOT HQ because that's what you did with them when you weren't working. Fucking hell. He reached for the phone at his belt.

Just then, a man stepped out of the shadows, Christina's phone in his hand—and a gun in the other.

"Hello, Remy. We've been waiting for you."

"Let her go," Remy said, his voice a guttural growl Christina didn't think she'd heard before.

Ben continued to point the weapon at Remy's heart, and Christina squirmed on the bed, trying to work free from the restraints. But they were tight, and every movement of her body only seemed to make them tighter.

"Drop the fucking phone, asshole," Ben said. "And shut up. I'm the one who does the talking here."

Remy's jaw tightened. He held his phone for a moment longer—and then he dropped it, tossing it so that it landed on the floor and slid beneath the dresser. She could just see it peeking out from beneath the cherrywood.

"There's a set of handcuffs on the table by the door. Put them on."

Remy did as Ben said, and Christina wanted to cry. He wouldn't look at her, and that worried her. On the other hand, she wasn't sure she wanted him looking at her. Ben had forced her to strip, and then he'd tied her up in as humiliating a way as possible.

Legs spread, hands behind her back so her breasts thrust forward. He'd pinched her nipples, stuck his hand between her legs. But there'd been no tenderness in his touch, no reality. It was almost as if he'd done it to prove he could.

His eyes had been dead when they'd met hers. She'd asked him not to do this, to think—but he'd told her it was too late for that. That's when the doorbell rang.

"You've been naughty, Christina," Ben said now, glancing at her while he kept the gun trained on Remy. "Fucking this guy every night. And wow, the things you say to him in bed—if you'd talked to me like that, maybe I wouldn't have had to look elsewhere for some excitement."

"You hypocritical asshole," she snarled, but it came out unintelligible because of the gag. And then a chill slid through her as she thought of the implications of his speech. He *knew* what she said to Remy in bed?

Ben laughed as he came over to rip the gag from her mouth, his gaze still on Remy. It pulled out a few hairs that had gotten caught in the knot. Her scalp stung, but it was better than wearing a gag any day.

"You won't need this anymore now that he's here," he said. "Couldn't let you warn him, could I?"

"You okay, Christina?"

She looked at Remy and found him watching her now. Her eyes filled with tears. Happy tears that he was here and she wasn't alone. Furious tears that she'd landed him in this predicament. She knew he was a badass, but how in the hell were they getting out of this one? He was cuffed, his hands hanging in front of his body, and Ben had a gun.

"Yes," she said, because she knew he meant physical health. And she was fine as far as that went. Mentally, she wasn't so sure. She was scared. And angry. So damned angry.

She glared at Ben. "How do you know what I say to him?" she demanded.

He laughed again. The sound was maniacal. Cracked. Oh God, what had happened to this man? She'd loved him once. He'd been normal once. Sane.

He was clearly not sane now. When had that happened?

"You can buy some interesting surveillance equipment these days," he said. "Don't even need to get inside to plant microphones. But you do have to get inside to plant cameras."

He went over to the vase on her dresser where she'd stuck a few willow branches to remind her of home. Then he bent down and said, "Hello, Benjamin old boy."

Christina's heart turned to ice. He'd been filming her and Remy? Filming everything they did together? Oh dear heaven, what was he planning to do?

"This is a mistake, Ben. You don't need to do this. Let us go and everything will be okay."

Ben straightened again. "Let you go? I don't think

so." He waved the gun. "I asked you to talk to me and you wouldn't. I told you that we could start over, be the political couple we were meant to be. We could found a dynasty, Christina. But no, you had to go and get all hot and horny over this guy. You've ruined everything!"

"You ruined it, Ben, not me."

His eyes flashed as he stuck his face on a level with hers. "Fucking whore," he snarled. And then he lashed out and slapped her, knocking her head sideways and making her ears ring.

"Touch her again, asshole, and I *will* kill you," Remy growled from where he stood with his wrists locked together. But he seemed closer than he had been before. Was he moving in the split seconds when Ben's attention was on her?

Ben barked a laugh. "How? I'm the one with the gun. You aren't superhuman, no matter how big and gorgeous you are, stud. A bullet through the brain will lay you out flat and put an end to any ideas you might have of stopping me."

"You can kill me," Remy said, "but you still aren't getting out alive."

Ben's brows drew together at that announcement. Then he reached out to wrap a hand in Christina's hair and jerk her toward him. He laid the gun against her temple, the barrel flush with her skin.

She closed her eyes and prayed that he wouldn't pull the trigger. There was so much she hadn't done yet. So much she wanted to do. If she died now, she would never see Remy again. Never know what it was like to kiss him one more time.

She snapped her eyes open and met his anguished

gaze. Whatever she was to him, she was clearly important. That thought comforted her a bit. She tried to smile for him, her mouth shaking at the corners as she did so.

"She dies first," Ben said. "Whatever happens. So think long and hard about what you intend."

CHAPTER THIRTY-ONE

REMY'S HEART BEAT so hard it was near to bursting. This was not how a Special Operator reacted to a crisis, but goddamn, seeing Christina smiling at him with a gun to her head made him desperate.

He wasn't letting that motherfucker shoot her. He'd failed Roxie, but fucking hell, he was *not* failing Christina. He couldn't.

Because if Ben shot her, Remy would die. He blinked as the realization hit him, but yes, he would die if Ben killed her.

Because he didn't want to live without her. Because she righted his world and made him happy. He hadn't been unhappy before her—but he would be now. Now that he'd had her, if he lost her—God, he couldn't think about it.

Her ex-husband was clearly insane. Whatever had happened in his head to crack it wasn't Remy's concern. Keeping them all alive until someone got here to help him was.

He'd dialed Cash's number before he'd thrown the phone down. If everything went according to plan, Cash had heard enough of the conversation to know what was going on. Remy could have dialed 911, but he didn't trust that the dispatcher would put the pieces together in time. Not to mention the sirens would alert Ben Scott as to what was happening.

No, far safer to dial his guys. They'd take care of it. Somehow.

Come on, you lovely motherfuckers. Need help.

Christina lived in DC. HOT was in Maryland. Cash and the boys could get here, but it was going to take some time.

"You don't want to hurt her, Ben," Remy said as soothingly as he could. "You want to keep her safe. She's your ticket to the governorship, right?"

Christina had said something to him about Ben wanting to run for governor of Louisiana. Ben wasn't from Louisiana but she was, and her father had always played a part in Louisiana politics. Ben had thought he would sail in on the strength of the Girard name and some crafty fundraising, no doubt.

Well, Remy wasn't against playing on the guy's fantasies if it bought them some time.

Ben's eyes narrowed. And then his arm went slack, the gun falling just a little bit from Christina's temple. If it fell a little more, Remy would make his move. He hadn't snapped the cuffs closed when he'd put them on himself as directed, but they still added split seconds to the timing. He needed to get to Ben fast, and he needed to disarm him. It could be done without hands, but with hands was better.

"I'd be a great governor."

"You would, man. I'm from Louisiana. I'd vote for you."

Ben's mouth hardened. "Don't lie to me. I'm not stupid."

"Well, I'm not real happy with you right this moment, but yeah, you can't do any worse than the other governors we've had. I'd give you a chance. Then if you didn't make things happen, I'd vote for the other guy the next time."

"She has to marry me again. That's important."

"Yeah, I know. Christina, you hear that? You need to marry this guy as quickly as possible. Get things back on track. We need a good governor."

He held her gaze, willing her to climb on board with him. He should have known she wasn't an idiot and didn't really need any encouragement.

"He hasn't asked me," she said softly. "He's only told me what I had to do. A lady likes to be asked."

"True," Remy said. "Ben, my man, you need to get down on one knee and propose properly."

Ben looked thoughtful for a second. Geez, the dude really had lost it. Irrational one second, almost childlike the next. Remy would have felt sorry for him if not for the fact he was holding them hostage.

"What about him?" Ben asked Christina, jerking his head toward Remy.

Christina swallowed. "What about him? He doesn't mean anything to me. I… I just wanted to make you angry. I wanted to get back at you for hurting me."

Remy knew she was playing the game now, but it hurt to hear her say those words.

Sadness crossed Ben's features. He reached out and ran his fingers along Christina's jaw.

“Prove it to me,” Ben said. “Prove he means nothing to you.”

Christina’s lashes fluttered. “I, um, okay. What do you want me to do?”

Ben lifted his head to stare at Remy. Then he slipped the fingers of one hand into his belt and started to undo it while keeping the gun trained on Christina.

“Blow me,” he said. “Right here in front of him.”

Christina licked her lips, but it wasn’t a sexy move. It was nerves. She shot Remy a look, her brows knitting, her mouth tightening. Fucking hell, he didn’t want her to do this. He couldn’t watch such a thing. And yet it would distract Ben enough that Remy could take him down.

Still, he couldn’t let it get that far. No fucking way. He wasn’t watching his woman blow another guy even if it saved their lives.

“I… I can’t,” she said. “It’s too personal.”

Ben’s gaze hardened. “I’ve watched you fuck him repeatedly. I’ve watched you blow him, and I’ve listened to you beg him for more. If you can do that with him, you can do it with me.”

Christina was afraid she’d be sick, but how could she refuse? A refusal meant they had to move on to whatever came next in Ben’s twisted mind. And that might mean the end for Remy. She couldn’t let that happen.

Because she needed him too much. She met his gaze,

her stomach flipping at what she saw there. He was furious and sickened, but the knowledge he couldn't stop this from happening was there in his eyes. He had no power, and she knew that made a man like him crazy.

"You have to untie me," she said, trying as hard as possible to think her way through this.

"Not happening. You can suck my cock without your hands."

"At least untie one leg. I can't get to you otherwise." She leaned toward him, demonstrating the point that he was out of reach.

Ben looked thoughtful.

"There are scissors in the end table," she continued, hoping he'd get them out and then leave them lying where she could reach them.

He opened the drawer and took the scissors out. Then he sliced into the scarf around her left ankle. He must have decided that having one leg tied was sufficient because he then slipped the blades between her wrists, surprising her. A moment later, her arms parted and her back stopped screaming with pain as her muscles relaxed.

"On second thought, I want your hands on me—but Christina, don't forget that I have the gun. And I *will* shoot your lover if you give me provocation."

"I don't care about him," she said. But the words hurt and she knew they weren't true. She did care. A lot.

Ben put the scissors back in the drawer and closed it. Then he thrust his hips forward. "You know what to do. Get busy doing it."

Christina reached for the belt he'd started undoing, her fingers shaking. Next she unzipped his pants and, as slowly as possible, unhooked the waistband.

How many times had she seen Ben's dick in her life? How much had she once thought he was the right man for her? They'd never had the kind of spectacular passion she had with Remy, but what they'd had had been enough for her back then.

She'd felt safe with Ben. Ironic.

She closed her eyes. She *could* do this. It wouldn't be the first time. She'd given Ben oral sex far more frequently than he gave it to her—but the idea was absolutely reprehensible to her now. Especially since he'd cheated on her. Was he safe? Clean?

She'd tested clean, but that was months ago and who knew what Ben had been up to since?

"Tell me how big my cock is," Ben ordered, and her heart skipped a beat. He'd listened to her and Remy make love. He'd heard everything. He'd watched everything.

Helpless anger surged through her veins. But she had no choice. Not if she wanted to live.

"Huge," she said softly, pushing his trousers open and lifting the custom shirttails out of the way. "I've never seen a bigger, more beautiful cock. It's everything a girl wants."

"Damn right," he said. "Everything a governor needs. Big cocks get shit done."

"Yes. Definitely."

"Suck it, Christina. Show this asshole who has the bigger dick. Show him who you really want."

She slipped her hands into his briefs and encountered a half-hard penis. "You, baby. Only you," she whispered as she freed him.

Remy made a sound and she squeezed her eyes tight, forcing herself not to look at him. If she did, she wouldn't be able to do this. She held Ben's penis and moved closer, swallowing down bile as she did so.

"Fuck this shit," Remy growled.

Christina's eyes snapped open in time to see Remy launch himself at Ben. At the same time, something shook the house, but she didn't know what it could be and she didn't have time to think about it.

Ben's arm came up, the gun aimed at Remy. Christina shoved with all her might, trying to knock Ben off-balance.

It happened in slow motion—Ben windmilled backward, Remy sailed through the air, and Christina scrambled in the drawer for the scissors so she could cut herself free or stab Ben or something, anything.

But she wasn't fast enough, because there was a deafening kaboom—and Remy dropped to the floor like a stone.

Her hand closed around the scissors as Ben lifted the gun again. She had no time to cut her last remaining restraint. Instead, she slashed upward with the scissors, felt them sink into flesh. Ben screamed.

Remy stretched out his cuff-free hands—how had he done that?—and then grabbed Ben's ankles, jerking his legs out from under him. Ben went down hard, his head cracking against the floor. He didn't move again.

Christina cut the last restraint with shaking hands as footsteps pounded up her stairs, then scrambled from the bed to rush over to where Remy had rolled onto his back. Blood gushed from a wound beneath his chest and his breathing was labored.

She pressed her lips to his. They were cooler than they should be. "Remy, oh Remy. You promised you wouldn't leave me. You promised."

His eyes rolled in his head and then focused on her for a brief second. He raised a bloody hand, dropped it again. "Not leaving. Promise."

"Jesus H. Christ," someone swore. Christina turned her head and saw four SEALs through a blurry lens.

"Help him," she said. "Please."

Because if he died, life wouldn't be worth living anymore.

"We got this, honey, don't you worry."

Cash McQuaid ripped the blanket off her bed and came over to wrap her in it while Alex Kamarov, Cody McCormick, and Corey Vance went to work on Remy.

"Is he going to be all right?"

Cash gently escorted her over to the bed and set her down on it while Cody lifted his phone and dialed 911.

"Of course he will, honey. SEALs are tough."

But there was something in his voice that said he didn't quite believe what he was saying.

CHAPTER THIRTY-TWO

"IS HE GOING to live?"

Christina couldn't stop shaking. Her body simply would not take the cues to stop. She was dressed now, so she wasn't cold. And she was free, so she wasn't afraid for her life.

But she was afraid for Remy. He'd been brought to the hospital over an hour ago and there'd been no word since. The SEALs in the waiting room with her exchanged looks before Viking, who'd arrived shortly after they'd reached the hospital, said, "Remy's tough. We have to wait and see."

Remy's entire team was here, and they all kept saying he was tough. But that wasn't the answer she wanted, so she kept trembling and praying and trying not to lose her shit.

The doors to the waiting room blasted open just then and Matt came striding in, Evie on his heels. Christina got to her feet and stumbled toward him. He wrapped her in a hug, and she started to sob.

"Honey," her brother said. "It's okay. You're okay."

"B-b-but Remy's not," she wailed.

Evie joined the hug, enveloping her from the other side. The three of them stood that way for a long minute, Christina crying and Matt and Evie just holding on.

Oh how she loved these two.

But she also loved Remy. She knew that now. Stupid, stupid, stupid idiot not to realize that's what she felt for him. It took watching him drop after taking a bullet for her to know that she loved him like she'd never loved any other man. He was her other half, the missing piece that made her feel complete.

And she might lose him before she ever got to tell him that. Why hadn't she told him before he'd passed out from the blood loss and shock? That thought only made her cry harder.

Matt steered her over to the chairs and sat her down in one. Evie dropped beside her and took her hand. "Do you need anything, sweetie? Something to drink or eat?"

"No," she whispered past the razor blades in her throat. "Nothing."

She looked at the men gathered there, her heart aching so hard. They would blame her for this. And why not? She blamed herself. She could have done more to make sure Ben didn't hurt anyone. If she'd only realized that he wasn't himself anymore, that he'd lost any semblance of reality he'd once known. Something in his head had twisted irrevocably.

She didn't know what had happened to him after the ambulance came for Remy, and she didn't really care. Not right now. Whatever it was, she hoped he spent a very long time in prison.

The doors opened and a surgeon came out. He was wearing green scrubs, but that's not what caught her attention. It was the smile on his face that made her heart soar with hope.

"Who's here with Remy Marchand?"

"We are," Viking said, indicating the whole group.

The surgeon looked at them all and then cleared his throat, choosing Viking to address his remarks to since he seemed to be the leader in that moment.

"We expect a full recovery. The bullet passed between two ribs and…"

Christina didn't hear what else the doctor said. Her brain swam and blackness crept into the edges of her vision. She must have made a noise because Evie patted her back.

"It's okay, sweetie. He's going to be all right."

"Oh God," Christina said, pressing her hand to her mouth to prevent a wail from escaping. Heaven help her, she was as uncontrollable as Penny had been back in Qu'rim. "I want to see him."

She didn't remember standing, but she was. Standing and facing the doctor, her hands clenching at her sides. She had to see him right this minute or she would burst.

"I'm sorry, ma'am, but no visitors tonight. If you come back tomorrow—"

"Mattie," she said, turning to her brother. "Do something. Please."

"Chrissy—"

"No, *do* something. Call someone. I'm not leaving here."

"Honey, we aren't next of kin. Mrs. Doucet can't do

anything," he said, referring to the Girard family lawyer. They had a lot of lawyers working for Girard Oil, but Mrs. Doucet was the best. She looked like someone's idea of a Hallmark Channel-movie grandmother, but the woman was a shark.

And to hear she couldn't do anything? That made Christina want to crumple. Except that she couldn't. She had to fight for her right to see the man she loved.

"Baby," Evie said, sliding into view. "You have other people you can call. The colonel, or even Garrett Spencer."

Christina's heart hammered then. Garrett "Iceman" Spencer was one of Matt's coworkers—or teammates, more appropriately—whose father-in-law was the newly elected president of the United States. Hell yes, the president-elect could get her in to see Remy.

"Please, Mattie," she breathed.

He took his phone out. "No promises, but I'll try. Give me a few minutes."

It was dark when he awoke, though not pitch-black. There was a pain in his side. A dull, throbbing pain that sent lightning bolts through him when he shifted. Remy blinked and stared at the ceiling. Then he turned his head and spied the screen that recorded his vitals.

That's what the fucking beeping was. Jesus, he'd been fighting that sound for a while now, thinking it was a bomb about to go off. But of course that had been a dream and the bomb was simply the hospital equipment doing its job.

Thank God, because no matter how he tried, he couldn't find the bomb. He shifted, groaning at the searing pain in his side.

"Remy?"

Someone touched him. Cool fingers on his forehead and cheek. He knew those fingers.

He reached up with the hand that didn't make his side ache and caught them.

"Christina?"

She came into view, hovering over him, her dark hair flowing over one shoulder as she did so.

"Yes, it's me." She squeezed his hand. "How do you feel?"

"Like I got hit by a truck."

She made a noise that he couldn't quite identify. "I'm so sorry. It's my fault."

He didn't know what she meant. And then it hit him that she was here with him, and she was safe. Jesus, the last thing he remembered was jerking Ben Scott's legs out from under him. He hadn't known whether the fucker was still alive or not, but he'd known his team had arrived because of the vibrations of their footsteps pounding up the stairs and through the floor upon which he lay. He'd only prayed they'd get to Christina before Ben could get off another shot.

Which they had, apparently.

"What happened?" he croaked. "And why does my throat hurt?"

She reached for something across the bed and then

put a large cup with a handle and a straw into his hand. He took a drink of water.

"Your throat is still raw from the breathing tube they used during the surgery. The doctor said you'd need to hydrate."

"Hydrating," he said, taking another sip.

"You got shot," she said. "Ben w-was trying to m-make me..."

He squeezed her hand, fresh anger flooding him at the thought of what her ex had been forcing her to do. Seeing her tied up like that, so vulnerable and helpless. God, it had nearly killed him. "I remember."

"You threw yourself at Ben. He shot you. But I stabbed him with the scissors—though it was only a flesh wound—and you knocked him out when you jerked his legs from under him. Your guys arrived after that." She swallowed. "Cash put a blanket over me. I was terrified you were dead, and I'd just stabbed Ben—though I didn't know it was a flesh wound. I was hoping he was bleeding out on the floor, quite honestly, while he was knocked out cold."

Remy's mind whirled at everything she said. "You stabbed him."

"Yes. But he shot you—and it's all my fault, Remy."

He thought she was crying, but he wasn't sure. "How is it your fault? I launched myself at him. But Jesus Christ, honey, I couldn't let him do that to you. You were going to do it for me, I know—but I couldn't watch. I couldn't let it happen."

"I should have known there was something wrong with him when he came to see me again. I should have gotten a restraining order."

"And what good would that have done? He was still going to do what he did tonight. It's not your fault, baby. Not your fault."

She sucked in a breath. "I love you, Remy. I know you don't love me, that we're still just figuring out this relationship—but I love you. When I thought you were dead—oh God, I thought I would die too."

Remy frowned. Was he still dreaming? Was this just another part of the twilight sleep he'd been experiencing?

Because, damn, he couldn't think of anything he wanted more than to have Christina Girard telling him she loved him.

"I love you too," he said, in case this wasn't a dream and she really was there. He would never forget for as long as he lived the way she'd smiled at him with a gun to her head. As if she'd been trying to reassure him. *Him,* when he was the one who should have been reassuring her.

He'd been willing to die to save her. He still was.

"I— Did you really just say that to me?" She sniffed. "Oh, right, it's the remnants of the anesthesia. You won't remember this tomorrow, but that's okay because it feels so lovely right now."

He tugged on her hand until she had to bend down over the bed, her face so near his. His side ached, but it was important that he see her eyes. Important that she see his when he said this to her.

"I'm not drugged, Christina—well, I am I guess—but not so much I don't know what I'm saying. I love you. I've loved you from the first moment you said hello to me. I don't know why—hell, I didn't know that's what was going on, believe me—but it's true. Since the instant you spoke to me at your brother's house, I've been yours."

Something hot and wet hit his skin, cooling quickly. He reached up again, swept his thumb over her face. It came away wet.

"*Cher*," he breathed. "Don't."

"I'm happy," she said. "These are happy tears, Remy Marchand. Don't you dare try to stop them either."

"Tell me you love me again."

She bent and kissed his cheek. He turned his head and met her mouth. It wasn't a sexy kiss considering the way he felt, but it was a wonderful one. He'd never kissed a woman knowing that she had his heart before.

"I love you," she whispered. "I was scared to love you, scared to try again—but I'm so happy my heart knew what to do even when I didn't."

"When I get out of here," he growled. "I'm showing you everything I feel until you never doubt it for a second."

She laughed a tear-filled laugh. "I don't doubt it now. Not anymore, Remy. Not ever."

"Jesus," he groaned as a sharp pain lanced through him.

"Shh, honey," she said, reaching across him and tweaking something on the tube going into his vein. "I'll be here when you wake, promise."

He instantly felt the silvery glide of morphine sliding into his veins, and he knew she'd hit the pain pump on his IV. Damn her. Bless her. Love her.

He fell asleep soon after and felt no more.

CHAPTER THIRTY-THREE

Two months later...

CHRISTINA COLLAPSED ON the bed, her entire body going limp as the power of her orgasm slammed through her. Remy thrust into her relentlessly, dragging out the pleasure until his own release caught him and propelled him over the edge.

He rolled off her and lay beside her, breathing heavily. She turned and propped herself onto an elbow, running her fingers over his magnificent chest. The angry scar of the bullet wound in his side always made her heart clench.

"It's okay," he said gruffly, capturing her fingers and dragging them to his mouth. "I'm alive."

"I'm still sorry it happened."

"Of course you are. We both are. But honey, don't you know I'll do it again if it means you stay safe?"

Christina frowned. "I don't want either of us in that position ever again, okay?"

Watching Remy recover from a bullet wound hadn't been fun. He'd been weak at first, and then he'd been in pain. When they'd let him go from the hospital, she'd insisted he stay with her. The SEALs and Matt's team had gone through her place with a fine-tooth comb. Ben had only had one camera in there. She'd discovered how he'd gotten inside. He'd gone to the neighbor she'd left a key with for emergencies, and he'd said he was with the gas company. The neighbor had let him in and he'd placed the camera. He'd recorded video and sound from it, but he'd also sat across the street from her house with a high-powered microphone aimed at her house and listened in that way as well.

It hadn't been the most sophisticated plan, but then Ben's mind wasn't working particularly well anymore either. She'd considered selling the place and moving, but then she'd gotten mad and decided that no way was she letting him affect her life so profoundly again.

Ben was currently in a mental hospital receiving treatment for schizophrenia. If he ever got out, he was going to trial for kidnapping and attempted murder. She wasn't afraid of him going free anytime soon.

"Me neither, baby," Remy said.

He hadn't been on a mission since he'd left the hospital, though he had returned to work. Though it was farther from her place to the military base, he'd stayed with her instead of going back to the apartment he shared with Cash. She liked that. She felt safe with him here. More importantly, she was happy.

She'd had to go to Houston a couple of times, but she'd turned over the international traveling. After the deal with Sheikh Fahd, her father and the board of directors had made her the head of business development. She had an entire team that she could send to make the deals she set into motion. It was working too. Business was up and Girard Oil was growing.

Remy got out of bed. She watched his naked ass, sighing that all that gorgeousness belonged to her.

"We need to get dressed, Christina. We're supposed to be at your brother's place in thirty minutes."

She stretched, her body still glowing in the aftermath of their lovemaking. "I know, but it's so much more fun just being with you."

He snorted. "Honey, everyone's beginning to think we don't like them anymore. Or that we're obsessed with each other."

"Aren't we?"

His eyes gleamed hot as they raked over her. "Yeah, we are. But get up, because we have to go."

"Fine," she grumbled.

Christina tried to distract him in the shower, but it didn't work. Well, mostly didn't work. He still lifted her up and fucked her hard and fast against the tiled wall.

She came too quickly, however, and he didn't prolong it. So now they were getting into his truck and she was grumbling at the idea they had to go anywhere at all.

When they reached Matt and Evie's place, there were cars up and down the street and in their driveway. Christina sighed. She wasn't the frightened introvert she used to be, but she still had to gear herself up for crowds.

Remy squeezed her hand as they stood on the sidewalk. "We don't have to stay for hours, promise. I know that wears you out."

She smiled and touched his cheek. "And I know you're an extrovert who likes people, so this is your time to recharge. It's probably getting boring just hanging out with me."

He blinked. "Are you kidding me? It's never a dull moment with you, Christina. You're the funniest, hottest, most beautiful woman I've ever known. You surprise me on a daily basis."

Okay, so she preened inside. No one had ever said she was the *most* anything. Well, maybe the most quiet. She'd gotten that one a lot as a kid.

"What did I do to deserve you, Remy Marchand?"

He pulled her into his arms right there on the sidewalk. "Do? All you had to do was be you. You're the air I breathe, the sun on my face, the energy in my veins."

"Wow," she said, her throat tightening. "You say the most amazing things sometimes."

He grinned. "All the time. Every word out of my mouth is amazing."

She knew he was trying to make her laugh so she wouldn't cry and ruin her mascara.

"Hey, stop molesting my sister on the fucking—I mean fire-trucking—sidewalk and get the heck in here," Matt called out.

Remy frowned. "Fire-trucking?"

Christina laughed. "Evie's making him clean up his language before the kids are old enough to pick it up."

Remy snorted. "Good plan."

Remy nursed his beer and kept stealing glances at Christina. She was sitting at the massive kitchen island with Alpha Squad's wives and fiancées—plus Ivy Erikson, Viking's wife—laughing about something someone said. She was radiant, her dark hair long and loose down her back, her slender form graceful in jeans and a white button-down shirt.

He loved her, and that made him feel a calmness inside that he'd never realized was missing from his life. It was pretty incredible to love someone and know they loved you in return.

"You treating my sister right?" Matt asked, snagging his attention.

But he was smiling, one eyebrow lifted in question, and Remy relaxed. "Like she's the most important thing in my life," he said, utterly serious.

Matt nodded. "That's good, man. Glad she has you in her life."

"I want to marry her."

Matt's eyes widened a fraction. "You've only been together a little over two months… you sure about that?"

"Yeah, I'm sure. And though I know that bastard stole all her money, I know she'll have more from your family trust, plus there's Girard Oil. I'll sign a prenup. I don't want anything except Christina, and I want you to know that."

Matt blinked. Remy knew he hadn't been happy when Christina confessed that Ben had bled her trust dry, so he wanted Matt to know he didn't care about the money. The Girards had a lot of money and she was entitled to her share according to Louisiana law, but he didn't want any of it.

"Jesus, dude—that's not up to me. It's between the two of you."

"I don't want you to think there's anything motivating me other than the way I feel about your sister. She's safe with me. Her heart is safe. I promise you that."

Matt held out a hand and Remy clasped it in a firm grip. "You took a bullet for her. But even if you hadn't done that, hell, the way she was in the hospital waiting room—well, that told me a lot about her feelings for you. She's herself with you. I never realized how contained she was with Ben, but it's so obvious now. You're good for her, Remy. I'll be happy to call you a brother-in-law as well as my Special Ops brother."

The two shook firmly and then went in for the bro hug. When Remy looked over at Christina, she was watching them, a question in her eyes. Remy took a swig of his beer and set it down.

"Nothing like the present moment," he said. "Wish me luck."

He strode over to the kitchen island. The ladies shot him sidelong glances. One of them, and he wasn't sure which one, said, "Here we go again, girls."

Grace Campbell Spencer, the president's daughter, laughed. "Yes, I believe you're right. Garrett had much that same look on his face in Buddy's Bar that night."

Christina looked at the women in confusion. "What? What are you talking about?"

"Christina," Remy said, taking her hand and ignoring them. When he had her attention, he dropped to a knee. She gasped. "Will you marry me?"

"Told ya," someone said. Glasses clinked.

Christina's eyes were wide. She put a hand over her

mouth. He began to believe he'd committed a grave error. She hadn't even been divorced a year. Her last husband had treated her horribly and broken her trust. And here he was asking her to marry him. *In public*. Putting her on the spot.

Shit, he was an idiot. An utter idiot.

"It's okay if you don't want to," he blurted, trying to give her an out. "We can take it a day at a time."

"And now he's backing out. Awkward," Ivy Erikson singsonged.

Remy turned to glare at the women, who stared down at him with looks of interest and amusement on their faces. They held their wineglasses as if this was a drinking game or something. Hell, he wasn't sure it wasn't.

"I am *not* backing out," he growled. "I'm giving her a graceful way out because she might not want to get married again." He turned to gaze up into Christina's eyes, which were suspiciously shiny now. "Which I understand, *cher*. Really. If you don't want to get married, I won't press you."

She surprised him, sliding from the chair and standing over him. She cupped his jaw in both hands, tilting his face up.

"Yes," she said softly. "I will marry you. Tomorrow or next year or whenever you want. I'm ready. Because we're *us*, Remy. Because I trust you with everything I am. Because you make me believe in the fairy tale."

She leaned down and kissed him then, and he squeezed her to him, kissing her back with all the joy he felt in his soul. He stood with her in his arms, and she yelped as her feet left the ground. Then she laughed and he slid her down his body, kissing her again before letting her go. Much more of that and he'd be sporting a massive hard-on in his jeans.

Everyone converged on them, offering congratulatory hugs and kisses from the women and handshakes from the men. Money shook his head as he gripped Remy's hand.

"Another good man down. Gonna miss having you as a roomie."

"I haven't been back in two months. You don't miss me at all."

Money laughed. "Nah, not really. I've been keeping busy."

"Yeah, I can just imagine. Careful, or you'll be the next one planning a wedding."

Money's eyes practically bugged out. "No way, bro. Not me. I am definitely not a one-woman man."

Remy's gaze slid to Christina. "You'd be surprised how that happens."

"Yeah, sure. Not me."

They stayed a while longer. Evie broke out the champagne, though she couldn't have any because she was breastfeeding the babies, and Matt didn't drink at all. After all the toasts and congratulations, Remy was ready to have Christina to himself. Especially when the talk turned to wedding plans. Good God, he wasn't about to discuss bridesmaid dresses or lace or any other fucking thing that went with weddings.

It took another twenty minutes to extract them, but soon they were in the truck and on the way back home. Christina was quiet, and that worried him.

"I'm sorry I put you on the spot," he said.

He could feel her eyes on him in the darkened interior. "I love you, Remy Marchand. I want to be with you forever. And I don't care who knows it."

He pulled into a parking lot because he couldn't wait another minute to hold her when there was no one else around. He unclipped her seat belt and dragged her over the console and into his lap.

"I fucking love you so much. I want you to be happy. I'll do whatever it takes to make that happen. If it's lace and bridesmaids and a fucking orchestra at our wedding, then that's what you're getting."

She twined her arms around his neck.

"I really don't want any of that, Remy." She chewed her bottom lip for a moment. "Do you think we could run away to Vegas and get married?"

He blinked. And then he laughed. "If that's what you want, hell yes."

"Then let's do it. I don't want to disappoint everyone, but I've had the wedding with all the trimmings. The wedding isn't what matters—it's the person you marry."

His heart swelled with all the love he felt for this woman. "Vegas it is then."

"Viva Las Vegas," she said, laughing.

"Viva Remy & Christina," he replied.

"I'll drink to that."

"We don't have any drinks."

"Then you'd better get me home and take me to bed instead."

He broke the speed limit complying with that order, but he soon had her spread out on the bed naked and moaning his name. Licking her into a frenzy was sweet, but sliding into her body was even sweeter.

"Remy," she gasped as he thrust slowly and surely. "I love you."

“I love you more.”

She laughed even while she moaned. “Not possible.”

He stilled and forced her to look into his eyes. “I know.”

And he did know. She loved him for who he was. It hadn’t been easy for her after all she’d been through, but her love was his greatest treasure.

He was going to spend a lifetime making sure she knew it too.

ABOUT THE AUTHOR

LYNN RAYE HARRIS is the *New York Times* and *USA Today* bestselling author of the HOSTILE OPERATIONS TEAM SERIES of military romances as well as 20 books for Harlequin Presents. A former finalist for the Romance Writers of America's Golden Heart Award and the National Readers Choice Award, Lynn lives in Alabama with her handsome former-military husband, two crazy cats, and one spoiled American Saddlebred horse. Lynn's books have been called "exceptional and emotional," "intense," and "sizzling." Lynn's books have sold over 3 million copies worldwide.

Connect with me online:

Facebook: https://www.facebook.com/AuthorLynnRayeHarris
Twitter: https://twitter.com/LynnRayeHarris
Website: http://www.LynnRayeHarris.com
Newsletter: http://bit.ly/LRHNews
Email: Lynn@LynnRayeHarris.com

Join my Hostile Operations Team Readers and Fans Group on Facebook:
https://www.facebook.com/groups/HOTReadersAndFans/

Made in the USA
Middletown, DE
10 November 2023

42354059R00170